Psychotherapy with Ghosts

Female Academy

Joseph S. Covais

NewLink Publishing
2022

Henderson, NV 89002
info@newlinkpublishing.com

Line/Content Editor: Dave Hardin
Interior Design: Jo A. Wilkins
Cover: Janelle Evans
E-Book Design: Richard R. Draude
Interior picture comes from the archive and collections of the Albany Academies

p. cm. — Joseph S. Covais / Paranormal
Copyright © 2022/ Joseph S. Covais
All Rights Reserved

ISBN: 978-1-948266-10-9/Paperback
ISBN: 978-1-948266-32-1/E-Pub

1. Fiction / Ghost
2. Fiction / Fantasy / Paranormal
3. Fiction / Fantasy / Romantic

NewLink Publishing
Henderson, NV 89002

Info@newlinkpublishing.com
Published and printed in the United States of America

1 2 3 4 5 6 7 8 9 0

This book is dedicated
to the class of 1841

Psychotherapy with Ghosts

Female
Academy

Chapter 1

Early September 1971

It took about five hours to drive from Manhattan to Willsboro, a village on the shore of Lake Champlain. In nice weather it was a beautiful drive. Mostly a thruway, the route took David up the Hudson River valley and through the Catskills. To him the peculiarly rounded mountains, worn down by eons of geology, the Hudson cutting through them, had an old soul, an enchanted quality, which inspired an entire movement of romantic landscape painters. In daylight it was easy to see why. After sundown those same mountains, full of goblins and secrets, were situated between him and the stars.

On this particular night David Weis drove home, lost in thought. Juggling two women wasn't easy. That one of them was a ghost certainly complicated things, but it also had its advantages. For example, awkward encounters at the supermarket or suspicious phone calls were most unlikely.

Of course, none of this would make any difference to Angela were she to become aware of the reason for his divided attention. Did it really matter? His interest in Almira was a mere fantasy. He knew it. The idea that this lovely young woman of the 1840s would have a romantic interest in him, a washed-up, twentieth century psychologist turned antique dealer, or that any mutual attraction could be advanced in any way, was simply absurd. Almira had no future. She dwelt in the past and, well...*his* past was ruined, a time he never wanted to return to.

While the logistics of maintaining his conflicting relationships were manageable, the tension boiling within him, wasn't. On one hand, it felt genuinely good to be together again with Angela. He'd missed her. Missed her caustic remarks, her intelligent observations; missed her warm, voluptuous and responsive body.

On their last night of this, their most recent visit, after an evening devoted to Chinese take-out and love making, they'd showered together. Later, skin to skin, Angela's body soft and powdered, David had breathed her in by the lungful. At such moments he loved to comb out her long, straight black hair. He'd done it before, but this night was different. On a whim, he wove her tresses into two long braids.

In the morning, she brushed out her hair as usual, but the crimped waves aroused some kind of animal desire in him. So much so that David carried her to the bedroom and took her twice more in quick succession.

"Wow." She gasped, as they lay entangled, spent and catching their breath. "What the hell got into you?"

That was then. Tonight, once he left Manhattan and merged onto the thruway, David's attention focused on Almira. Nail biting rumination ran amok. What if, thinking him gone forever, Almira had simply disappeared? Vanished into the ether. With no clear idea of where she existed when not materialized in the Quiet Room, how would he find her?

The thought of being unable to find Almira was, as they used to say in Dr. Koenigsberg's office, *anxiety provoking*. It stirred up emotions and desires. All of them, professionally problematic—possibly unethical.

David reflected on the difference between her time, long past, and his complicated present. Almira came from a world in which doing the proper and selfless thing, chastity and respect, weren't just platitudes. They carried real societal weight. The contrast made clear the features of life in 1971 which turned him off—cynicism, materialism, hedonism, nihilism. All these fashionable *isms* were destructive. They cheapened everything.

But Weis also had legitimate professional interests. In their last session Almira seemed to have turned a therapeutic corner. A deep well of guilt, anger, and jealousy had been revealed. That was good, but Weis knew presenting symptoms often indicated far deeper problems. In fact, she'd hinted at something more, a secret that would require courage to face. Was Almira awakening to her dilemma, estranged from life and afterlife alike?

If that was the case, the therapeutic task was clear and profound— nothing less than the transition from life to death she had somehow failed to complete. Such a transition had to have a unifying principle, a name, but he still couldn't bring himself to call it God. Maybe, he mused, that should be his own therapeutic goal.

His first night back, David found Almira on the daybed, reading *The Knickerbocker.* She put the magazine down, looked up and smiled. "Dr. Weis, it pleases me to see you have returned. I've missed your visits terribly."

"Is that so?" he said, arranging the klismos chair and settling in.

"Yes, it is. In truth, I feared you might not return, you were gone so long a time. Where were you?"

Weis suspected the question was borne of frustration. Does she feel neglected and unhappy with my absence? "There were some things I had to attend to in New York City. Important business and personal affairs. I was gone longer than usual, you're right, but now I'm back. We can have a nice, long talk."

Almira seemed immersed in the cover of her magazine, but Weis noted the slightest hint of a smile flicker in the dim light. "That would please me," she said.

3

Eager to recapture the therapeutic momentum of their previous session, he said, "You seemed more at ease when we finished our last conversation. You also told me there was much more you would say if you had the courage."

"Did I say that? Perhaps I did."

"I'd love to know what you meant."

Almira paused, appearing to weigh her response. "Though you have helped me see certain things, not all of them are easy to face. Indeed, I am finding that sometimes it is better not to know everything."

"That's an interesting idea. What are the things it's better not to know?"

She started to strobe like the image from a stop-motion camera. Damn. He'd been too quick, too much in a hurry. David tried to retrieve her, to calm her down, but within seconds Almira's voice became garbled. She flickered and was gone.

Chapter 2

September 1841

Almira sat in the sewing room with Emily Wilcox and Phebe Gardiner. The trio constituted an informal sewing circle of which she was the newest participant, and Phebe, though the youngest, was the most accomplished seamstress. She demonstrated her method of pleating the skirts of fashionable dresses. The fabric of her latest project, an evening dress of green watered silk, lay draped across the padded table. Phebe sewed four parallel lines of running stitch along what would become the top edge of the skirt.

The efficiency with which Phebe applied the needle always seemed like an extension of her poised and cheerful demeanor, but not today. Her aim was off, and frustration born of imperfection spoiled her ordinary countenance. Searching her face, Almira wondered what might be weighing on her. Phebe pursed her lips and wrinkled her nose.

"For mercies sake, I've skipped a stitch."

"I don't think it will show," said Almira.

"No, no, it's all wrong." Phebe yanked the errant thread out as if extracting a barb.

"You seem tired," Emily said. "Maybe we should stop for today."

"No, really, I'm fine." It took Phebe only seconds to thread a new needle and perform the correction with great efficiency.

"There. That's better." She appeared satisfied, took a deep breath, and ran the flat of her hand across her work. "Now, to resume, lest your pleats be uneven, it is essential that the running stitches be perfectly aligned, one above the other and all of equal length. You will both also notice that I have quit the lining even with the folded edge. It makes for a more delicately formed skirt, one in which the fullness is more discrete."

Emily excused herself to the water-closet. "But please, do go on, I'll be right back."

Phebe tried to resume her demonstration but seemed to have lost her way. When she noticed yet another very minor imperfection, her eyes welled up. Almira waited for her to say something, but Phebe remained quiet. Finally, Almira broke the silence.

"Phebe, is there something wrong? You seem distracted today."

"Do I? Forgive me. It is nothing with which I should burden you. *Rien du tout*, as the French would say."

"My mother always told me that true friendship allows us to halve our troubles and double our joy."

Phebe listened but said nothing. She threaded another needle, replaced the silver thimble on her finger, rectified the sewing error, then resumed pleating the skirt of her new dress. Suddenly, she spoke.

"You have no doubt heard gossip about my older sister Mary and Professor Horsford."

"Yes," Almira said. "Naturally, one overhears the other girls conversing, but I hope you don't think I've indulged their bad habits."

"I do not. But it's no matter," said Phebe. "Idle talk about who is engaged to whom is an easy thing, and normally it's simply the anticipation of joyous news."

The room grew uncomfortably quiet. Phebe pulled the parallel threads, drawing the fabric together into dozens of small, accordion-like pleats, as if by magic. "That was what we expected, but I received a letter from my sister yesterday." Phebe smoothed her work to even out the gathers. "Mary tells me our father has rejected Professor Horsford's request for permission to court her. She tells me that father feels he is unsuitable."

The possibility that Eben Norton Horsford would be deemed unworthy of any girl was unthinkable to Almira. "How can that be?" she said. "Professor Horsford is a learned man as well as a gentleman."

"I agree," said Phebe, "but our father says he is of modest means. He says Professor Horsford's pursuit of the daguerreotype is a fool's errand, and his position at the academy will not support Mary in the way she is accustomed. Apparently, he and Mary had quite an argument about it before she left for Providence."

"Surely Mr. Gardiner must know he will progress in his earnings."

"He does, but there's another thing. The Horsford's are a new family from the western counties of the state. Where I'm from, on the eastern tip of Long Island, there are some very old families. Some, like mine, have been there more than two hundred years. The Smiths, the Huntings and L'Hommedieus, the Osbornes, and we Gardiners. Mary would gain little socially from a marriage outside of our circle."

All this sounded familiar. A perfectly honorable man, intelligent, and with the purest of intentions, denied his true love by a father for whom only wealth and status mattered.

"My dear sister is very upset and embarrassed, as you might expect. And I shudder to think of the humiliation Professor Horsford must endure. By now you know that their expected engagement has been an open secret among the girls at this school."

Phebe placed her hand on Almira's and looked into her eyes. "I have said too much for decorum's sake," she said, "but I sense I can trust you, though I haven't long known you. Is that strange?"

"No," Almira said. "I'm expert at keeping secrets."

Chapter 3

September, 1971

"Hey, get this," Angela said. David looked up. She held *The Young Lady's Friend,* turning its pages as if tickling a baby. She flipped back a page and started reading. "'What a pity it is that the thousandth chance of a gentleman's becoming your lover should deprive you of the pleasure of a free, unembarrassed, intellectual intercourse with other single men of your acquaintance.'" She glanced up, arched a penciled eyebrow and went on. "'Yet such is too commonly the case with young ladies who have read a great many novels and romances, and whose heads are always running on love and lovers.'" Angela grinned at David. "More?"

"Sure."

Man, David thought, Angela looked sexy with a book in her hand, turning pages. With any other book he would be enjoying the show, for Angela read with style. It could be something of a performance. Unfortunately, this time she was handling Almira's book, *The Young Lady's Friend.*

"Okay, let's try this one," she said, paging ahead. "'Someone has said that matrimony is with women the great business of life, whereas

9

with men it is only an incident. An important one to be sure, but only one among many to which their attention is directed.'"

David smiled. "What do you think of that?"

"I hate to say it, but I think there's some truth to it," she said.

Without revealing his discovery of Almira's trunk, her memorial, and confessing his conversations with her, there was no way for David to address her observation truthfully. He'd kept his involvement with Almira to himself and wasn't willing to change that—not yet anyway. After all, how do you explain to your girlfriend that you're up all night with an attractive twenty- year-old doing psychotherapy, especially when she's a ghost?

"Where did you get this?"

David scolded himself for having brought the book downstairs in the first place. He should have left it in the Quiet Room. "I found it in the attic," he said, and left it at that.

"Well, this book is a gas, that's all I can say." Angela laughed from time to time as she continued thumbing the pages. "I can't believe some of—oh, David, look, there's a note in here."

"Give me that," he said. She shot him a look. He'd been too abrupt.

"Do you know what it is?"

"No, of course not, I'm just, you know, intrigued," he said, recovering himself. "What does it say?"

"It's kind of hard to read."

David leaned closer so he could see it too. The handwriting was inelegant and the spelling inconsistent, but to him it was legible. Angela began reading...

"'Darling Almira, I send this by way of Sandborne—be on the lookout for a candle in his window. It is the signal that I have come for you. That night you should meet me at midnight once you are sure everyone is asleep. I will wait for you by the carriage house. Do not pack anything you can't wear or put in your pockets. Trust me for this is my plan. With God's help we will be husband and wife very soon. I am yours forever and ever, Daniel Dwyer'"

10

The room was silent, but for the ticking of a clock.

"Wow," said Angela. "It sounds like someone had plans to elope."

David tried to play dumb. "Yeah, I know. Can you believe the weird stuff you find in old books? It makes you wonder who these people were, doesn't it?"

Angela agreed. "It's kind of romantic though," she said. "Honestly, I feel like we shouldn't be reading it."

"Well, whoever wrote it is long gone."

Perusing the book, Angela hummed something familiar he couldn't quite make out, before speaking again. "There's something about it that's sort of appealing. It's innocent, you know, because these people really believed this crap. They believed there's a way that things ought to be."

Angela lay with eyes wide open, staring into the darkness. Their lovemaking had been poorly synchronized. David came early and having climaxed seemed to lack the motivation to bring her the rest of the way, so she had faked it. Now he lay sound asleep. If she was quiet, made sure to bite her lip and swallow back any groans of pleasure, she could finish herself and he'd never notice.

Release brought satisfaction, but it was fleeting. She plumped her damp pillow, then plumped it again. Her mind raced. It was impossible to set aside what she'd read in the old advice book, not to mention that secretive note hidden inside—what was the story behind that?

At two-thirty, she gave up. She got out of bed and went into the living room, switched on a lamp, and settled herself into the sofa where she'd been earlier. Except for the hum of the refrigerator in the kitchen and the ticking of the antique clock on the mantel, the house was silent.

Angela picked up *The Young Lady's Friend* and looked through the table of contents. At the chapter titled "Behavior to Gentlemen" she started reading. One paragraph jumped out at her.

> *The credulity of women on the subject of*
> *being loved is very great. They often mistake*
> *a common liking for a particular regard and,*
> *on this foundation, build up a castle in the air*
> *and fill it with all the treasures of their bright*
> *hopes and confiding love, and, when some*
> *startling fact destroys the vision, they feel as if*
> *the whole creation were a blank to them, and*
> *they the most injured of women.*

Something about the phrase, "all the treasures of their bright hopes," made her both sad and anxious. Her mind raced with questions. Was she mistaking their mutual love of sex and companionship for what she had convinced herself was love or, as the book put it, "a particular regard?" Would he be sleeping just as contentedly if he'd made love to another girl tonight? Was she building castles in the air hoping they would have a wedding someday and children to follow?

She hoped not, because ditching her relationship with David and starting over would be a drag. In fact, before she met David the whole dating scene had gotten to be one big fat drag. Superficial guys. Stupid guys. A lot of them were good-looking but boring, interested in only one thing. Sure, David was no matinee idol. He was self-absorbed and often emotionally distant, but he wasn't stupid. No, he kept her interested. A deep thinker who took life seriously, the way she did.

Angela mulled over all the possibilities. Would he respect her more, maybe be more apt to propose, if she wasn't always sexually available to him?

She turned another page. The author cautioned against allowing oneself to fall in love foolishly and spoke of unrequited love as a syndrome one should, and could, take steps to avoid.

> *Since women are prone to think much of love,*
> *to read books of sickly sentimentality, and the*

12

poetry of amatory bards, since girls will put it into each other's heads that they are in love, or that someone is in love with them, it is desirable that they should understand the first symptoms of the disorder and take early and vigorous measures to stop its dangerous course.

She heard the toilet flush. David shuffled into the room. "Hey," he said, scratching himself, his voice gravelly. "What're you doing in here?"

"I couldn't sleep, so I got up to read."

He held out his hand. "C'mon. Come back to bed."

That sounded good, so she did as he suggested. Cuddled against him, she fell into a deep slumber. Sometime later, Angela woke with a start. A glance at the clock told her it was barely five a.m. She rolled over and tried to go back to sleep. Outside, birds chirped, and that meant dawn was about to break. Despite having only a few hours' rest, her mind felt alert. She got up and went to the bathroom, reconciling herself to the fact that there would be no more sleep that night.

The yoga classes she and her roommate Tina had been taking came to mind as she washed her face. Yoga at dawn seemed like a good idea—spiritual too—but where? David was still asleep in the bedroom, and she didn't want to use the living room. That stupid advice book would be a distraction. It had already cost her a night's sleep.

What about going upstairs to what David called the Quiet Room? That sounded compatible with yoga. At least it was clean—no paint rollers or power tools scattered around. Angela scooped up a throw rug and went up the back stairway, feeling the temperature rise with each step to the second story. It wasn't yet full daylight.

The door to the Quiet Room loomed in the darkened hallway. She sprang the latch and slipped inside. At first, it was hard to make out objects, but sunlight would soon splash high against the wall opposite the window, chasing away the last vestiges of night. She looked around. She took in a chair, trunk, and the refurbished daybed David was so proud of. That was all. The cleanliness and uncluttered Zen ambience would be perfect for a peaceful yoga session.

Just as she and Tina had learned to do in their class, she positioned the rug in the center of the room, then sat cross legged. The routine started with deep meditative breathing, followed by stretching and warm up. Assuming the different postures came next, but halfway through downward-facing-dog, the feeling that someone was watching seized her. Angela knew that couldn't be the case, so she tried to ignore it, but it was no use. The feeling only grew stronger. This room wasn't peaceful—but downright unnerving.

Repeating one of the seated poses, Angela turned her head, touching chin to shoulder on either side. She took the opportunity to check every corner of the room until satisfied this was nothing more than the hangover of a horrible night's sleep.

Suddenly, a chill pressed against her, trying to envelope her from above and behind. Angela leaped to her feet, and for the briefest instant came face to face with someone—a young woman. She yelped, but even before the sound died away the image vanished.

Abandoning the rug, she rushed out of the room, down the back stairs, and into the kitchen, flipping on the light as she entered.

Angela started a pot of coffee and straightened the counter— carefully aligning the salt and pepper shakers. There was a pack of cigarettes on the table. She took one and lit it from the burner, noticing that her hands shook. The last ten hours hadn't gone very well. That stupid book, the cryptic note, being up all night, and now this. It was all too much.

She smoked and sipped coffee. In an effort to collect her nerves Angela took inventory of what she had felt and seen upstairs. A female figure. Young, dark haired but otherwise lacking detail which she could remember. The vision had simply been too brief. The emotion, the vibe, whatever you wanted to call it, was the stronger of the two. It communicated an easily resurrected sense of desperation.

Yeah, the encounter had been spooky, like the way she supposed being face-to-face with a ghost would be, but not threatening. If anything, it evoked pity. Had she actually seen a ghost? Possibly. But by the time she'd lighted her fifth cigarette with the fourth, Angela still wasn't sure. She'd always said this place looked haunted, but it was always meant as a comment on the building's run-down appearance, not any real belief in the supernatural. Until now.

Chapter 4

September, 1841

Almost overnight, Almira had gone from living an isolated life in Willsborough to sharing accommodations with nine other academy girls boarding with Mrs. Bright, the proprietress, and two domestic servant girls, Rose and Matilda.

Mrs. Bright was a prim, middle-aged widow who wore her blonde curls piled high on her head, in the old-fashioned style. Her rooms were on the ground floor, while the domestics lived together in the attic room, leaving the second and third floors reserved for the boarders.

All the upstairs bedrooms were painted white. A few of them had a border of stenciled drapery running along the exterior walls but were otherwise plain. One or two framed pictures were the only other decoration. Most were commercial prints, but a few theorem paintings had been created over the years by previous occupants. A still life, a bowl of fruit painted on white velvet hung in Almira's room.

Boarders were given a bed and a bureau on which sat a dressing mirror, pitcher, and bowl. There was also a writing table and chairs. The majority of girls shared a room with someone else. A few enjoyed

17

private accommodations, a luxury for which their parents paid extra.

The home itself was a handsome brick structure, mustard yellow with red shutters and ornamentation. Located on Maiden Lane, it stood less than four city blocks from the academy, an easy walk in pleasant weather.

House rules at Mrs. Bright's were simple. Everyone was expected to be out of bed by six a.m. Breakfast was served from seven to seven-thirty—usually hard-boiled eggs, porridge, or cold meats, with bread or pie. If they wished, the girls were welcome to take a lunch composed of whatever leftovers or other edibles were on hand that day, wrapped in wax paper. Supper was served promptly at six. And by ten p.m., everyone should be settled in their rooms.

"I do not know what has been asked of you at home," Mrs. Bright said at the commencement of their first supper together. "But since a girl's education should include the duties of a wife in maintaining a household, each of you will lend a hand one Saturday each month in some part of the housekeeping."

The girls looked nervously around the table. Who among them might have been raised in such pampered circumstances?

Mrs. Bright crossed off a few items from the top of a list she prepared, then continued her well-rehearsed monologue. "Absolutely no gentleman visitors are allowed, excepting with prior permission and with myself or a chaperone present at all times, and then only on Sunday afternoons or very special occasions. Lady visitors are welcome to the downstairs parlor. There is a fresh candle in your room now. When you need a new one, you will come to me, and I will instruct one of the girls to bring you another—likewise with coal once the season is turned. In this way, I will know if you are being wasteful."

Almira didn't dare raise her head but undertook a close study of the bone china plate before her on the table.

"Are there any questions?" Mrs. Bright expected none but paused a moment to allow for the possibility.

"Very well, I trust we will be a happy family together. Now, who will lead us in saying grace? Susannah, would you be so kind?"

It was indeed a family of sorts, and a happy one in those early days. As with any collection of strangers living under the same roof, Mrs. Bright's boarders sorted themselves out by seniority, common interest, and shared tastes. Those younger girls on the third floor included Susannah Platt, an awkward if sincere girl, desperate to adopt the mannerisms of her older schoolmates; the Skinner twins, Hannah and Sarah, together with the youngest, little Betty Wheeler from Vermont. All were nice girls, but still children, with a tendency to giggle amongst themselves late into the night.

The older girls, besides Almira, included Emily Wilcox, Harriet Ames, Phebe Gardiner, and Rebecca Carvalho.

Phebe had her own suite of rooms at the end of the second-floor hallway. When the older girls wished to be alone, they would gather in her more spacious quarters.

Almira shared a room with Emily, whom she learned was from Orwell, Vermont, directly across the lake from Willsborough. At twenty-one, she was the oldest boarder in the house and a teaching scholar to the girls in the younger departments. In Mrs. Bright's eyes, the position gave her a semi-official ranking.

Miss Wilcox had her own secret. "My first name is Thankful," she said, confiding to Almira one night before snuffing out their candle. "You may see it written on my letters from home. It is a dreadfully old-fashioned name, but I was the last of eleven children. Please don't tell anyone else."

Across the hall lived Harriet Ames, a Massachusetts girl, whose glib and cosmopolitan qualities Almira initially found appealing, until her competitive nature grew tiresome. It seemed no matter what Almira or anyone else said, Harriet was quick to match it with something bigger, brighter, more expensive, or more accomplished.

Occupying another room at the opposite end of the hallway was Rebecca Carvalho, without question the most exotic of the boarders.

At first sight, Almira thought she must be a Spaniard, with large sloe eyes, dark hair, and olive complexion suggesting an Andalusian background. But Rebecca was from Charleston, South Carolina. Not a word passed from her lips without that drawling accent—however softly spoken—it infused every syllable.

English spoken in the Southern manner was new to Almira. She thought it charming. Indeed, she was captivated by its phrasing, its cadence, and its musical inflection. There were other things about Rebecca which she found vaguely mysterious, but difficult to identify. Things said, things left unsaid alike, caught her attention.

Almira and her housemates were but a fraction of the girls attending the Albany Female Academy that year. Every morning, over three-hundred young women gathered in the chapel of the Greek revival edifice on North Pearl Street. Once they were seated according to their level of advancement, or department as it was known, a short invocation would be given, scripture read, a hymn sung, and general announcements made. The Sixth Department, which included the youngest students, many of them no more than twelve years old, were first to leave for their classroom. Next, came the Fifth Department, followed by the Fourth and so on. Almira was part of the Second Department, which meant that her classes included algebra and English composition in the morning, with French and botany in the afternoon. The schedule alternated with Grecian and Roman Antiquities, and English literature on Tuesdays and Thursdays.

At home, tutors had always treated Almira with deference. Mr. Descharmes, for example, never expressed the least impatience with her. But the instructors at the academy, whether male professors or female teachers and interns were different. They were intolerant of mediocrity and exacting in every detail. Especially daunting was the manner in which each girl was made to stand when called upon to recite aloud her answer to any question. Many of the girls could be seen to wipe away their tears and tremble as they stood to answer, voices quavering.

At the conclusion of the day's classes, Almira and the other girls from Mrs. Bright's would pass through the columned portico of the academy and pour down the steps to Pearl Street, a cascade of bonnets, parasols, and paisley shawls. Returning home arm-in-arm, they chattered amongst themselves.

On this particular afternoon the chief topic of conversation was a demonstration by students from Mr. Peck's Asylum for the Deaf. "I think it is quite nice that they are allowed out," said Harriet.

Emily nodded. "There is a blind girl in my hometown. She never leaves the house, poor creature. Who knows what will become of her once her parents are gone?"

Opposite the Baptist church, the girls crossed Pearl Street and made their way down Maiden Lane.

"The deaf girls were quite plain," Almira said, "though the young men were rather handsome—especially the one who'd told a story with hand signs.

"Maybe he could be your beau," said Harriet. "But whatever would you talk about?"

"The language of love is universal," Rebecca said. "Sometimes, when spoken gently it falls on deaf ears, but anyone who listens can understand it."

Betty and the Plattsburgh twins tittered amongst themselves. Looking out over the city below, Almira mulled over the remark. What a mysterious thing to say. That was when she saw him. Daniel was walking toward them, not more than fifty feet away. Could she trust her eyes? But there was no mistaking his lanky stride, sandy hair and, now that he was closer, cleft chin. Even the checkered vest and gray roundabout he wore were familiar.

Almira panicked. She couldn't let him go by without catching his attention. Recalling a ruse she'd read once in a novel, she pulled a glove from her basket and let it drop discretely to the planking at her feet. As she and her classmates drew near, he stepped aside.

"Good afternoon, ladies," Daniel said, touching the visor of his cap as they passed.

"And to you, sir," said Emily. The other girls nodded but remained quiet.

Almira's heart pounded. How she wanted to throw herself against him, but she knew better. Breathless as she looked up, she and Daniel locked eyes. He smiled at her in that same way he had smiled so many times before, when it had been unsafe to acknowledge their true feelings openly.

Then, as quickly as the encounter had begun, it was over. Almira's head swam. She had already surmised that Daniel was somewhere in the city. After all, he'd told her he would follow her there, hadn't he? But Almira thought she would have received some kind of written communication first. She'd told him about Sarah Rawson, that he could communicate to her through her new friend. Perhaps he hadn't been able to meet with Sarah yet.

"Mirie, did you hear me?" said Rebecca, standing with arms outstretched.

"What?"

"I was suggesting this afternoon we study our algebra together."

"Excuse me, miss."

Almira whirled around, delighted to again find Daniel's grinning face before her.

"Pardon my intrusion, miss, but I think you've dropped this glove."

"Oh, um, yes, thank you very much, sir, for your kindness."

"My pleasure, miss," he said, as he extended the glove to her.

Almira made as if to take it, but he held firm for a second. "It would be a crime for a hand as pretty as this to be left unprotected."

She would have stood there, not saying anything, but Rebecca, with whom she'd been walking, pulled her along.

"My goodness, Mirie, I do believe you're blushing."

Chapter 5

September, 1971

When David came into the kitchen and kissed Angela's cheek, he must have noticed all the fresh butts in the ashtray. "Rough night?"

"You have no idea," she said, but left it at that. There's a pot of coffee on the stove. It's hot. Would you like me to get you a cup?"

"No, don't get up. I'll get it."

Angela watched him shuffle to the counter, take a mug from the cabinet, and commence his coffee routine. Four sugar cubes, evaporated milk—the same every time.

"David," she said once he sat down, "let's not stay in today. Let's get out."

"Sure." He stirred his coffee, the sound fraying her nerves like blue jays pecking on glass. "I'm sorry you didn't sleep well.

Angela shrugged. Her eyes burned. She knew her hair had to be a mess. "This house is weird."

"I know," he said. "It can get spooky at night." David reached out a hand. "Tell you what, we'll put the top down on the Ghia, go for a nice drive. If you want, we can take the ferry ride across the lake again, like we did over Memorial Day."

"Really? I'd like that." The tension in her neck and jaw drained.

"And tomorrow, don't take the bus. I'll drive you back to the city."

A cautious smile broke across her face. "Honey, that would be great. I have to work Monday morning, but Tina's out of town. We'd have the place to ourselves. You can sleep late and leave when you're ready."

David smacked a fist into a palm. "Perfect. Why don't you get ready while I check the paper? There might be some auction we can hit on the way."

Angela got up and went into the bathroom, stepped out of her night clothes, and turned on the water. She couldn't wait to wash the jarring experience of the previous day from her body.

The shower felt great, hot and soothing. The water pressure was so good, she found herself swooning under an impromptu massage. She soaped, scrubbed, rinsed, and did it again. The ceremonial quality made her mood brighter until the hot water started to run out.

Angela emerged through an alluringly scented mist of shampoo and fragrant soap. David loved it when she smelled clean and fresh. It was kind of a thing with him. She squirmed inside a thick white towel, adjusting the edge across her breasts. She felt completely refreshed and even a little sexy. She sat across from him, crossing her legs demurely. "Hey, what did you find?"

"Well, there's a big estate auction in Jericho. That's in northwest Vermont. If we're taking the ferry to that side of the lake anyway, we can check it out."

It was so typical of David, weaving some antiquing mission into what could be a day just for them, but she didn't mind. "All right. I think there's still some hot water left."

Angela loved driving his convertible on the open road, so after breakfast David tossed her the keys. Preparation was something she made a ritual of. First, she tucked her hair under a beret and adjusted her sunglasses. Next came the seat, then the mirrors. Following this, she palmed the wheel, the shifter, and touched all the pedals. David once told her the ritual reminded him of a World War I fighter ace preparing to take off on another mission.

One quick kiss and they were off. On the thruway, she had just gotten up to the posted cruising speed, when she stole a glance at him. David was studying a map, struggling to hold it still in the wind. He leaned toward her and shouted in her ear. "We follow the thruway all the way up past Plattsburgh. We take a ferry to the Vermont side from there."

"Aye aye, sir," she said, delivered with a mock military salute.

An hour later, Plattsburgh behind them, Angela discovered this end of the lake was enchanting. She had no idea. There were numerous small, forested islands, and mountains on both sides. If the panorama was sometimes less spectacular than the Maxfield Parrish poster in her bedroom, at least it was real.

On the ferry, they leaned against the fender and soaked up the September sun. David turned to her and said, "Hey, I'm sorry about how that whole Shelter Island thing went this past summer. I was a dope, I know."

It was the last thing she expected him to say. Angela assumed he had just put it all out of his mind. Awkward as it was, she found his apology touching. It made her happy, even as it reminded her of how hurt she'd felt at the time. Most girls would let him twist in the wind for a while, but that wasn't her style, not today anyway. "Forget it. I was just disappointed."

"I know, and I'm sorry. Let's plan on taking that trip next summer. What do you think?"

"Be careful Weis," she said. "Don't make promises you can't keep." She hoped David wasn't turning into one of those guys who repeatedly let you down, then expected forgiveness. Guys like that were a pain in the ass.

For the moment though, life was close to perfect—the weather, the enchanting landscape, and the company. She slipped her arm through his and cuddled a little closer. "This might be a nice place to have a summer cottage, but you still don't have me sold on living up here."

"I think you like it more than you let on."

"Maybe," she said with a little smile. "Maybe not."

The ferry docked and the first cars rolled off onto the Vermont shore. Angela suggested he take the wheel. The rest of the ride was a groove. Jericho turned out to be a storybook village nestled at the foot of the mountains, with all the requisite features—a village green complete with gazebo, a white, steepled church, and a general store which looked as if it had been there for a hundred years.

A few miles outside of town they found the auction down a dirt road. Angela could already hear some guy with a megaphone calling out bids as they parked the car and walked onto the property. The estate was a large white farmhouse, a barn, and outbuildings. Another dairy farm gone under, she supposed.

A crowd of about a hundred people were already there, some actively bidding and others milling around, examining items yet to be placed on the block. They appeared most interested in dairy machinery and not antiques. She knew that would please David. All the while, short-haired farm boys, in jean jackets emblazoned with their chapter of Future Farmers of America, carried furniture and cartons of household goods from inside and sat them on the lawn.

This was David's territory, his world of old stuff. They started picking through ranks of wooden crates and cardboard boxes. He went a lot faster than she did. She envied David's ability to assess and judge value so dispassionately. For her, each item had to first be identified and then considered on its own merit, but he seemed to disregard almost all of what he saw. He could be like that with people too.

Twenty minutes later she noticed him up ahead, burrowing into the contents of a cardboard box. He's on the scent of something, she thought.

"What are you looking at?"

"Cased images," he said. "These are photographs from around 1840 to about the end of the Civil War."

They were bound in small leatherette containers with tiny brass latches—much the same dimensions as a cigarette case. She picked one up and opened it. The red, crushed velvet lining the inside surprised her. It even had a bright brass mat around the otherwise unimaginative, black and white portrait. "Pretty fancy. They're all like this?"

"Yeah," he said, "with variations that help to date them. Like that one you're holding. It's a glass plate image called an ambrotype. Typical of what was being done around 1860."

David took out another cased image from the box and, before handing it to her, dropped his hand, like a conductor silencing an orchestra. "This is the one I'm after," he whispered.

She opened the cover. It was a mother with a young child, supine on her lap. Tilting it back and forth, Angela remarked, "That's so weird. It's like a photograph burned into a mirror."

"Right. It's called a daguerreotype. It's a silver coated copper plate, an earlier process. It dates from about 1850 or earlier. See how the whole package is simpler, the matte, the cushion, it's all a little more primitive."

Angela tried to inspect those details, but her eyes were drawn back to the image itself. She felt as though the picture of mother and child were sucking the life from her. "David, there's something weird about this picture."

"Well, it is a post-mortem."

Confusion clouded her face. "What do you mean, a post-mortem?"

"I mean the kid on her lap is dead."

Angela glanced down. Now it was obvious. The look of grief on the mother's face and the toddler's eyes slightly open but vacant and sunken in. She slammed the case shut and pushed it back into his hand. "Okay, Dr. Frankenstein, I'm going to keep looking around. Hope you find some more pretty pictures." She walked off, shaking her head.

Bidding on the smaller items wouldn't start for another hour. There had to be something in all these cartons that wasn't such a downer. Then Angela discovered a dozen or more volumes from a children's series.

"These books are so cute," she told David when he crouched down beside her a moment later. "I love these titles. *The Motor Car Girls at Coney Island, The Motor Car Girls at the Grand Canyon, The Motor Car Girls on the Western Front.*"

As the auction proceeded, David won the bid on a pair of Art Deco lamps and the daguerreotype, along with all fourteen volumes of *The Motor Car Girls* for prices that had lots of mark-up potential.

"How much do you think you can get for those lamps?" Angela said, flipping through a book as they walked toward the car.

"About three hundred, maybe a little more. Pretty good return on an eight-dollar investment."

"And that creepy picture? What about that?"

"There's a guy I know with a shop in Albany. He likes that sort of thing. I think I can get thirty or forty from him."

"Just keep it away from me."

David smirked in that paternalistic way of his, put the car in gear, and backed up.

Angela stretched, extending her arms in a lazy letter Y. "I'm starving. Is there any place to eat around here?"

Probably not, but we're going through Burlington on the way home. We can get something there. I'm pretty hungry too."

On the outskirts of the city, they found a busy Lum's. David parked the car. She helped unfold the canopy and lock it down. Once they settled into a booth, Angela removed her sunglasses while the waitress took their order.

"Did you notice that old couple at the auction," David said. "The ones sitting in lawn chairs under the tree. I think they were the owners."

"I did notice them, yeah. They looked a little shook up. Like they were watching their whole lives being auctioned off."

David only nodded, gazing out the window.

"God," she said. "That's so sad. They seemed like a sweet old couple. They must have been married for a million years." The long arc of a marriage flashed through her mind—children, grandchildren, holidays, tragedies, and joyous homecomings.

"Well," David said, after a moment. "At least they have each other." He fiddled with the sugar packets.

"Exactly. It's nice to see an old married couple like that. Don't you think so?"

"I think it's nice to see two people who are happy together, but I doubt being married is what makes them happy. I mean, does a piece of paper make such a big difference if two people love each other? I don't think it corresponds to happiness in anyway."

"You don't think so?" Angela leaned away, eyeing him through a squint. "You don't think the legal status and all that, in-the-eyes-of-God, part matters that much?"

"No—especially if there's no God."

Later, on the road south of Burlington, Angela's mind drifted back to their conversation. The way he'd copped such a blasé and detached attitude about marriage and God had annoyed her to no end, and it was kind of aggressive. She didn't like it. Distraction was what she needed, but there was nothing on the radio. She reached behind the driver's seat and brought out the daguerreotype. In the waning summer light, she studied the stricken mother and her decomposing child. It felt ghoulish but equally difficult to resist, like the urge to stare when driving past the scene of an accident.

"How could they do that," Angela said. "Take photographs of their dead kids. It's sick."

Not unexpectedly, David had a different view. "You have to remember that photography was brand new then. I think the realization that it was possible to preserve a moment overpowered any morbid thoughts. They called it the annihilation of space and time. Until then, children who didn't survive—and there were a lot of them—would become a vague memory and fade away as years passed. The daguerreotype changed all that."

During the final leg of their journey back to Willsboro darkness fell. They grew silent, Angela lost in her own thoughts. She wondered what David could be thinking. The drone of the engine was hypnotic. The unsettling events of the previous night reasserted themselves. She was about to fall into an uneasy sleep when David posed a question.

"What would it be like if we were married?"

"Huh?" Angela perked up, taking in the sweep of the headlights on the road ahead. Had she heard him correctly?

"You know, how exactly would it work?"

She turned to face him, alert as a sentry. "It's simple. We'd be a couple. We'd live together and someday have kids."

"How many?" he said. "I'm not crazy about children."

"But you'd be crazy about *these* kids. I mean, they'd be ours. Loving them would come naturally."

David worked a thumbnail across his lower lip and stared straight ahead. "I don't know. What about the living together part? I mean, I really like it up here."

Angela could sense how uptight this topic made him. For a psychologist, David was a pretty messed up guy. Oddly, rather than being frustrated by his reclusive habits, as would ordinarily be the case, she felt pity. She knew raising these questions was a big deal for him. Maybe one or two of her own, carefully worded, could draw him out.

"How far is your place from Syracuse? I'd have my degree finished and maybe I could get a position at the university there."

"Forget that. Syracuse from Willsboro is a day's drive. It's way the hell on the other side of Albany."

"Oh." She bit her lip, considering. "That's assuming we lived in the house, but we could live somewhere else, couldn't we?"

"I don't know. I don't think so. I'm pretty attached to the property. It's not just a crash pad for me."

The house in Willsboro had a clear hold on him—she could see that. He probably loved it more than he loved her.

David smiled and patted her hand. "Okay. I'd like to be able to talk to you more about this again sometime, but I'm apt to clam up, so let's just—"

"See what happens?" Angela said, finishing his sentence for him.

"That's right, see what happens."

The drive around the lake and the sunset ferry ride had calmed her nerves. And the way David raised the question of a long-term future together allayed her insecurities. She also thought about the unsettling experience in the Quiet Room and concluded that before they left for the city, she would have to reassert her presence. After all, if she couldn't separate David from that house, then she had to make it hers too. Rooms out-of-bounds to her would only make it easier for David to isolate himself.

Returning to the Quiet Room alone would take courage, but she knew it was absolutely necessary. The following morning David was outside, getting the car ready, the sun already peeking over the trees. She went up the back stairs and found herself standing at the door to the Quiet Room. She hesitated, hand on the latch. It was hard to imagine having felt so frightened the last time she was here. She stepped into the room. Except for the unusual, stenciled walls, it was just one of many empty rooms in the big house. And any trace of what was there last night was gone.

Angela stepped inside. The trunk caught her attention immediately. She'd noticed it before but hadn't given it much thought. Presumably, David picked it up on one of his antiquing trips. Or had he found it in the house?

Her nostrils flared imperceptibly, like a deer alert to danger. Kneeling, she had a premonition that whatever was inside would introduce another uncontrollable element in their already complicated relationship. She took the heavy brass lock in her hand and lifted it from the hasp, then pulled the top of the trunk back on its hinge.

The contents weren't surprising at first. It was just an old trunk packed with very old things. She was relieved, but digging deeper, realized there was more to the collection than met the eye. Scanning the items, she noticed a dried twig, clothing, a couple of large, old-fashioned hair combs, books, and what Angela now recognized as a cased photograph.

It was free of dust, as if it had recently been wiped clean. Angela picked it up and unlatched the tiny brass hooks. What she saw inside made her catch her breath. The image was of a young woman, the same young woman with whom she'd come face to face. This time seated, the young woman wore a plaid dress and bonnet. Angela was sure from the way the photograph reflected daylight that it was what David had called a daguerreotype. But unlike the one at the auction, this image seemed so deep and lucid as to invite her in. There was even a hint of color to the flowers in her bonnet.

Studying the face, Angela felt the same sense of desperate loneliness as before. The hairs on her neck stood at attention. *She's pretty, but she doesn't seem happy.* The poor girl, whoever she was, was posed as if facing the whole world rushing at her. It seemed to Angela that something terrible had happened to her.

The downstairs screen door slammed. David. Angela closed the case, returned it to the trunk, lowered the lid, and hurried downstairs.

"Hey," she said as she reached the kitchen. "I was just checking that I didn't forget anything."

Chapter 6

September, 1841

A fortnight since her arrival at the Albany Female Academy, and already there were secrets for Almira to keep—her love affair with Daniel, her knowledge that he was in the city, what they'd done on their last night together in Willsborough, and how they'd pledged themselves to each other under a shooting star.

The elation of her chance meeting with Daniel was still with her, brightening each morning with the chance of another encounter. Almira took secret pride in having told him all about Sarah and Ezra Rawson in Whitehall. How clever of her, for now Daniel could secret letters to her within Sarah's correspondence. Most of all, Almira hoped that she and Daniel would soon cross paths again since she took the same route to and from the academy every day.

Almira could hardly think of a time when she'd been happier. Aside from her relationship with Daniel, life at the boarding house agreed with her. Every morning she was awakened by a housemaid's light knock at the bedroom door. She and Emily rose immediately, going in turns to the water closet, and then return to begin their toilet. They would tighten the laces of each other's stays and fasten the hooks and eyes of the other's chosen dress for the day. On most mornings, Emily would turn her attention to reading a passage from her bible. Almira preferred to devote extra attention to her hair.

A structured schedule was, judging by her unusually strong appetite, a healthy regimen. Inspecting her corseted profile in the mirror, Almira noticed an unmistakable womanly fullness to her girlish figure. It pleased her.

At the breakfast table, there were lively dialogues with her classmates sharing expectations for the day's academics. In French class, lessons in letter writing commenced. Algebra still confounded her, and a series of special lectures on the science of phrenology were delivered by the popular young Professor Horsford.

Another week passed. On Saturday, Almira, Emily, Rebecca, and Susannah ambled to Broadway where they spent the afternoon shopping. The girls admired a fine display of fur muffs, and Almira found some plaid ribbon she had to have for her bonnet. They stopped at a stationers, then made their way to a bookstore and browsed the shelves where, turning pages, they traded comments on the fiction of the day. Almira would have liked to have found a new novel, but there was one left unread in her trunk and no time to read novels now.

"Look," called Susannah to the others. "Autograph books. Aren't these so pretty?"

She held up a red leather-bound volume, about six inches square, with the words *Mossrose Album* and a flower embossed in gold on the cover.

Rebecca clapped her hands. "We ought each to buy one. Then we'll always remember this day."

"I'd love to," said Almira. "But I've already spent too much on ribbon and peppermint candy. With ink and pen nibs, I'll have spent most of my monthly allowance."

Rebecca took the album from her hand. "Don't fuss now. This will be my gift to you."

"I couldn't. That's too generous, really."

"No, I insist," said Rebecca. Her large black eyes brooked no resistance. "You wouldn't want to refuse me this pleasure, would you?" Back at the boarding house, a pair of envelopes sat waiting on Almira's bureau. She snatched them up and glanced at the return addresses. One was from her father and Loretta. The other was from Sarah Rawson.

"News from a friend?" Emily had slipped quietly into the room behind her.

"I think so. It's from my friend in Whitehall, the one I met on the packet boat this summer."

In her last letter, Almira had shared the recent, upsetting events in her life: the terrible argument with her father and Daniel's dismissal from the household. Desperate for advice from her older, more experienced friend, she tore open the envelope, sat down on her bed, and started reading. Sarah began her letter by announcing that she was pregnant with Ezra's child and how happy they were to start a family.

Next, she turned to Almira's troubles. Sarah counseled that all families have their squabbles, that her father was a good man, if strong willed as many good men are, and that time would surely heal the rift between them. As far as Daniel was concerned, Sarah wrote, "Do not lose heart, my dear friend. If love is true, it will find its way."

Then Almira read something that made her heart leap. "Late last month, Mr. D passed through Whitehall and spoke to us. He asked that I allow him to communicate with you through our letters, to which I agreed. In any case, I did receive the enclosed note from him yesterday."

She unfolded a hastily written message on what was no more than a scrap of paper, but the news was monumental.

"My dearest Almira. I am boarding in Albany at the Temperance House on Hudson Street and have obtained a situation in Horsford & Cushman's Daguerreian Gallery. I can be found there most days of the week."

Almira gasped in delight.

Emily, who was reading her own correspondence, looked up from her letter. "Mirie, is everything all right?"

"Yes," she said. "Everything is absolutely, utterly, wonderfully all right."

After she'd read the letter a half dozen times, Almira sat, biting her lower lip, ruminating over the letter's implications. Danny was already working as a daguerreotype artist. He would soon have father's approval and respect. He could court her openly, and she could entertain him in Mrs. Bright's parlor on Sunday afternoons. Maybe they could go, with a chaperone of course, to one of the balls her classmates talked about. Let the other girls go on about their beaus at home. Soon they would be talking about her and Daniel.

But how was this supposed to happen with so much of her life supervised and controlled? Almira enjoyed being at the academy, but it was impossible to be out alone. No matter. She somehow had to arrange a way for her and Daniel to meet. First of all, it would have to be under conditions Mrs. Bright would condone and which would not seem contrived. Something that wouldn't attract the censure of the academy or the premature attention of her father. Almira's mind raced. Fighting the impulse to throw on her bonnet and run to Horsford & Cushman's gallery, the solution dawned on her.

The following evening, most of Mrs. Bright's girls were gathered in the parlor, signing names and sincere sentiments into their new autograph books. As Almira finished another inscription, she said, "While we were shopping last Saturday, did anyone notice the daguerreotype gallery?" The question was directed to no one in particular, but its intention was pointed as a needle.

"I certainly did," said Susannah. "I should love to have my miniature made someday."

"Us too," the Skinner twins said in unison.

Rebecca, who was well traveled, commented that she'd seen a

daguerreotype. "I must say, it was amazing. Just like a looking glass, except that someone else was staring back. I would gladly sit for my miniature if given the chance."

"All of you should," Almira said. "It's such fun."

All heads in the room turned toward her.

"You have had your miniature taken? When?" asked Harriet.

"Yes, here in Albany this past summer."

Harriet pursed her lips and cast her eyes down.

"I can assure you Harriet, it is not the least bit painful or a terrible inconvenience, unless one considers the cost. It is expensive."

"And how much does it cost?"

"Three or four dollars, I think, though I don't well remember. Father told me that if he was always able to see my likeness, the cost was inconsequential. Wasn't that sweet of him?"

The twins sighed. Emboldened, Almira embellished the lie.

"My stepmother's cousin lives in Baltimore. Their daughter attends a very fine school there. Well, according to her all the smartest girls are crazy over sitting for miniatures. Some do it with their friends as a memento. Can you imagine that?"

A gleaming Chinese teapot on the sideboard drew Harriet's attention. "I've made up my mind," she announced, as she poured herself a fresh cup. "Expensive or not, I know my parents would want a portrait of me too."

The Skinner girls looked at each other. "We have to go. We could sit for our image together."

Harriet proposed a plan. "I think we should go as soon as we can, first thing Friday at the conclusion of classes."

Emily reached for her autograph book. "Yes, it would be fun to have our miniatures made, but at three dollars apiece, it's far too expensive for me."

The Skinner girls were beside themselves with excitement, pleading, "Please Emily, Mrs. Bright won't let us go alone, but she trusts you, you're the oldest."

Emily relented with the hint of a smile. "Very well, I will ask her and go along if she has no objection, but don't expect me to spend money on this vanity."

There followed a discussion about what clothing to wear, how they would set their hair, and whether it would be better to pose with or without a bonnet. As the only one in the room who'd ever had her daguerreotype taken, Almira was regarded as something of an expert and enjoyed the prestige that came with that distinction.

"Now you will come with us, won't you Miss Mirie?" Rebecca said. "You have been there. You are our Indian guide."

Almira couldn't believe she'd managed to bend them to her will so easily, yet she dared not betray her excitement. "If you insist," she said. "Yes, I suppose I could tag along."

At the end of the week, Almira, Emily, Harriet, and Rebecca hurried back from the academy, changed into their finest dresses, and prepared to leave for the studio. Mrs. Bright had told Susannah, Betty, and the twins that they were too young to go. Phebe stayed behind too, explaining that she'd already had her portrait painted on ivory by the artist, Mr. Mount of Stony Brook.

As they left, the crestfallen younger girls loitered about the parlor, sullen and restless. The Skinner twins voiced their opinion that Mrs. Bright was being terribly unfair, while Susannah said, "I shall write to my mother and father. They will give their permission, and then Mrs. Bright must let me go."

A short carriage ride later, Almira led her friends up the stairway to Horsford & Cushman's top floor gallery. Even from the first landing, the familiar chemical odor evoked memories of her first visit to Albany. How much had changed since then. Immediately upon entering the showroom, she searched for Daniel. He was at the counter, writing out a receipt for a middle-aged couple. The woman's attention was fixed on the daguerreotype in her hands.

"If only we didn't look so stern, dear, it would be our perfect likeness."

"Madam, the serious expression will be seen as poised reserve," said Daniel. A look of recognition flickered in his eyes as Almira raised her chin slightly, standing among other girls in the anteroom. "If the ladies will have a seat, I'll help you directly."

The man shook Daniel's hand, declaring that the daguerreotype was, in his view, top drawer, altogether satisfactory.

With the couple gone, Daniel turned to the academy girls. "Welcome to Horsford and Cushman's Portrait Studio," he said. "I am Mr. Dwyer. How may I serve you?"

Harriet stepped forward at once and spoke. "I am Miss Ames, and I would have my likeness made."

"Excellent. And will the rest of the ladies be sitting for their portraits as well?"

Emily was still of the opinion that the whole idea was a frivolous expense, but Rebecca begged to differ, excited by the prospect of seeing her image etched into silver. "I'll sit for mine please," she said. "Mirie, you to."

"I'd love to, but my likeness was taken in this very studio last summer."

"Then," said Daniel, "I trust your daguerreotype portrait has been roundly admired. The camera cannot lie in the face of beauty."

Almira blushed. Harriet cut a glance in her direction, then interrupted. "Be that as it may, you will please explain your services sir."

While Daniel described details of the daguerreotype process to Harriet and Rebecca, Emily and Almira retired to one of the settees. The two made small talk. All the while, Almira observed Daniel closely.

He had cut his hair shorter than she'd ever remember seeing, but nicely combed with a bit of mascar oil. Except for his usual checkered waistcoat, her young man wore new clothes, new to him anyway. The brown woolen tailcoat was worn thin at the cuffs and elbows, but the broadcloth was nicely brushed, and the brass buttons were polished. He sported a white silk cravat, which looked new, as were his hounds-tooth trousers. Most surprising were his leather pumps. She'd never seen him so nicely dressed. At home, Daniel had always worn a workman's attire of jean cloth and heavy boots. It pleased her to find gentlemanly clothes sat naturally on him.

After a few minutes, Rebecca took him by the arm as he led her up to the roof where the artist was waiting with his camera. Harriet walked across the showroom to the settee. "I could tell Mr. Dwyer wants more time to consider how I should be posed, so naturally I let Rebecca be first. Besides, she's so excited to be sitting for her portrait, I don't think I could have held her back."

"It is exciting," Almira said.

"Indeed, it is," said Harriet. "And what do you think of Mr. Dwyer? He has a kind of rugged good looks, don't you think? I've half a mind to make him my next conquest."

Almira's dander rose but with Emily carrying the conversation, she said nothing and drifted off to view the sample daguerreotypes on the wall. Examining the largest one, a view of Broadway, apparently taken from the rooftop or an upper floor window, she noticed something strange. The street was completely, utterly deserted.

Daniel came down the stairs and entered the showroom. Almira looked his way and braved the briefest of smiles. Stepping up beside her, he cleared his throat. "You find this daguerreotype interesting, miss?"

"I do, very much so," she said. "But can you tell me why there is no one, not even a single carriage, on the street?"

"It is because the camera is unable to capture moving objects as they pass."

"Is that so?"

"Yes. On sunny days the sensitized plate must be exposed to light for nearly a minute. Anything moving across the lens in less time isn't recorded."

Though she already knew many of the answers, Almira posed a

few more questions. They chatted amiably for another minute, then he inquired, "May I ask your name, miss?"

"I am Miss Almira Hamilton of Willsborough, in Essex County."

"Daniel Dwyer. It is a pleasure, Miss Hamilton, to make your acquaint-ance."

The entire conversation was, of course, a sham, staged for the benefit of Almira's schoolmates. The performance wasn't wasted, at least on Harriet, who observed the pair with keen interest. She rose and inserted herself between them.

"Mr. Dwyer," she said, "are you sure that this miniature will agree with my unusually fair complexion and Titian curls?"

Daniel assured her that the process would be complimentary, and accurate to nature.

Harriet fluttered her lashes. "And the color of my eyes, will they be appreciated?"

Almira's face twitched with rage. She would have scratched out those eyes, whatever their color, if only she could. Fortunately, Rebecca returned with Mr. Meade and distracted everyone.

"Did your sitting go well?" Almira said.

"I wasn't allowed to move one itty bitty bit. I had to be just like a statue, but Mr. Meade said I was his most perfect subject. Now I'm positively beside myself with suspense."

"Well, go I must," said Harriet, who whirled around, snatched Meade's arm, and pulled him through the doorway, leaving the others behind.

"Come." Emily patted the settee cushion. "Sit here with me and tell me all about it."

Almira remained standing with Daniel. "Mr. Cushman was not the artist?"

"No, Mr. Cushman is sometimes indisposed," said Daniel.

The two went to the opposite end of the showroom. There was a window there. The clamor of wagons and pedestrians wafting up from the street below would allow them a chance to talk with a modicum of privacy. Daniel asked about her classes. She described her school until Daniel stopped her.

"I've got to go. I have to develop your friend's image," he said and, with a kiss on her hand, he was gone.

Almira took a seat near Rebecca and Emily. As she listened to their conversation her head swam and her heart burst with pride at having seen Daniel at work in a daguerreotype gallery. He was learning the profession and growing into the respectable gentleman she always knew him to be.

Presently, Harriet returned. "Well, Mr. Meade was ever so mindful of my exact posture," Harriet said. "I know he wanted to pay special attention to every detail."

After a short while, Daniel returned to the counter with two finished daguerreotypes set in cases of red Morocco leather. When the girls rushed to the counter, Almira took the opportunity to tuck one of her gloves between the cushions of the settee.

Presented for their inspection, the daguerreotypes were indeed true miniatures of their subjects in every detail. Even Emily was impressed. For her portrait, Rebecca paid in silver coin, but Harriet made a show of producing a gold-piece from her silk-knitted miser's purse.

Once the receipts were written, they bade Mr. Dwyer farewell and started back down the staircase. In light of the substantial expense they had incurred, Emily suggested they abandon hiring a carriage and walk back to Maiden Lane. Rebecca readily agreed. Even Harriet, who may have realized she'd just spent what amounted to a week's wages for most working men, agreed to a token effort at thrift.

Almira stopped dead in her tracks. "Wait, I think I've forgotten one of my gloves. I'll go fetch it. Please wait here."

Rebecca reached for Almira's arm. "I'll go with you."

"No, no." Almira was already pulling free and stepping away. "I'll be right back. Wait for me here."

"All right then, Mirie, but do hurry up." Harriet narrowed her eyes but made a show of nonchalance.

In a flash she was back in the stairwell, skirts gathered in her fists and ascending the steps two at a time. Along the way, Almira passed the well-dressed man as he descended. That was good. It meant there might not be any other customers in the gallery. She burst through the showroom door and flew into Daniel's arms.

Face to face, they held each other's hands. "Mirie," said Daniel. "I can't believe you're here and we're together, at least for a moment."

"Miss Ames behaved scandalously. I can't–"

He pressed a finger to her lips. "Never mind her. Mr. Meade will be back any second. I'll speak quickly. You must have gotten the note I sent to Sarah Rawson?"

"I did."

"Good. Then you know I'm boarding at the Hudson Street Temperance House. If you need to, you can write to me there. I work nights at a livery stable on Steuben Street, but you can always leave a message where I board. It's hard to believe I'm learning to make daguerreotypes, but I am."

Barely able to conceal her excitement, Almira said, "Danny, I'm so proud of you. Everything's going to be wonderful, isn't it?"

"It is," he said. "When I first came here, Mr. Cushman told me right off he had no need for another uneducated Irishman. He was about to throw me out. There weren't any customers, so I started shouting out each of the steps in the process and the names of the chemicals. See, I memorized it all from reading your father's newspapers. Professor Horsford must have heard me. He came out from the back room, bless his heart. He told Cushman it would be better to hire me than have me become competition. Now Mr. Cushman quite likes me, and he's showing me how to make daguerreotypes. Anyway, Mr. Cushman isn't in good health. So that means most days his assistant, that Englishman, Meade, is exposing the plates while I help prepare them for the camera and take care of the customers."

Someone called to Daniel from upstairs.

"Just a minute, sir," said Daniel over his shoulder. He turned back to Almira. "Listen, I read in the paper that there's going to be some kind of celebration in front of the statehouse this Sunday. I'll be there. Can you be there too?"

"I don't know. I can try."

"If you get away, we can be together for a little while. There'll be lots of people around, but we'll just make believe we're new friends. No one will know better."

Daniel paused. She looked into his eyes—the bluest she'd ever seen—and marveled at the course her life had taken.

"Mirie, how I love you," said Daniel. He kissed her hands and then kissed her again full on the mouth. "I know you have to leave. Just remember, try to meet me Sunday and write to me at the Hudson Street Temperance House."

Almira threw her arms around his neck and they kissed again.

"Dwyer, where are you!"

"I can't wait to be your wife," she whispered in his ear.

Almira was nearly out the door when he called after her, "Miss, you've forgotten your glove."

Chapter 7

September, 1971

On this first chilly night of autumn, David found himself in a session with Miss Hamilton in her sitting room. It didn't seem much like psychotherapy to him. Keeping a clinical perspective was wearing, and by now he wasn't even bothering to take notes.

Instead, their conversation wandered among the pleasantries of music and literature. She embroidered while he passed the time watching the movements of her hands and eyes, admiring the graceful curve of her coral encircled neck. Her mannerisms and voice soothed him, the archaic phrasing of her speech he found so endearing. David studied each of these things individually and together.

Even if Almira's personal story was troubled, her world of intact ideals was refreshing. Think of it, a time before cynicism was fashionable. Becoming part of her world and leaving this one behind was a fleeting temptation. David felt a chill cut through him.

"I can see you very clearly tonight," Almira said, casting a furtive glance his way.

David smiled. "Is that good?"

"I think it is, and though I do not quite understand where you come from, doctor, I do so enjoy our visits."

Her frankness stunned him. His heart jumped in his chest—desire at war with decorum. But above all, he didn't want to call attention to his arousal, so he played it cool. "I do too. I enjoy our talks very much."

Almira pressed her lips together. He waited as she worried the inside of her cheek with her tongue. "Might I ask of you a personal question?" she said.

"Sure. Go ahead."

"Have you someone to converse with, as I do with you?"

The question was clinically important. Almira hadn't shown any interest in his life before. Doing so would have been impossible without disturbing her protective curtain of denial.

Experience had taught David that acknowledging her misplacement from conventional reality caused her to dematerialize. This, he believed, was because the dissonance made her manifestation too difficult to sustain. As long as Almira remained immersed in her own time, reminiscing, reading, writing letters, or sewing, she seemed calm and most concrete. Did her question mean she was coming to accept his reality and, with it, her own failure to pass on?

"Yes," he said. "I do have someone whom I talk to."

Almira pulled a length of yellow floss through her needlework. "Would it be improper of me to presume this is a lady? Is she a special friend?"

"I would say she is, yes."

"Is this the lady who has been here?"

David froze. "You know about her?"

"She has been in this room, I have...sensed her. Sometimes she is with you, but not always."

"Do you mean you've met her?" David said, his fingernails skewering the palms of his hands.

For a moment Almira sat, letting her head sway from side to side. "No, not as you and I visit. But I know of her."

The very idea set off alarm bells in his head. David liked to keep friendships compartmentalized. They were easier to control that way. Certainly, he didn't want to share Almira with anyone—especially Angela.

She reset her needle and pulled it through, the slightest curl of smile on her lips. "This lady, she cannot be as engaging as I am. That should be quite impossible."

David's face flushed with a surge of excitement. The thought that Almira had developed a romantic interest in him, however innocent, was more appealing than he wanted to admit. Keep it professional, stay focused, he reminded himself.

Comparisons were unavoidable. Angela was more educated and almost certainly more intelligent. She had the ambition, the earthy awareness, and the appetites of a man. This made her bold in bed, unafraid to ask for what she wanted, though this often came at the sacrifice of her sweeter qualities.

Almira spoke, shaking him free of his thoughts. "Are the two of you betrothed?"

David flinched. "No. Not exactly."

"And why not? Aren't you in love with her?"

"I might be, I don't know."

"Forgive me, Doctor Weis, I am prying into your personal affairs. It is indiscrete of me to ask these questions."

I don't mind," he said. "But in return, can I ask about you and Daniel?"

Her brow furrowed, her laughing eyes gone suddenly guarded. "That," said Almira, poking the divan cushion with her needle over and over, "is something I am obliged to keep confidential."

"Sure, that's all right. But I do want you to understand that all our conversations are private. Nothing we say here ever leaves this room. Not a word. Ever."

47

Almira looked up. "Like me?"

David kicked himself for the lapse. "I'm sorry. I didn't mean it that way."

"It doesn't matter, Dr. Weis," said Almira. She resumed embroidering the braces which never seemed to reach completion. "There are so many secrets to keep."

David yawned into the receiver, and not for the first time in this conversation.

"Honey, you sound exhausted," said Angela. "How about if I call you back on Thursday?"

He stifled another yawn and rubbed a hand across his face, noticing the kitchen table could use wiping. "I'm sorry, I haven't been getting much sleep lately."

"Is there something on your mind?"

"Just, I don't know, preoccupied I guess."

No sooner had he spoken before David knew he'd said too much. If he wasn't careful, she'd unravel his story. Angela had a talent for intuiting these things.

"Somethings bothering you," she pressed.

"No, of course not," David said. He sounded guilty. Angela must already smell blood.

Footsteps. It sounded like Angela was pacing back and forth in her apartment. He pictured the receiver clamped between her head and shoulder, heard the strike of a match, the crackle of a cigarette, imagined her extinguishing the flame with a flick of a wrist.

"David, what's going on? You've been kind of secretive for the last few months. Is there something I ought to know about?"

"No."

"Don't lie to me, Weis, I'm smarter than you think. So, is there something I ought to know about?"

There was no putting her off once she wanted an answer. She'd drag it out of him eventually. In a way, he was glad.

"Well, it's hard to explain," he said at last.

"Try me."

"I don't think you'd believe me if I told you."

"Look," said Angela, "is there someone else?"

"No, not exactly. No."

"Come on David. *Not exactly* is a lousy answer to that question. Don't play psychologist head games with me. Be honest. I'm a big girl. I can take it."

David weighed his options. He'd been well trained to refrain from conversations about patients. But Almira had been dead for over a hundred years, and so was everyone who ever knew her. Confidentiality was moot. He took a deep breath and said, "Okay, get ready for this. I've been talking to a ghost—therapeutically, I mean."

"A ghost?" she said. "You're putting me on, right?"

"No."

David thought he detected a note of relief in her voice. He certainly felt that way. For a long time now, he'd wanted to talk to her about it. But because Almira was both supernatural and at least technically a patient, he'd always felt reluctant to do so. Now it was out.

"Alright," Angela said. "I never told you this, but I was up in your museum room one morning when the sun was coming up. You were still asleep. I was trying to do yoga, but I kept getting this weird vibe like I was being watched. Then I saw someone. It scared the hell out of me. I mean it freaked me out."

"Yes, that would be her."

"So, you're not kidding."

"I'm not kidding."

"And you're not scared?"

"No, it doesn't bother me," he said. "In fact, I sort of like it."

"Okay, who is this ghost you're talking to?"

"Well..." David took two deep breaths and closed his eyes. "...I think it's the ghost of a girl who used to live here. For some reason, she's unwilling or unable to leave. She's not a very happy person."

"You have conversations with this girl? Do you know her name? How old is she?"

"She calls herself Miss Hamilton. I think she's nineteen or twenty, something like that. Pretty young anyway."

Another mistake. Details would only peek Angela's curiosity.

"And you can see her?"

"Oh yeah. It's quite remarkable."

"What does she look like?"

Oddly, David relaxed. It felt good to get this off his chest, even if it opened a world of complications.

"Dark hair, very well dressed. Pleasant features. Kind of attractive, actually."

"And you talk about what?" Angela said.

"Things in her life, or her after-life—as the case may be. She's depressed and confused. I'd even say she is having a dissociative reaction—except I don't think that diagnosis applies in this situation. Anyway, it's pretty interesting from a clinical perspective."

"And she just appears?"

"Only in the one room," David said.

"Your museum room, right?"

David frowned. "Yeah, the Quiet Room. That's the place. If you've seen her too, why didn't you say anything?"

"I could say the same."

Silence landed like a hammer. David felt the goodwill of confession evaporate. After many minutes, Angela spoke, her voice that of an interrogating cop.

"So, you're dead on your feet because you're up all night doing psychotherapy with a dead chick?"

"Well, she's troubled, Angie. She needs help."

Ignoring him, Angela continued her line of inquiry. "This ghost, she writes you a check, or does she carry some kind of ghost insurance?"

"Come on, it's not funny. I feel really bad for her."

"Oh. My. God."

"What?"

"You're in love with her, aren't you?"

"No, no," David said, too quickly he realized too late. "Don't be ridiculous."

"Ridiculous? Come on, David. She's young. She's fascinating. She's beautiful. She's tragic. She's the perfect answer to your classic rescue fantasies."

God, Angela's good. She should have gone into psychology—or the law.

"Well?"

"Stop it," he said, hoping to pull the ripcord on the conversation.

"David, I'm serious. This kind of stuff has gotten you in trouble before."

"Look, this is different. I'm not in love with her." He noticed he was on his feet pacing the length of the kitchen but couldn't remember standing up.

"Don't bullshit me, or yourself for that matter."

"Believe me, I'm not bullshitting you or anybody else."

"Well," Angela said, "at least she's already dead."

After a curt goodnight, David leaned against the wall for a moment. His heart raced with the realization of what he'd just revealed. Almira had become the principal catalyst in his life. If he were honest, he'd admit that everything was secondary to her and being with her.

He needed to retreat. The desk was where David felt safe, most at ease, but before leaving the kitchen, he poured a tumbler of Slivovitz. Moments later, slumped in his office chair, he sipped his drink and tried to quiet his mind. On the wall above the typewriter hung Almira's memorial. He regarded the depictions of black silk, white marble, and weeping willows. *Gone but not forgotten.* The iconography of mourning helped focus his thoughts.

Balancing Almira and Angela, reconciling the temporal and

51

the spiritual, had suddenly gotten much harder. He couldn't afford to lose control of his life as had happened before. Last time, it cost David his psychology career. If he screwed things up again, he'd lose more—the business, the house, Angela. He would wind up teaching at a junior college somewhere. All over something supernatural—or quite possibly a figment of his imagination.

The Slivovitz kicked in, calming his nerves, rounding the jagged edges. Perhaps the conversation with Angela hadn't gone so badly. Really, it felt good for once to be forthcoming about the Almira situation. Trying to act like there was no one else in the house occupying his attention was wearing and phony, and David didn't like it.

He got up to refresh his drink. On the way back to his desk, the urge arose to update his clinical notes. He made a detour to the magazine where he'd hidden them.

Notes in hand, David sat and took a long drink. He clicked his pen and started jotting ideas onto paper as quickly as they came to mind.

I can't comprehend the nature of these apparitions. Patient seems physically real. Brings with her objects as well. Whenever in the Quiet Room, entire interior comes alive too.

Empty whale oil lamps give off light. The fire in the hearth gives off no heat. Nothing more than a visual representation of flame? The colors of the frescoes are brighter when she is near to them—as if recently painted. Objects Almira handles appear solid, including the daybed she sits on. Ghost furniture?

There is a dream-like quality to these sessions. Hours pass without being aware of the passage of time. Example: Almira might appear at one a.m., and after what seems like a thirty-minute conversation, I discover the sun rising. My perception of time is grossly distorted. Is the Quiet Room a parallel reality in which time flows at a different rate? How does that happen? How does she do that?

Chapter 8

September to October, 1841

The bustling city of Albany hummed around her, but Almira's mind whirled with excitement. Except for the shameless way Harriet had behaved, her plan had gone perfectly. On Sunday, she and Daniel would be together again, openly and as friends. Arm-in-arm with Rebecca, they lagged behind to avoid Harriet's irritating babble.

"What's it like there, where you're from in South Carolina?" she said.

After a moment or two, Rebecca said, "Well, our part of South Carolina is known as the low-country. It's flat land with rice plantations. It's very warm in summer, and we rarely see snow even in the coldest month. Did you know we call it Yankee cotton?"

Almira laughed and tried to imagine a winter without snow. Crude woodcuts of palm trees in the Sandwich Islands came to mind.

"My family doesn't have a plantation," said Rebecca, who seemed pleased to have been asked to share details of her life. "Daddy is a cotton and rice broker, so we live in Charleston. It's a beautiful city, with white houses and flowers all year round." She paused as if carefully considering how much to disclose. "There are many people of my background there. We've been there since before the revolution, so as you might imagine, I have a good-many cousins."

What an unusual remark, thought Almira. Another mysterious allusion among many, but before she could ask just what was meant by *her background*, Rebecca changed the subject.

"Well, Mirie, it seems to me that whenever you're around that young daguerreotyper, you can't hold on to your gloves."

"What do you mean?"

"Wasn't Mr. Dwyer the same gentleman who found your glove a few weeks past? You remember. We were on the way home from school."

Almira's eyes flashed a panicked glance at her friend. "Please Rebecca. If anyone hears about—"

"Don't fret yourself. The other girls didn't notice, and my lips are sealed. But now, in payment, you must tell me who he is."

At breakfast, Almira asked if anyone had heard about a celebration at the statehouse planned for Sunday.

"That is our city's annual commemoration of the Battle of Saratoga. It is quite an event," said Mrs. Bright.

Predictably, the Skinner sisters asked if the boarding house girls couldn't all go. Betty Wheeler and Susie Platt joined the chorus. Almira quickly added that she thought it was an excellent idea.

"Very well," said Mrs. Bright. "If the weather is nice, we shall all go and make a picnic of it."

So it was that after church on Sunday, the four younger girls, as well as Phebe, Harriet, Rebecca, and Almira, all shepherded by Mrs. Bright, made their way up State Street in a hired carriage. Disembarking near the capitol building, they made their way across the park. The housemaids Tildie and Rose brought up the rear, carrying picnic baskets and a folding camp stool for Mrs. Bright.

A reviewing stand had been erected on the grounds in front of the statehouse, decorated with a portrait of George Washington, and draped with red, white, and blue bunting. Nearby, a brass band played "Hail Columbia." A crowd of over a thousand had already gathered. Gentlemen and ladies of all ages made themselves comfortable on blankets or stood in small groups.

The weather was superb, the temperature just right for fine merino shawls. Rose spread two large blankets on the ground beneath a sugar maple in the first blush of autumn display. Once everyone had settled themselves, Mrs. Bright asked Tildie to open the basket and set out the fried chicken, pickles, and an apple pie.

Hoping to be visible from a distance, Almira kept her parasol folded. Rebecca nudged her.

"Isn't that your young man?"

Almira had only just spotted Daniel making his way toward them when Harriett sprang to her feet, waving a handkerchief and calling, "Oh yoo-hoo, Mr. Dwyer, it's us ladies from the academy."

As he drew close, she ran to meet him, linked her arm with his, and escorted him to the picnic. Seeing them walking together, Almira suffered a wave of jealousy. *He ought to be walking with me, not with that brazen hussy.*

"Mrs. Bright, may I introduce Mr. Dwyer. It was he who prepared our miniatures last Friday."

Doffing his top hat, Daniel bowed to the matron and kissed her hand.

"You are the miniaturist?" she said.

"No ma'am," Daniel said. "I'm afraid that I am still learning the art under Mr. Cushman's guidance."

"Well, the likenesses are indeed striking, young man. You are evidently learning from a master."

Rebecca patted the blanket between her and Almira. "Mr. Dwyer, do sit here between us."

Daniel looked for Mrs. Bright's permission, which was granted with a nod.

After taking a seat, Daniel said to the matron, "One of the gentlemen teaching me the photographic process is from the academy."

Mrs. Bright, her curiosity piqued perhaps, said "Our Albany Female Academy?"

"Yes," said Daniel. "Professor Horsford. He and Mr. Cushman are partners in the art of the daguerreotype."

"Professor Horsford, why he's my professor of natural philosophy, and quite a gentleman," Rebecca said.

Almira saw an opportunity to reassert herself. "All of us from the academy are well acquainted with Professor Horsford. He's a great favorite among us girls."

Mrs. Bright laid a finger to her chin. "It is a small world," she said, almost to herself. Looking up, she added, "I remember seeing notices in the newspaper for their public lectures, though I admit, I did not attend. To be truthful, I thought the daguerreotype a lark, but I can now see it is more than that. Professor Horsford is a much-respected gentleman at the school. I doubt he would be involved in something silly. So, you know the professor then?"

"A little, yes," said Daniel. "I've helped prepare and process experimental plates with him and Mr. Cushman."

"Experimental plates?"

"Yes, the daguerreotype is a sensitive and complicated procedure. There is much trial and error involved in its perfection."

It was only with difficulty that Almira kept her pride hidden. The band stopped playing. A gentleman standing on the platform announced that the citizens of Albany would now see a demonstration by the Emmitt Guards. Almira leaned in toward Daniel and whispered, "That is a very nice beaver hat you're wearing."

"Thank you. It's borrowed from Mr. Meade," Daniel said under his breath.

The crowd parted as a formation of perhaps sixty men advanced in close order, firelocks balanced vertically against their shoulders, blue uniforms with many buttons, smartly trimmed in yellow worsted lace.

There was scattered applause for the militia as it deployed into a line of battle. Bayonets were fixed. A series of choreographed movements with arms were demonstrated. The Emmitt Guards loaded their muskets with blank charges and fired a volley into the air. The crowd was delighted, girls jumped, men clapped, boys cheered, and more than one baby wailed. A cloud of sulfurous black powder smoke spread across the park, and tufts of wadding lay smoldering in the grass.

When the mayor of Albany rose to address the crowd, Daniel saw an opportunity and requested Mrs. Bright's permission to escort the misses Hamilton and Carvalho about the grounds. The three rose quickly, making their escape before the mayor's speech got underway.

As they sauntered off, Phebe remarked that Mr. Dwyer seemed a very nice young man. "His acquaintance with Professor Horsford speaks very well of him."

"It does, at that," said Mrs. Bright.

As the mayor's address commenced, the trio strolled along the perimeter of the festivities. Beneath a chestnut tree, an old woman sold cockades of red, white, and blue ribbon for a penny. Daniel bought one for each of the girls, which they pinned to each other's dresses.

Rebecca whispered into Almira's ear and they struck a tableau vivant—balanced on one foot while crossing their folded parasols high, like swords. "Saratoga and Victory," they proclaimed in unison. "Let's give the haughty British their due!"

Daniel clapped his hands. "Bravo. Aren't you a couple of good American girls."

"We are, we are," sang the pair.

Exuding a sense of frolic, they drifted to the far side of the statehouse where it was much quieter.

Turning to Rebecca, Daniel said, "You know, Mr. Meade was quite taken with you and your southern ways."

"Was he then?"

"Oh yes, I could tell he was smitten. You were all he would talk about after we closed the gallery that night."

Rebecca looked away, a smile on her lips. After a beat, she turned to Daniel and said, "Mirie tells me you and she are special friends, is that true?"

Daniel flashed his sweetheart the terrified glance of a man exposed.

"It's all right. Rebecca is my friend. We share each other's secrets, and she knows we are in love. You can trust her."

"Well, it is true," Daniel said. "Almira and I are together, and have been, though it's better for the present if that cat stays in the bag."

"I understand completely. You two go ahead without me," she said with a sweep of her hand. "Go on now, be off. I'll catch up in a little while."

Grateful for privacy, Daniel and Almira walked to a park bench where they sat, knees touching. The chance to spend unsupervised time together was a found treasure.

"I think Rebecca and I are already just like sisters," said Almira.

"She's a lively girl."

"Ah, the great game of love." She sighed, closing her eyes and lifting her face to the sun. "Isn't it superb?"

Happy just to be together again, Almira and Daniel listened to the distant sounds of martial music and people applauding from beyond the statehouse. A breeze rustled the leaves above them.

She cuddled closer. "Somehow this reminds me of our meeting place on the clover hill."

"Does it now...the same only in that we're sitting side by side again. But how our lives have changed otherwise. Do you ever miss Willsborough?"

"I do miss the lake, but here there's always excitement of some kind or other." She took everything in—the grounds, couples walking together, a pack of young boys roughhousing. "I miss Wigwam. Sandborne too. I even miss little Egbert, but I miss our riding lessons most of all."

Savoring the implication perhaps, Daniel squeezed her hand. "Me too. Even though we had to be careful, it was the Lord's own blessing that we were brought together. Wasn't it easy when we could see each other every day? It's hard, but it will get better. Right now the important thing is that Mrs. Bright seems to like me."

"She keeps a close watch over us boarders," said Almira. "But on Sunday afternoons, we're allowed to receive gentleman guests with her permission."

He struck an exaggerated pose of formality. "Would Miss Hamilton wish to receive Mr. Dwyer some Sunday?"

"I'm quite sure she would love it," said Almira. She brought her free hand across and traced the line of his jaw with a finger. "Danny. Harriet gives you a lot of attention. You don't fancy her, do you?"

"Miss Ames? Heavens no. That girl is a fly in my face."

"Good," said Almira. "That's what I wanted to hear. Next time I'll bring a fly swatter."

Pleased that she'd made him laugh, Almira thought it might be a good time to raise a concern. "I heard some girls say that the chemicals used in the daguerreotype are all deadly poisons. Is it true?"

Daniel scratched his nose and squinted at a distant line of trees. "There are dangerous chemicals," he said, forming his words carefully. "Mercury, bromine, chlorine. But these only make a fellow sick if he's careless."

"Like Mr. Cushman? Is he careless?" asked Almira.

Before he could answer, Rebecca stepped up. "I thought you two had run off to Alabama. Well, I'm sorry to disturb you, but we better get back to the others."

The three continued their circuit of the capitol building. Soon they approached the blankets where Mrs. Bright's girls waited.

"Mr. Dwyer," said Harriet as they stepped up to the picnic. "You have allowed the misses Hamilton and Carvalho to monopolize your time. I insist that there be a rematch in which myself and Phebe shall be your principal devotion."

"I beg your pardon, Miss Ames," said Daniel. He turned away from her and squared his shoulders. "Mrs. Bright, might I have permission to call on Miss Hamilton some Sunday afternoon?"

"Yes," Mrs. Bright said. "You may write to me at thirty-six Maiden Lane. I will notify you of the arrangements."

Almira tried to control the urge to gloat, but with limited success.

Chapter 9

Late September, 1971

The New York Public Library was a good place to think things through, unless avoiding reflection was one's true intention. In which case, it was the last place to be.

During her long shift, Angela replayed over and over her unsettling conversation with David. "He's talking to a ghost," she murmured among the stacks. "Doing psychotherapy with a ghost."

It was bizarre. Really weird. *Thinking* you've seen a ghost—as she had herself—is one thing. But having conversations with a ghost night after night is quite another. And to top it off, the ghost obviously turns him on.

Or maybe David was losing his mind. She'd seen him come unglued before, after his patient committed suicide. And being cooped up in that house all alone made matters worse—of that she was certain. Withdrawal from human contact was unhealthy. Anyone who'd taken a basic psychology class knew that.

Healthy or not, she'd seen the ghost too. Admitting this, shifted things between them. If the ghost was real, a real presence anyway, was she going to lose him to it—to her—to that house? It kind of looked that way. Which would be too bad, because David was different from all the other guys she'd been with.

That night Angela took the subway home, a decent enough neighborhood on Staten Island, like she always did. She tossed the mail on the counter and walked to Tina's room. Her roommate was packing for her regular overnight to London.

"You look like shit," Tina said, glancing up from her open suitcase.

"Just tired."

Tina closed the closet door, a slinky dress draped over her arm. "Are you and David having trouble again?"

Her question was direct. Very typical of her.

"I don't know, maybe. It's hard to explain. I can tell you having a relationship when you're living far apart is a real hassle."

"Not when you're a stewardess. I've got one boyfriend in London. He's a barrister or something. I'll see him tomorrow. And there's Klaus, this German businessman. He's married, so we meet in Paris. And I'm not even counting the occasional pilot. The point is, you're on the pill. Enjoy it. There's lots of great guys out there. Really successful guys. David's an oddball, if you ask me. You should get rid of him."

Angela studied Tina's uniform, a sky-blue blazer and skirt, nylons, white blouse and red scarf with the TWA insignia pinned to it. How would she look dressed as a stewardess? No, it wasn't her style.

Tina opened and closed bureau drawers, tossed lacy underthings into her suitcase. Angela stepped out of her way. "I just feel like David and I are drifting apart."

"Are you guys getting it on?"

"That's all you ever think about," Angela said. "But yes, he's as interested in sex as ever. He just seems…distracted whenever we're, you know…doing it."

Tina paused, hip cocked—make-up perfect, blue eyeshadow, nails, the whole come-fly-with-me package. "You're not forgetting anything, you know, in the sex department," she said, bending to her vanity mirror and reapplying her lipstick one last time.

"No, I'm not forgetting anything. I don't think so anyway."

"Good. Because sometimes guys want special treatment and if you don't give it to them, they find someone who will." Tina zipped up her luggage and hoisted it effortlessly. "Men are simple. They're like puppets when you know which string to pull."

Chapter 10

September, 1841

It was after eight. Emily and Almira sat in Phebe's suite studying French, as was their habit on Thursday evenings. After a short while, Rebecca and Susannah joined them, wearing only petticoats and corset stays.

"Why are you two half-dressed?" Emily said.

"Susie and I are experimenting with new ways to set our hair," said Rebecca. "We don't want to soil our clothing."

"Yes, we've come in search of advice."

"That's right," Rebecca said. "Do y'all know a good way to set ringlets so they don't come all apart before noon?"

The question was tossed around. Phebe asked if Almira might have an idea.

"My mother taught me to wet the last six inches of my hair in water with a little milk. I like to mix in a bit of lavender water too, so your hair won't get a sour smell."

The erstwhile hairdressers thought it an excellent idea. They were about to leave when Harriet walked in, announcing that she had just concluded another piano lesson with little Betty. "It will take time," she said, "but I think she has potential."

Seeing there would be no further French lessons that night, Phebe suggested the study group put away their books.

"If we had a fiddler, this would be a grand cotillion," Emily said.

"Not without at least two gents for each of us," Almira said to everyone's laughter.

The impromptu party brought a general discussion of dances and balls. They all watched Rebecca and Phebe demonstrate the waltz steps.

"It is a German dance, you know," said Phebe. "According to my governess, it is very popular in Europe."

"Here, let me demonstrate the part of the gentleman," she said. "Rebecca, you are the lady."

Phebe's instructional manner wasn't diminished for being both younger and smaller than her partner. She placed her right hand at the small of Rebecca's back and proffered her left, palm turned upward.

"Rebecca, let your hand rest ever so lightly upon mine. I will begin to step backward and turn and sway. You will step with me. Are you ready?"

Someone tapped on the door. "Miss Rebecca, you in there?"

"Yes, Tildie, come in."

"You want me to put out your things for tomorrow?"

"Yes, my green dress please, thank you."

"Yes, miss," Tildie said. "If there's nothing else you need, I'll say goodnight."

Perplexed, Almira wondered about Tildie's connection to Rebecca. Why did she give her special attention, putting out her things, bringing her a pitcher of warm water every morning, and a hundred other pleasant trifles?

"You will forgive me Rebecca," Harriet said, "but I am embarrassed by your peculiar Southern institution."

"Pardon me?" Rebecca seemed taken off guard.

"How do you and your coreligionists justify this outrage against equality?"

"Harriet, I don't have the least clue what you're talking about," said Rebecca, stepping away from her dance partner.

"Oh, I think you do."

The room went quiet, save for the faint sound of the Skinner sisters playing upstairs.

After a long moment, Rebecca nodded. "No, in fact I do. Pardon me. Please, I feel a headache. I feel indisposed." Head down, tears hidden behind her hands, Rebecca pushed her way past the other girls and rushed out the door.

Phebe let go a great exhalation and threw her hands up. "Harriet, how could you. That was terribly unkind and, I might add, a presumption on my private chambers."

"Phebe's right," said Emily. "How could you treat a sister scholar that way?"

Harriet crossed her arms and rose on her toes. "Is she not a descendant of money lenders, a daughter of Judah?"

Befuddled by the strange references, Almira looked from Harriet to Phebe and back again.

"That has never been a problem for us," said Phebe, rising to Rebecca's defense. "You know that."

"I do not think girls of Rebecca's persuasion ought to be allowed among us," said Harriet. "But besides being a Christian institution, shouldn't we agree that our Albany Female Academy is also a good abolition school."

With all these obscure references, Almira was bewildered by the confrontation. More so was she distressed to see Rebecca, her closest friend, humiliated, her feelings so obviously hurt by Harriet's remarks. If only she understood the argument, Almira would have rushed to her defense. But lacking that understanding, she could only think to sooth Rebecca's wounded feelings. Almira turned from the others and slipped out of the room. She made her way down the hall and tapped on Rebecca's door.

"Who is it?" said a flat, affectless voice from inside.

"It's me, Mirie. Won't you let me in?"

"Go ahead, the door's unlocked."

Almira entered. The room was dark, except for Rebecca standing at the moonlit window overlooking the back yard, her petticoats and corset glowing white.

"Are you here to convert me?"

"I don't know what you mean."

"Never mind," said Rebecca, who remained gazing through the panes. Almira drew closer.

"At home in Charleston, my father keeps roses. From my bedroom window I look out on rose gardens. On summer nights like this, they are quite beautiful."

"Rebecca, what does it mean, what Harriet said about you being a daughter of Judah?"

She laughed and turned toward Almira. "Is that what she said?"

"Yes."

"You truly don't know?"

"No. Should I?"

"Harriet was referring to my family background."

"Yes. You're Spanish, are you not?"

"That," Rebecca said, "is nearly correct. The Carvalho family is Portuguese."

"But why would Harriet object to that?"

"Because we're Jewish. She hates Jews."

"But...but, you attend church with us every Sunday," said Almira.

"Yes, I attend your Christian church. My parents told me it would be better that way while there's yet no synagogue in Albany. So, Mirie, I am a Jew, though obviously not a very observant one. I hope you're not disappointed."

"And what about Tildie?" said Almira.

"Tildie is my servant, a slave if you insist."

Mouth agape, Almira said, "But isn't she white?"

"No. She's quadroon. That means she's one quarter black, so she's still a negress."

"My God." Almira covered her mouth and fell back on the bed.

"Come now, don't act so shocked. If you haven't noticed, this world is full of masters and slaves." Rebecca went to her bureau and rearranged toiletries. "You think it repulsive, I know, but what if Tildie were free? What would happen to her? Where would she go? Surely you know the carnal appetites of men. How long would it be before she was forced into the most compromising of situations?"

Almira let her hand drop to her lap. "But, but, Rebecca, isn't...is slavery not wrong?"

"Wrong?" said Rebecca with a dismissive laugh. "Did you know Mrs. Bright pays Tildie for whatever she does beyond attending to me? Did you know that? Do you know that I give her pocket money myself? No, you didn't know that either. Well, you Yankee girls don't know much, do you? Certainly not about our way of life."

Almira looked up at her. "Tell me, please."

"Since coming north, no one has ever asked me about the Southern way. Instead, Yankees have condemned me without curiosity. But I can see that you are sincere, so I will tell you.

Tildie's been with me nearly all her life, and she knows I'll never abandon her, not as long as it's within my power. I'm sure you think I should let her go, turn her out into the world. Well, you don't do that to your people."

"Your people? Rebecca, she's a slave. Don't you appreciate what that means?"

"Oh yes, I appreciate it. Don't forget my people know what it means to be slaves. Did you ever wonder why I've come from so far to attend school in Albany? It isn't as if we don't have girls' academies in the South—it's because this school allows Jews like me to enroll."

Almira didn't know how to respond, all of it too much to comprehend. Her head swam with strange new contingencies. Rebecca sat beside her on the bed. Pressed together, bathed in moonlight, they made a luminous pair. Her friend seemed calmer now, emboldened. Rebecca took one of Almira's hands in hers. She turned it upward and lightly traced the palm with a fingertip, pulling it to her face. The heat of Rebecca's breath playing across her hand and between her fingers thrilled Almira. She inhaled sharply. At the sound, Rebecca raised her eyes and held Almira's gaze.

"You're so innocent," Rebecca said. "So beautiful." Her voice grew softer, like secrets whispered across a shared pillow. Rebecca pressed in closer. She brushed her lips across Almira's cheek, ending in a long, lingering kiss. "Tildie's black. I love her. You're white. I love you too."

Chapter 11

September, 1971

Sleighbells hanging from the door jingled. The proprietor behind the long counter looked like an old hippy, with a potbelly, mustache, and gray ponytail.

"Davey," he said, looking up from his magazine. "Hey baby, what's happening?"

"You tell me," said David, going along with their ritual greeting that never varied.

He had been friendly with Larry Greer for a decade. The friendship had grown out of the repeated bidding wars between them at the same auctions up and down the Hudson Valley. After one of these encounters, Greer walked up to David with two paper cups of vile concession coffee. He had suggested that instead of running up the bidding, hurting both of them, why didn't they work things out beforehand.

Since then, Larry's store on Lark Street was someplace David enjoyed visiting whenever he came to Albany. It held a nice selection of vintage fine arts, early furniture, and one-of-a-kind curiosity items—his kind of shop.

The storefront had been a bar until sometime in the recent past, which lent an absurd atmosphere to the establishment. Even with the stools and tables all gone and the mirror behind the bar mostly concealed by shelves of books, the scent of stale beer and cigarette smoke betrayed its former life as a saloon.

"How's business?" David shook Larry's hand. "You come across anything special lately?"

"No. Not like I should. What about you? Any more dead babies? That last one you sent was pretty nice."

"I'm glad you liked it, but no. No more post-mortems." David was eager to leave the small talk behind and get to the subject at hand. "Larry, you know a lot about daguerreotypes," he said. "I want you to take a look at these enlargements of one I found in my place in Willsboro."

David placed a manila envelope on the bar, opened it, and pulled out five, eight-by-ten black and white prints of Almira's portrait.

Larry took the prints to his desk, sat, and switched on a gooseneck lamp. After taking a long look at the first portrait in its leatherette case assembled with the brass matte, he set it aside. Next was a photo of the plate removed from the case without the matte.

"Very cool," said Larry, "the way you can see reflector panels to the side."

He placed the print to the right of the first one, assembling what would become a fan of enlargements.

The third view was a close up of Almira's face, neck, and shoulders. This, Larry placed at the top of the arc. Print number four was another of the entire daguerreotype, and the fifth was a detail shot, zooming in on the hallmark at the bottom edge of the plate. With a loupe screwed into his eye like a monocle, Larry said, "William Butler, he was one of the really early dealers in photographic supplies." Greer sat upright and removed the loupe. "Somebody ought to write a good book about this shit."

"You know enough about it," said David. "You should do it."

"The hell with that."

Larry surveyed all five prints together and then again picked up the one displaying the hallmark at the plate's edge. "Seriously though, see the way the corners on this plate aren't clipped? That's a sign of a very early dag. I think they started clipping them early on, so the corners didn't tear whatever they were buffing the plates with."

"So, when would you date this?"

"Oh, given the style of the case, the matte, the whole package, probably before '45, '46. It's hard to say exactly."

"And they started taking these things in 1839, right?"

"Yeah, but late in the year. I don't think there were commercial galleries until well into '40, and then only in, say, New York City and Philly.

"What about here in Albany?" David asked.

"The earliest operators I know of around here were the Meade brothers of course. The Meades and one or two others, but I didn't think they were around until later, like '43 and '44." Larry pivoted in his wooden swivel chair, got up and went over to a bookshelf behind the counter. He withdrew a thick volume. "Check in here, it's like a city directory. It dates to 1849, but it's close."

David thumbed through a heavy, leather-bound book titled, *The Annals of Albany*. Sure enough, Larry had the date of publication spot on. That shouldn't have surprised him. Greer was one of those guys with an eidetic memory David envied.

As David checked the index for references to daguerreotype studios, Larry picked up a magnifying glass. "You still running around with that girl, what's her name, Angela?"

"Yeah, we're still an item."

Larry continued scrutinizing Almira's portrait. "Who is this chick? Do you know her name? What do you know about her?"

"I'm pretty sure her name is Almira Hamilton. If that's so, then she once lived in the place I bought in Willsboro."

Larry leaned forward in his chair—eyes fixed on the image. "Man, this girl's pretty cute—have you noticed that?"

"Yes, she's attractive."

"No shit. Well, she kind of resembles this go-go dancer I used to date. She was double jointed. A very talented girl, if you know what I mean."

David didn't like the smutty insinuation, so he redirected the conversation back to history. "This Hamilton girl, she went to the Albany Female Academy in '41. Have you ever heard of it?"

"Yeah, sure. It was a high-end finishing school in those days. I have a Wedgewood plate with a transfer of that place on it."

"Anyway, that's pretty much all I know about her, except she told me she lived in a boarding house on Maiden Lane."

Larry folded his arms and grinned. "Oh, did she now? That's nice."

David winced, caught himself, and grinned sheepishly. He didn't want his relationship with Almira divulged to anyone. He waved a hand in dismissal. "I mean, from what I've read in family papers that came with the place."

"Sure," said Larry. "I know what you mean." The old hippy eyed him carefully. "Anyhow, Maiden Lane is still there. It's a little alley just north of State Street in the old part of downtown."

"Hey," said David, pointing to the open book. "Here's Meade brothers listed, along with two other guys, Churchill and Bissou."

Larry slapped the heel of his hand to his forehead. "Of course," he said. "Churchill and Bissou."

"Well from what I can figure out, the girl in this dag died late in 1841, meaning that she was only here for a few months the previous fall."

Larry leaned all the way back in his chair. He stroked his mustache, anticipating David's next question. "And you're wondering if this image could have been taken that early?"

"Exactly."

"Well, it's possible," said Larry. "I didn't think there were galleries in Albany then, but, unless this is a post-mortem, which it obviously isn't, who knows. It is a very early dag, I'll say that."

David took in the information with no small amount of pride.

Larry rocked in his seat, waiting in vain for David to respond. "So what's the deal. You want to sell or what?"

"No, I'm gonna hold on to it. It sort of goes with the house."

Greer collected up the prints and returned them to the envelope. "Well, I can't say I blame you, man, but if you change your mind, I'd like first dibs."

"Hey, you said you had a Wedgewood plate from the school?"

"Oh, yeah. It's over there, on that display case in the corner."

David found it immediately, displayed on a wire support. "Check it out," Greer called from behind the counter. Larry couldn't help but narrate the piece. "Pretty standard flow-blue Wedgewood, around 1850 or so. It's got the usual crazing but no major cracks or chips. A nice piece with a cool transfer."

The composition was a view of a columned Greek revival building. Where had he seen it before? That's right, on one of the photostats he got from the archivist at the Albany Academy for Girls. David turned the plate over in his hands. He didn't know a lot about Wedgewood, but he knew enough to recognize the markings as appropriate.

David didn't bother to dicker over price. The Wedgewood plate would be worth more than Larry would ask.

Greer hummed as he wrapped the plate in newspaper. "That building, it's still there you know."

David cocked his head. "The one on the plate?"

"Yeah, the one on the plate." Larry regarded David—an eyebrow arched. "It's pretty run-down, and there's no columns anymore, but it's the exact same building."

"No kidding. How would I get there from here?"

"Okay, go out here to Washington Street," Larry said. "Take Washington toward downtown, past the public library to State Street. Stay on State and North Pearl will be on the left a couple of blocks down."

David, who'd been finning his hand right and left with every step of Larry's directions, repeated them back.

"You got it," Larry said. "Anyway man, that building is still there, up on the left. Maiden Lane intersects right around there. I think the last time I drove by it—it was a liquor store or something."

A handshake later, David was back in the Karmann Ghia, but before pulling into traffic he unwrapped the Wedgewood plate and set it on the bucket seat beside him. The directions from Larry were accurate. Using the plate as a guide, he saw the building at once.

Greer was right, the columns were gone, but after a quick comparison with the plate on the seat, he was certain this was it. He had to park to take a closer look. Half a block further up, David pounced on an empty parking spot. It was tight. Relieved he wasn't driving the truck in the congested city, he grabbed his camera bag, put the plate in it, pushed two dimes into the meter, and gave it a crank.

North Pearl Street was still a principal business avenue. It was clear however, that the commercial heart of the city had moved on. The neighborhood was made up of retail stores, office buildings, and bars catering to the people who worked in them. Like he'd seen in Burlington, one of those detested urban renewal projects was already underway, hollowing out the old downtown and replacing it with bland, sterile architecture.

David found himself standing across from the derelict structure. Pulling the Wedgewood plate from his camera bag, he looked first at the building, the plate, then at the building again, hoping all the while that he was mistaken. He wasn't. There it was, four stories, distinctive windows, steps across the front, although it looked like a few had been removed. The scene was heartbreaking. The Greek temple pictured on the plate, with all the hopes, ideals, and aspirations it once embodied, was reduced to a decayed tooth begging to be pulled.

With his camera already loaded, David took shots of the building. It was lunch time, so clusters of secretaries poured onto the sidewalks. All high heels, nylons, long cigarettes, and green eye shadow—a lot of girls named Sharon and Teresa, he supposed. They eyed him suspiciously.

Putting away the camera, David crept out from between parked cars and loped across the street. Standing in front of the building, he read the signage for a discount grocery and liquor store, but most of the lower windows were boarded over. A notice, *Condemned Property*, was taped to the front door.

Too bad. Too, too bad. It must have been beautiful when it was new. He took a few more pictures, but the whole situation was depressing, so he put the camera away. He stepped up to the building and touched his fingertips to the structure. He thought of the spirit in which this building was put up, imagining the ideals it embodied, envisioning the intelligent, young women who passed through its doorway, their lives still ahead of them and full of promise. The only ones who lingered here now were the sinister dwellers of the night.

Trash littered the once proud portico, cigarette butts, pull tabs from soda cans, an empty bottle of cream ale. If he were to clean up the refuse, acknowledge this proud building's nineteenth century ideals, perhaps the decay of the present might, in some small way, be reversed–if only for a moment. He gathered up what he could, but the effort was useless. There was a battered garbage can nearby. He dumped the litter into it and walked away.

Maiden Lane intersected North Pearl just above State, but it was so narrow David at first mistook the street for a service alley. Before he turned into the narrow passage, he snapped a few more pictures; the site of the academy as seen from the corner, another view looking down Maiden Lane toward the Hudson River. It was obvious the street was now used for overflow parking and pedestrians and wasn't open to vehicular traffic in any practical sense.

Looking back toward the academy two blocks away, David reasoned Almira must have walked this street every day during her time in Albany. Though he was trying hard to imagine how it would have been in 1841, it wasn't easy. Few, if any, of the structures she would have passed still stood. Except for the academy building, just about every square yard had been replaced long ago with apartments and offices. In truth, the condition of the old female academy was jarring. Seeing it left him feeling rotten and reminded him of everything he hated about the present.

A couple of blocks further down Maiden Lane a sign in a tavern window advertised sandwich specials. David ducked inside. The smoky interior, full of office workers on their lunch hours, had a few open seats at the bar. He took a stool, stowed the camera bag between his feet, and ordered lunch.

After a few minutes, the barkeep set a Rueben sandwich, fries, a pickle, and a glass of iced tea in front of him. The sandwich was good; surprisingly good. To his left, a couple of guys in business suits were having an animated conversation about real estate. On his right, perched a woman in a sleeveless dress. Smoke from her cigarette swirled around the cocktail in her hand.

She'd been throwing sideways glances his way. "You some kind of photographer or something?"

David set down his glass. Judging by the make-up and perm, he figured her to be an executive secretary or low-level bureaucrat. "Not really," he said. "Just taking some photos of the neighborhood."

"Oh yeah? Around here?" She smirked, blowing smoke through her nose. "What for?"

"That old building up on Pearl Street. It's historic you know."

"Oh," said she, sounding already bored with his answer—with him. She looked to be in her early forties but was probably younger.

"Is that what you're having for lunch?" He nodded toward her gin and tonic.

"What's it to you?"

"Nothing," he said, and slid his basket of French fries down the bar. "I can't eat all these. Why don't you have some?"

Chapter 12

October, 1841

Following Rebecca's humiliation, Mrs. Bright sensed the atmosphere in her home was disturbed. The years of keeping a boarding house for the Albany Female Academy had sharpened her intuition, making secrets impossible for the girls to conceal from her for very long.

"You do understand that I cannot allow members of my household to be upbraided on account of their religion," she told Harriet one afternoon in her private office.

"But Mrs. Bright, it is not only that Miss Carvalho is of the Hebrew persuasion," said Harriet. "That is secondary. The greater offense is that she belongs to a slave holding family and has brought her horrid institution among us. If she is allowed to perpetrate this injustice, are we not only condoning it, but degrading both races in the process?"

As if she'd just concluded a brilliant legal argument, Harriet held her head high, secure that her irrefutable logic could not go unrecognized.

Mrs. Bright leisurely sipped her coffee. "What you say is true enough, but this academy has always allowed members of her race to be enrolled on the understanding that they accept this as a Christian institution, which she has done entirely. As for the other matter, Matilda's status is one over which we have no control. I have asked Miss Carvalho to be discrete in the display of her relationship to her servant, and in my opinion, she has been altogether compliant with that request."

Harriet looked crestfallen to find her position supported so half-heartedly. When she tried to rearticulate her complaints, Mrs. Bright raised her hand.

"Please listen to me. Though you may find both these arrangements personally objectionable, and you may not be alone in this sentiment, the institution of slavery is still the law in much of our republic."

"But as a true abolitionist, I must protest—"

"No, in that you are mistaken," said Mrs. Bright. "You will keep those sentiments to yourself." Tapping the tabletop between them with her stirring spoon, she went on. "Now listen closely. I have a responsibility to the school and to the other girls in this house that all are provided comfortable accommodations. I intend to do whatever is necessary to meet that responsibility. Henceforth, this subject is forbidden in this household, and that is my final word on the matter. Am I clear?"

"Yes, ma'am."

"Now, I expect you to offer an apology to Rebecca and the other girls who were forced to witness this unfortunate display. Tonight's evening meal should afford an excellent opportunity to set things right."

Harriet bit her lower lip but did not answer.

"Do we have an understanding, Miss Ames?"

"Very well, Mrs. Bright," she said with a quick nod. "If you insist."

That night, after grace was said, it was announced that Miss

Ames had something urgent to share. Harriet swallowed hard and expressed regret at her unkind remarks. Even though the apology was delivered woodenly, Harriet's eyes fixed on her plate, her words were accepted with feeling.

"Might I say one thing?" said Rebecca. "I do realize that my background is different, and some of the ways to which I am accustomed are not well regarded here in the north, but it was my parents' decision to have Matilda accompany me to this place from Charleston, not mine, and I am sorry if her presence disturbs anyone."

The younger girls seemed confused, only vaguely aware of what had taken place a few nights before, but Phebe and Emily were visibly relieved to have the ugly event behind them.

"Then the matter is settled," said Mrs. Bright. "We will speak no more of this subject but regard each other's differences with tolerance from this point forward."

With peace restored to the household on Maiden Lane, Almira's first quarter at the Albany Female Academy was nearly finished. She'd kept apace with the other scholars. To be sure, algebra still plagued her, but she enjoyed antiquities and French very much. The most demanding subject was English composition, as the other girls had predicted.

Yet Almira had discovered that outlining her essays, rewriting sentences with the various phrases and clauses rearranged, brought new meanings buried within the words. It was tremendously rewarding. Indeed, her brightest academic moment occurred when Miss Meigs instructed her to stand before the class and read from her assignment.

> *"Man is a wonderful being. He has a moral nature, which enables him to distinguish between right and wrong. He is surrounded by temptations to sin, but this is his unerring*

83

guide to truth. As virtue to him is attainable, this points him to objects worthy of his noble endowments. It restrains his grosser passions, illumines the pathway to another world, and raises the heart, with grateful emotions, to the source of all good."

At midnight, the bells in the city's numerous churches announced the passing of one day into the next. After another night's work at the livery stable, Daniel trudged back to the Temperance house. He wore his jacket buttoned tight against the steady wind which blew up from the river. Compared to this life, his days at the Hamilton home in Willsborough seemed so easy, though, beyond stealing every moment he could to be with Almira, purposeless.

Now his days were consumed with purpose. There was room for nothing else but immersion in his chosen trade. He would learn the art of the daguerreotype, and with it become a man with a respectable profession. Soon he'd have something to offer, as Mr. Hamilton had put it. But right now, he didn't feel that way. His boots smelled of manure and his clothes of horses. His shoulders ached, and his hands were calloused from manual labor.

Turning the corner onto Hudson Street, Daniel saw the glow of the camphene lamp above the doorway of the Temperance House, a reminder to the residents that abstinence was their guiding light.

At the door Daniel scraped his boots on a cornhusk matt and stepped inside. The smell of coffee and tobacco washed over him. Someone always kept watch at the front desk through the night. Usually it was Jack de Groot, sitting with his feet on the table, smoking his pipe and reading the *Rip-Snorter*, his favorite penny comic.

"Good evening, Jack."

The watchman put down his reading. "Danny Dwyer, you hard working son of a buck. Sit with me."

"I think I will," said Daniel, collapsing with a groan. The two smoked their pipes and made small talk—the weather, a new steamboat named the *Eureka*—until Daniel asked, "Jack, have you got a spare piece of paper? I haven't had time to go to a stationer."

De Groot got up and rummaged through books and ledgers on a nearby desk.

"A pen and ink too, if you can. I'll pay you back."

Handing Daniel a small sheet of foolscap and a pen to write with, Jack said, "When you get some paper, put a sheet back."

Daniel nodded, pressed the paper out flat on the table, dipped his pen and began writing.

> *Dearest Almira,*
>
> *I've just returned from the livery where I keep Marcus. Poor fellow, he feels like a prisoner in his stall all day. I take him out for a ride when I can, but I know he's unhappy in the city. Either I keep him there and work for his board or I shall be forced to sell him as a carriage horse, and I cannot bring myself to do that.*
>
> *At the portrait gallery I help Mr. Cushman prepare plates to be exposed. Though he did not want to hire me, we have become quite friendly. We apply the chemicals and buff the plates until customers begin arriving about 8:00 a.m. Depending on the day, I assist either Mr. Cushman or Mr. Meade, holding reflector panels, exposing plates to mercury vapors, or I simply wait on customers until closing at 6:00 p.m. Twice I have gone with Mr. Cushman to the home of a deceased person to take their portrait in death. Most days I assist in producing more than twenty daguerreotypes,*

85

> *so you can imagine I am becoming quite*
> *proficient at it. Afterwards I return to my*
> *boarding house where I eat some stew and*
> *change into my work clothes. Then I go to the*
> *livery until midnight.*

Daniel imagined Almira holding this very paper, reading it in privacy. Making her understand what his life was like now was important if she were to understand what their life might be like in the future. Daniel wrote a final paragraph.

> So, my dearest Mirie, as you can see, I work all day and most nights. *Only on Sundays have I free time to attend to personal business and go to church. A few times I have walked past Mrs. Bright's at night. I stand outside and wonder behind which window you are sleeping. Someday soon I will have enough money saved to get a presentable suit of clothes. Then I will ask Mrs. Bright if I may pay you a visit. I think of you every day, all day, and it is only the thought that I will soon see you again that gives me the strength to go on. Remember that I love you above all else. You are the Almighty's own comfort to me.*
> *Yours forever,*
> *Daniel Dwyer*

He folded the letter together with one to Sarah Rawson, then sealed it with candle wax. Tomorrow, he would place it with Mr. Meade's outgoing mail, but for now he needed to sleep.

Daylight was already illuminating the window as Almira opened her eyes. Her nose felt colder, the room chillier than on any previous morning. Autumn was giving way to the first whispers of winter. She nuzzled further into the blankets, bringing them close around her face. Her bed felt deliciously warm. She luxuriated in the moment, knowing that it could only last a few seconds more.

Overhead, the padding of small feet signaled that the younger girls had already begun their day. She pulled her arms out from under the covers, balled her hands into fists, stretched her entire body, and sat up. She could see Emily had already risen and was first at the water closet.

Meanwhile, from down the hallway, Rose was knocking on bedroom doors—first Harriet's, next Phebe's. By now, Matilda would be attending to her mistress, having brought Rebecca a pitcher of warm water and set out her dress for the day.

Almira swung her feet to the floor, pulled her wool shawl from the bedpost, and stood at the fireplace, trying to soak up whatever remnants of heat still radiated from the coal grate. She turned her back to the hearth and let the shawl slip to her elbows. The warmth felt good. In the growing light of day, Almira noticed a spatter of blood on the floor, then another, and another still. Tracks led from the door to Emily's bed. The covers were turned back, and a bright red medallion marked the center of the mattress.

It could mean only one thing. With a sickening start, Almira realized it had been a long time since she herself had been *in her flowers*, as Mrs. Bright's girls put it. How long exactly? Eight weeks– no. No, it was ten, maybe longer. Her courses had always been predictable. Now they were long overdue. Almira's stomach clenched with fear and dread.

She sat, eyes fixed on the tell-tale sheets and floorboards. Emily appeared in the doorway holding a ball of lint in her hand. "Oh dear," she said, shoulders slumping. She immediately knelt to wipe up the blood. "Well, it looks like Auntie Flo is visiting again."

"What did you say?" Almira said.

87

"I said, Auntie Flo is visiting," said Emily, as she got up from her knees. "What do you call it?"

"I don't call it anything. I've never lived with other girls."

Emily went to her trunk, removed a knitted pad on a belt and put it on, tucking fresh lint in place as she did so.

Meanwhile, Almira performed her morning toilet in a daze. Even removing her curling papers seemed beyond her, and lest she miss breakfast, Emily felt the need to hasten her. It didn't matter, she'd been too nauseous to eat anyway recently. She feared the reason was all too clear.

"Well, Mirie," Emily said, as she closed the door behind her, "I shall see you at the table. Do hurry."

Alone now, Almira studied her features in the mirror. She did look different, whether or not anyone else could see it. She raised a tentative hand to examine the face of this stranger. As her fingers slowly explored chin, mouth, cheek, and nose, her mind raced. What would happen to her once her condition became obvious? She would be expelled from the academy in disgrace, she knew that. Father would be furious beyond reason. Daniel was her only salvation. But how could Daniel still want her with her shame on exhibit for all to see?

"Mirie," Rebecca called out as she tapped the door. "Are you coming?"

"I'll be right there," said Almira, taking a deep breath.

"I'll wait for you downstairs, but y'all step lively now, everyone else has left already."

Almira went to her cowhide trunk and opened it. There at the bottom, untouched since she'd packed them in August, were her own belts and pads, placed beside a novel she'd had no time to read. Thinking that perhaps her body needed a gentle reminder, she took one out, gathered her petticoats around her waist and put it on.

At the foot of the stairs Rebecca waited loyally, a bit overdressed in an ankle length cape and ermine muff. They kissed good morning.

Rose approached. In her meaty hands, two small waxed-paper packages.

"Miss Rebecca, Miss Almira. Take these sandwiches with you. You both eat like birds."

They thanked her, grabbed their baskets, and stepped through the door. The weather outside was blustery. Almira was glad. She could stay sheltered behind the brim of her bonnet most of the time. Besides, they were late and had to hurry, so conversation was necessarily limited.

That entire day, she was preoccupied with her predicament. It was impossible to concentrate on her lessons. Twice she made her way to the water closet in hopes of evidence her body, reminded of its duties, was responding accordingly. She saw no sign that such was the case. Even writing a letter to Sarah Rawson during a study period was more than she could accomplish.

Walking back from the academy, among her favorite times of the day, was equally frustrating. Phebe insisted on speaking French, and even Rebecca's stories, usually so amusing, seemed intolerably trivial. How strange and terrible, she thought, to feel alone while walking arm in arm with friends.

A few hours later, after a supper of lamb stew, Harriet was busy giving Betty another piano lesson. A couple of other girls were still in the parlor, but most, including Almira, had retired to their studies. For once, it felt good to be in her room, sitting at the table she and Emily shared, having better success at a desperate letter to Sarah Rawson.

Her roommate sat across from her, preparing instruction notes for her Fifth Department students. When she winced, Almira asked, "Are you all right?"

"I am, yes. It's...turbulence."

"I'm sorry," said Almira, returning to her letter.

"How old were you when you started?" Emily abruptly asked.

"Pardon me? What did you say?"

"How old were you when you began your courses?"

The room swam. Had she been discovered? Was it her frantic scribbling which betrayed her?

"Fourteen, ah, nearly, um...fifteen," she said, looking down at her letter.

"You were young. But I've never heard you complain of it. Your seasons must be gentle on you."

"Yes, I am blessed," said Almira. Relief spread through her. It was clear Emily did not know her secret.

Emily made a face that reminded Almira of an ill-tempered old woman. "Well," she said, "were that I was married with children, then I wouldn't be so bothered."

Almira watched as Emily slashed a line through a student's composition and scrawled criticism in the margin, ending with the stab of a period.

"Those girls in the Fifth Department are nitwits."

Almira tried to ignore her roommate's outburst.

Emily rose and started gathering her lessons. "It's late," she said, barely suppressing a yawn.

For a moment Almira felt sorry for Emily, then was drawn back to her letter. "What can young ladies do when this change is upon them, yet they must resume nature's ebb and flow?"

She folded her missive into a small envelope, addressed it to Sarah in Whitehall, and dribbled a spot of candle wax on the flap.

Now Almira was ready to retire as well. Troubled as she was, it had been an exhausting day. She was still desperate to talk to someone older who could offer guidance but feared her exhausted roommate would be easily vexed.

Emily turned, presenting her back. "Would you mind?"

"No, of course not." Almira stood and unhooked her friend's dress, eighteen flat brass wire hooks and eyes. She counted them.

"My shoulders are covered with freckles," Emily said. "I don't like it. It's ugly."

"You're being silly."

"No, it's true. I am a plain girl. Men are not drawn to me as they are to others. I know that. That is why I'm fitting myself for a teacher."

"Don't say such things," said Almira, though she thought it true. "You will soon have a husband of your own. I'm sure of it."

Emily ignored the comment, stepped out of her dress, and hung it on a peg. "You, on the other hand, are beautiful. Finding a husband will be easy for you. That tall Irishman from the daguerreotype gallery for example. It was obvious you captured his fancy."

"Do you really think so?" said Almira, relaxing the laces of her friend's corset.

When the job was done, Emily sat on her bed. "Come," she said, patting the mattress. "Sit here beside me. I will unfasten yours."

After Emily finished unhooking Almira's dress, she glided a hand across the younger girl's shoulders. "Your skin is flawless, like porcelain."

It felt awkward to have her own beauty pointed out, so Almira said nothing. She rose and squirmed out of her stays, went to the dressing table where she kept her brush, let down her hair, and began her nightly grooming ritual. She could see her roommate behind her, reflected in the looking glass.

"Emily," Almira said, choosing her words carefully. "How long, I mean...when a woman is carrying a child, does she know it straight away?"

"I think most do, yes," said Emily, crawling under the blankets.

"And do they know if it is to be a boy or girl?"

"My mother said she knew all along I would be her only daughter. That's why she named me Thankful. Why do you ask?"

"No reason. Idle curiosity."

The two said their goodnights as Almira snuffed the candle, leaving only the faintest glow from the fireplace. She wanted to continue their conversation but held back. Speaking about the problem would only make it more real.

That night she could not sleep. Searching for a comforting image, Almira tried to summon recollections of her mother—not as she lay dying, but as the healthy and cheerful woman she once was. Suddenly, an incident resurfaced from deep in her reservoir of forgotten memories. It had been morning, sometime in the summer of 1837, and they were alone in the parlor embroidering matching black aprons.

"Don't be frightened, Dolly," her mother had said. "It is only moon blood. That is what all the van Elst women call it."

Chapter 13

September, 1971

"Good afternoon. My name is Doctor Weis. I have a three o'clock appointment with Mrs. Holding."

"Yes, Dr. Weis," the receptionist said. "Mrs. Holding told me to expect you today. If you'll please have a seat, I'll let her know you're here."

David made a show of examining his surroundings without seeming to. The lobby was elegant. The wingback chair he sat in, plush. Across from him, a wall of glass looked out on an enclosed courtyard. Nearby, oil portraits of people he guessed were past academy presidents and important alumni adorned the walls. Most of the furnishings arranged around the room appeared to be genuine antiques, while those that weren't, such as the chair he was enjoying, were very high-end reproductions. Best of all, he saw an antique microscope on display on the ebony sideboard immediately to his left. He regarded the perfect marriage of highly polished brass, wood, and glass for what it was—a masterpiece of nineteenth century optics.

"Doctor Weis?"

David turned toward the voice. Before him stood an impeccably dressed woman, mid-to-late sixties he guessed—older, but not elderly. Wearing glasses and a pearl necklace, she projected the very embodiment of a classic doyenne. Extending a hand, she said in a soft-spoken but confident voice, "I am Thelma Wade-Holding. It is very nice to meet you. If you'll come with me, I have some material for you that I think may be of interest."

Mrs. Holding guided him toward the hallway to their left. On the way, they passed a life-size bas relief of a young woman in profile. The marble portrait captivated David's attention. He took in her delicate features, feminine jawline, and chignon of abundant hair gathered at the nape of her neck. Her lovely face and serene poise stopped him in his tracks.

"You are taken by the portrait?"

"Yes, I am...taken."

"On first seeing it, many visitors are. She is quite beautiful."

"Who is she?"

Mrs. Holding took a step closer. "Miss Mary Mather, class of 1845. Miss Mather stayed on at the academy and taught after her graduation. She died a few years later, beloved by the students and faculty alike. Afterwards, the alumnae association commissioned this portrait in marble."

They moved down the hallway. A few students uniformed in hunter green skirts and blazers passed, then, beyond the headmistress's office, Mrs. Holding directed Weis into a small conference room.

"I'll have Miss Lamar bring us the material. Please wait here."

Mrs. Holding disappeared through a paneled door, and then returned with a student carrying six large and very old ledgers.

"Margaret, dear, please place the books on the table. Thank you very much. I'll call you when we're finished."

Once alone, the archivist sat to David's right and touched her fingertips to the top volume. "This record book includes a listing of tuition paid during 1841. Beneath it is a listing of students for the same year. You are welcome to examine all these books for signs of your ancestor, though I must remind you they are fragile. Consequently, we cannot make photostatic copies. You may, however, make notes with the pencil and paper Miss Lamar left with us. No ink pens please, for reasons I'm sure you will understand."

The ledger was tall, about fifteen inches, but only about six inches wide, with a heavy, marbleized cardstock cover. It had a leather spine and outside corners.

David placed it on the table in front of him. Once opened, the distinctive, musty scent of old paper rose from the pages, which were covered in careful, cursive penmanship.

He saw a random list of men's names followed by amounts of money, he assumed tuition payments, mostly in ten, fifteen, or twenty-dollar increments. Evidently, the names were recorded in the order received. Scanning the listings for George Hamilton's would take time.

Meanwhile, he and Mrs. Holding chatted. Her initial reserve evaporated, and he found her to be pleasant enough company. He told her about his place in Willsboro, embellishing the truth to give the impression the property had been in his family for generations. Shifting the subject, David commented on the school's long and impressive history.

"I am from the class of 1926," she said. "Of course, in those days, we were in the building on Washington Avenue."

"When did the academy leave the North Pearl Street site?" he said.

"The Classic Columns building, as we call it. That property was abandoned in the nineties, when we were still called the Albany Female Academy."

David's gaze stopped short. "Here it is," he said. "George W. Hamilton, fifteen dollars. It appears to have been paid sometime in August 1841."

Mrs. Holding leaned forward and adjusted the glasses balanced on the end of her nose. "So it is," she said, a twinkle in her eyes. "Don't you think we should look at the student listings at once? I'd rather not wait."

The second book was wider, and not so tall. In loose alphabetical order the girls were listed. To the right of the names were six columns. David studied the page. Within each of these columns the names of courses, French, astronomy, chemistry, and so forth, were written in the tiniest script imaginable. Skimming rapidly through the next dozen pages, David read some of the names aloud, "Catherine Bois, Jane Bullions, Adeline Carr, Emily Foote, Mary Gardiner."

David slipped his hand under the next leaf and turned the page. It occurred to him that he was holding his breath. With the turn of each successive page, he might uncover what he'd come here to find. Suddenly Mrs. Holding spoke. "There she is. Almira Hamilton."

His heart raced. This was as close as he had—might ever come— to tangible evidence that Almira had once been a real human being.

"Well," the archivist said, her face beaming with evident pride, "it seems clear that your ancestor was one of our girls after all.

Nodding, David agreed. "Yes, and if we're right about these columns representing departments, then she began her time here in the Second Department."

Mrs. Holding turned the page and glanced over other names before returning to Almira's record. "I must say, this does speak well for the record keeping of our academy."

David penciled Almira's courses on paper. Mrs. Holding said, "Doctor Weis, may I ask how exactly it is you are related to Miss Hamilton?"

Scrambling to come up with a plausible answer, Weis blurted, "Through my mother's side of the family." He didn't like to lie but, having gained access to the archives through the ruse, like most lies and prevarications, had to be perpetuated.

Though the pair scoured the remaining account books, they were unable to find any further references to Almira.

"That isn't unusual," Mrs. Holding said. "Many girls attended for short periods and, for various reasons, did not complete through to graduation."

"Is there any other set of records I ought to check?"

Mrs. Holding shook her head. "No, I don't think so. The only other source might be the records of the alumnae association. We are the oldest women's alumnae association in the world, you know, but since Miss Hamilton isn't listed as a graduate, I doubt we would find anything there."

It was clear that the visit to the Albany Academy for Girls had run its course, at least for that day. Miss Lamar was summoned. She collected the assorted books and left. After a few more minutes of idle conversation, David and Mrs. Holding walked back up the hallway to the lobby, where he stopped to take a last look at the marble portrait.

"What happened to her?" he asked.

"I must admit that I don't know," Mrs. Holding said, with a hint of embarrassment. "Give me some time. I will look into this matter and contact you. It is something I should know about."

Outside, David made his way to the Ghia. It was the end of the school day. The weather, that of a beautiful, Indian summer afternoon. Groups of girls in hunter green clustered in front of the academy, waiting for their rides while a few walked with friends to their own cars.

Across the street, students from the boys' academy in gray uniforms were doing the same, while another group practiced close order drill on the athletic field. Watching them, David folded down the top of his convertible.

On the way back to Willsboro, David couldn't help but be excited, imagining Almira's pleasure when he told her about his trip to Albany. The Wedgewood plate would be like bringing home a trophy. He was nearly all the way back to Whitehall when he remembered Angela's warning about Almira. Beautiful and tragic, she'd said. What did she call it? A classic rescue fantasy. She was right, and that tragic quality begged for protection.

Dr. Koenigsberg had also cautioned him about indulging such ideas, knowing all this countertransference was ill-advised from a therapeutic standpoint. Without question, he was straying from professional conduct. The heart of the dilemma, he had to admit, was that he didn't so much want a therapeutic relationship with Almira. Not primarily—not anymore. What he wanted was something different, something intensely personal and intimate.

Chapter 14

October, 1841

Mrs. Bright guided George Hamilton into the parlor. He'd arrived from Willsborough the night before by packet and taken rooms at the Albion, as was his habit when in Albany on business.

"It is such a pleasure to meet you," she said. And it was, for Hamilton had made an impression on the woman the moment he'd stepped through the door of her boarding house. "I was pleased to receive your letter of last week."

"The pleasure is all mine, madam," he said with a bow. "My visit remains a surprise, I assume?"

"Of course. Almira has no suspicions, but until she returns from school, please do have a seat." Mrs. Bright directed an aproned maid to bring them coffee as she settled herself into the chair opposite.

"Are you in Albany on business or simply to visit your lovely daughter?"

"Both actually. She will be nineteen years old on the sixteenth of next month. Since I have business in the city, I decided to surprise her with an early birthday visit."

"Ah, is that not a parent's joy?" matron Bright said. "Your daughter tells us that you are engaged in trade along Lake Champlain. According to her, you're quite the sea captain."

Laughing off the compliment, Hamilton said, "I'm afraid Almira exaggerates, though I have captained a vessel or two over the years. Now I mostly own the ships and leave sailing to the younger men."

As they made small talk, Mrs. Bright studied his face, trying to discern some family resemblance or shared mannerisms. She saw little of either, except a look in the eyes that suggested the same stubborn determination she'd seen more than once in Almira's.

A tray was placed on the table between them, and the maid poured each a cup. "You want cream and sugar, sir?"

"Yes, that would be nice."

"Will there be anything else, ma'am?"

"No, Tildie, but do remind Rose that she needs to trim the wicks before sunset."

Hamilton stirred his coffee with a miniature spoon, then took a long sip. "Ah, that is good."

The two continued their conversation, mostly about the Albany Female Academy. Before she'd realized it, Mrs. Bright had recounted her entire association with the institution, and much about her own past. For her, Hamilton was strangely easy to talk to. His personality was arresting and impossible for her to ignore. What was more, the immaculate grooming, rugged features, and graying red hair were all evocative of her late husband. He even shared Jonathan's habit of lacing his fingers on his knee. How many years had it been, she thought, reminded of how lonely she was?

"Please tell me, how is my daughter?"

"Very well, I should say. Almira gets on famously with the other boarders and is a pleasant companion to us all. She tells me she enjoys her classes, and it's clear to me that she takes a great interest in them."

"It does my heart good to hear all this, madam," Hamilton said.

"Parents are always delighted when they learn that their daughters are doing well."

"No, it is more than that. Allow me to explain. The last year or more has been trying for Almira. When her mother was taken from us, the girl was grief-stricken, took it badly. She was inconsolable for weeks, months. Frankly, since then it has been a difficult time for all of us. My daughter is changed. She has become sullen and sometimes willful in ways she never was before."

"The poor thing," said Mrs. Bright.

"I tell you all this confidentially, of course. But I imagine you already have more experience guiding girls into womanhood than I will ever have."

Mrs. Bright smiled and nodded, but inwardly she felt a flicker of excitement, already fantasizing that Hamilton would begin visiting his daughter more frequently during her time at the academy. As he spoke, she imagined the way their growing familiarity would blossom into friendship, and how Almira's eventual graduation would coincide with a proposal of marriage from widower to widow.

Hamilton took another sip of his coffee and continued. "To be honest, Almira was reluctant to come to Albany, but I felt it was important she be removed from the influence of certain situations at home in Willsborough."

Lost in her daydream of life as Almira's stepmother, Mrs. Bright said, "Of course."

Hamilton cleared his throat and went on. "In any event, it is my hope that the academy will expose her to a better class of, well, a better class of suitors."

She imagined them together, sharing domestic life, meals, quiet evening conversations—a large feather bed. It wasn't too late. She wasn't yet an old crone.

"I am like all fathers, I suppose. I would like to see my daughter make a good match. Marriage to a young man of ambition, of some means and strong moral standing, would please us a great deal."

"Us?" said Mrs. Bright. Reality, she feared, was about to reassert itself.

"Yes, I have very recently remarried. As a matter of fact, my new bride is a graduate of the academy. Class of '28, if I remember correctly."

At the stab of jealousy, Mrs. Bright silently chastised herself for entertaining such foolish, foolish, foolish ideas. Thankfully, the sound of a half dozen girlish voices engaged in as many conversations approached from the street.

"Sir, it sounds like Almira and her classmates have returned from their school day. Before they come in let me assure you that I understand your intentions completely. Do not be concerned. As you'll presently see, your daughter is both happy and well supervised under my care." She stood and added, "Come, let me introduce you to my girls."

Hamilton rose from his seat, adjusted his cravat and tugged once on the lapels of his tailcoat. As the door flew open, a whirlwind of bonnets, cloaks, and rustling skirts poured into the central hallway.

"I knew I should have worn my woolen dress today," one of the girls said.

Another girl shrugged her cape off into a maid's waiting hands, while the rest of them hung their cloaks and bonnets from pegs along the wall.

Girls today favor dark, somber colors, and flattened, oiled hair. Mrs. Bright sighed. They were so different from the girls of her own youth who had always tried to outdo each other in colorful dress and flamboyant ornamentation. The commotion from the hall brought her back.

From the parlor, Mrs. Bright announced, "Ladies, girls, do come in and meet Miss Hamilton's visitor."

Almira turned around in surprise with all the others, but then her hands flew to her face. "Father," she cried. "You are in Albany."

In her new knowledge of the details of Almira's life over the past year, Mrs. Bright thought she detected a welling of competing emotions—anticipation, disappointment, fear, and maybe even relief.

"I have waited long enough to see my dear Dolly." Father and daughter embraced. Hamilton held her by the hands at arm's length. "Let me inspect you, my city girl."

Everyone watched as Almira dabbed her eyes. The tears were unexpected, for no one had seen her cry before. Mrs. Bright was especially touched. She'd judged her to be a sensible girl, one not given to frequent outbursts.

Holding two of his fingers in her tiny fist, Almira turned to the others in the room. "Everyone, I would like to introduce my father, Mr. George Hamilton."

Hamilton found himself surrounded by an array of academy girls. As Mrs. Bright looked on proudly, Almira introduced each in turn.

"Father, this is Miss Gardiner of Shelter Island."

Phebe curtseyed demurely as Hamilton bent to kiss her hand.

"Miss Gardiner," he said. "It is an honor."

"And this is Miss Wilcox of Orwell, Vermont, Miss Ames of Quincy, Massachusetts; and, of course, you already know Susannah."

Hamilton bowed to each, repeating the ritual.

"These are the Skinner sisters," Almira said, indicating the twins in matching plaid dresses. "They are from Plattsburgh. This is Betty Wheeler of Vermont, and Miss Carvalho from Charleston, South Carolina."

Hamilton took Rebecca's hand and slowly kissed her drooping fingertips. "My, but you have come a long way," he marveled. "I do hope you find our northern life to your taste."

"I do, but you must promise me the weather won't turn colder than it already is. I thought I'd freeze walking to the academy with Miss Almira this morning."

"It's true, Papa. Rebecca was bundled up like January."

"Then my girl, you will see to it that Miss Carvalho is well supplied with flannels and furs," Hamilton said with the sweep of his arm. "I expect you to protect this rare southern flower from our harsh climate."

Rebecca, who was seldom speechless, concealed her face behind one hand. "Really sir, you flatter me," she said, nearly stumbling over her words.

So inspired was she by the perfect deportment of her charges, Mrs. Bright exclaimed, "Sir, you must join us for tea."

Phebe endorsed the idea, saying, "Truly, *monsieur*. We have so few gentlemen visitors. It would please us exceedingly if you would be our guest."

"Yes, Mr. Hamilton," said the twins, insisting. "Please do, please."

From the chorus of bashful titters, feminine smiles, and fluttering lashes it was obvious to Mrs. Bright that Hamilton was flirting with her girls and, what was more, quite successfully. Even the taciturn Emily, who was not given to spontaneous expression of any kind, seemed to have come alive under his masculine spell.

Raising one hand high, Hamilton said, "Ladies, I have dedicated plans already to dine with my daughter. May I accept your gracious invitation on my next visit to Albany?"

An audible wave of disappointment passed through the room. Hamilton told Almira he would return for her in two hours. "In the meantime, you should prepare yourself for an elegant evening." Turning to the others he bowed and said, "Until then I bid all you charming ladies, *adieu*."

At the entrance, Hamilton left amid a storm of farewells and delight at meeting him.

"Come on," Rebecca took Almira's hand. "We've got to prepare you."

As they ascended the stairs, a great drowsiness took hold of Mrs. Bright, so overcome was she with memories of long-ago girlhood. She retired to her bedroom and locked the door.

George Hamilton returned punctually at six-thirty. Almira was ready, though it had taken a community effort. She wore her own best silk plaid dress with matching pelisse, her hair had been freshly dressed by

Phebe, her hands warmed within Susannah's newly finished fingerless mitts. From her wrist dangled Rebecca's ermine muff. Even Harriet had contributed a daub of perfume.

Taking her father's elbow, they descended the front steps together and walked to a waiting carriage, where a uniformed footman held the door open.

"It will be good for you to have experience in dining, my girl," he told her as they settled themselves inside on velvet cushions. "The next time, you may be in the company of a proper gentleman. It will not do for you to appear uncultured."

At State Street the driver reined the horses to a stop. Peering through the carriage windows, Almira saw sidewalks teeming with people softly illuminated by gas light. One building was especially active, with candles in every window. She read a signboard swaying over the entrance, "Three Roses Eating House."

Hamilton escorted his daughter through an entryway where freshly caught game hung on display—two grouse, a turkey, and a large hare.

Inside, they checked coat, cloak, bonnet, walking stick, and top hat, and were led upstairs to a private room where a valet seated them at a round table. It was covered in an immaculate white linen cloth upon which napkins, silverware, and crystal goblets of iced water were perfectly arrayed.

Almira looked around wide-eyed. On a nearby sideboard were bottles of fine wines, spirits, and liqueurs in crystal decanters. Another, along the opposite wall, was laden with loaves of bread, bowls of nuts, and fruits of every variety.

Father," she said. "Aren't those oranges?"

"They are."

A uniformed waiter approached. "Sir, madam, our *carte du jour*."

Hamilton took the menu in hand without glancing at it and continued his conversation. "How many live at your boarding house?" he said.

Let me see," said Almira. "Nine of us girls, Mrs. Bright, her nephew, and the two chambermaids."

"Very well." He turned to the waiter. "Young fellow, while my daughter and I review your bill of fare, open a bottle of your best madeira. And my daughter will have...?" He tilted his head in Almira's direction.

"Have you any cocoa?"

The waiter nodded. Hamilton scowled.

"Almira, cocoa? You can't be serious. Have they taught you no ladylike ways at this academy of yours? Have a glass of sherry."

"Father, do you forget I am temperate?"

Hamilton rolled his eyes and turned his attention back to the waiter. "The lady will have cocoa. And one more thing. Do see to it that three-dozen oranges are delivered to the boarding house of Mrs. Bright at thirty-six Maiden Lane. See to that immediately."

After placing a full goblet before his guest, the waiter bowed and disappeared. Hamilton looked across the table at his daughter.

"Father," exclaimed Almira, "all those oranges will cost a great deal."

He waved it off. "It is of little consequence. Besides, I just this afternoon signed a lucrative contract with Commodore Vanderbilt." He took a drink of his wine and added, "Remember, in this life it does no harm to make a good-faith gesture."

Almira and her father placed their orders with another waiter— grouse for her and a beef steak for him. The meal began with turtle soup (which she thought tasted better than it sounded), breads, and a variety of cheeses. When her grouse arrived, she eyed the sauces suspiciously and was mortified to learn that the unknown side dish was escargot.

"That's snails to us," Hamilton informed her.

Noticing that his daughter had left much on her plate untouched, Hamilton said, "Dolly, you've barely touched your meal. Isn't it to your liking?"

"Surely it is, but it would be unladylike for me to consume more than half."

"Of course. How could I have forgotten."

With the main course whisked away, the Hamiltons were served a round of dessert. Almira asked for another cocoa while Hamilton ordered a glass of tawny port.

"I hope you've enjoyed your introduction to French dining. I know it isn't to our American taste, but such is society today. In any case, it's important that you be familiar with these things."

Almira studied him as he raised the glass of port to his nose and inhaled its smoky aroma. He took a sip, set the glass down and closed his eyes.

"It has been a long year, my girl. Things have changed so much since your last birthday."

Her father rolled the stem between his fingers. The port swirled, first one way, then the other. Thick as blood, it reminded her of the terrible secret she was carrying.

Almira felt pulled in so many directions. Her love of the academy life, with all its urbane excitements vied with her need to escape into Daniel's arms, to be alone with him in a life of their own. Soon, her terrible predicament would become known. Then it would be too late for choices.

"Yes," he continued, "much has changed. But we are well and together, celebrating your birthday once again, so we must be thankful for that."

"Do you think of her?" Almira said.

Hamilton opened one eye. "Your mother? Every day," he said. "An hour doesn't go by but that she comes to mind. I imagine it's the same for you."

"It is," said Almira. "Sometimes I awaken at night from a dream, and it feels like she is there in the room with me. Other times it is hard for me to remember her at all. That frightens me."

Hamilton reached across the table, taking his daughter's hand in his and holding it tightly. "Tell me about the academy."

"The academy is hard, so much more than my tutors at home ever were," Almira said. She wanted to confide more but didn't dare. The shame of her secret was too awful to reveal anything more, so she went on about her school. "Some of the classes confound me, but us girls study together, and I enjoy most all of them. We have wonderful instructors too, though I should say that the female teachers are harder on us than the gentlemen."

"I'm not surprised," he said, laughing.

Almira told her father about a visit her department made to the office of engraving. He nodded with approval, then asked her to tell him more. She described the visit by the deaf students and their way of finger spelling.

"And the other girls at Mrs. Bright's, what are they like?"

"They're very nice, mostly. They all come from the best of families. Susannah is a sweet child, as are the Skinner sisters and that little girl Betty from Vermont. I don't spend so much time with them."

"No? What about the rest of them?"

"Emily is a teaching scholar. She is my roommate and the oldest of us, I think already twenty-one. She is an excellent seamstress, as is Phebe Gardiner, though she is not nearly as old. Did you know Phebe is a cousin of Miss Julia Gardiner?"

"No," said Hamilton, as he put down his glass. "Should I recognize the name?"

"Most surely. Julia Gardiner is known as the Rose of Long Island, and the Gardiners are a very well-respected family."

"Of course, forgive me. And who is your favorite?"

"I should say Rebecca. You met her—she is the girl from Charleston. Didn't you like her Southern accent?"

Hamilton chuckled. "I certainly did. She makes an impression. She seems very nice though."

"Oh, she is. We have such fun together. Can I tell you a secret?" Almira leaned forward and whispered, "she is a *j-e-w.*"

Hamilton laughed out loud and slapped the table. "You don't say." He drained his second glass of port and added, "My dear girl, you're so innocent."

"Then it doesn't bother you?"

"For God's sake Mirie, no. I've done business with a Jew or two in my day. Good businessmen and I'd say a damned sight more trustworthy than your average Dutchman. These Albany square-heads will eat the cheese off your plate if you let them."

Assured now that her father wasn't offended by her choice of friends, Almira became more forthcoming. "One girl, that one from Massachusetts, thinks Rebecca oughtn't to be allowed at the academy."

"Why, because she's a Jew?"

"Yes, but also because her family owns slaves. Did you know the servant girl is Rebecca's slave?"

"You don't say," said Hamilton, his cheeks glowing like embers in the candlelight, his eyes gleaming like wet stones. "The dark haired one I suppose, not that fat Irish girl."

"No, that's Rose," she said. "The other maid. Rebecca told me she's only one fourth cast, but that still makes her a negress."

"Well, you are learning some things at that academy after all," he said, a little too loudly.

Hamilton tapped the rim of his crystal goblet. It was refilled at once. Almira watched as he drained half the glass. It was, she wagered, perhaps a good time to raise a question.

"Father, the academy offers a class in bookkeeping. Do you think I might take it? I think it would be an improvement in my practical knowledge."

Her motivation was indeed practical. During daydreams in algebra, Almira had imagined herself as an essential partner in Daniel's future daguerreotype gallery. She visualized keeping ledgers, corresponding with suppliers, and greeting sitters as they arrived. Maybe Daniel would teach her the daguerreotype process. Perhaps this would all take place somewhere out west; Buffalo or Cincinnati perhaps, but wherever it was, they would be working side-by-side, building a new life together.

Hamilton's eyes narrowed. "Bookkeeping," he said. "What does a lady need that for?"

"Well, you will recall the book you and Mother presented me on my last birthday, *The Young Lady's Friend?*"

"Yes, of course."

"I read in it that it's important for all ladies of the house to know how to keep thrifty accounts, lest servants and unscrupulous tradesmen take advantage of their gentle nature."

"There may be some truth to that. I'll consider it. But for now, my dear girl, we have one other item of business."

Hamilton turned to the waiter. "Fellow," he said, "bring that silver platter over here, won't you?"

The server placed the covered platter on the table and stepped back. Almira couldn't imagine eating more, her corset stays were already uncomfortable.

"Go on. Take a look inside," her father said. It was less an invitation than a command.

She raised the lid. At very first she thought what lay underneath must be yet another course to this meal, but then realized she was looking at a fur so black it had a bluish tinge.

"Well pick it up for God's sake."

Almira extended her mitted hand to stroke the fur, but her fingers disappeared within its exquisite softness. "It's a muff, isn't it?"

"I should say it is, and a damned smart one at that."

"Muffs are all the fashion," she called. "How did you know? And this one is so beautiful."

"Yes, my girl, it is. Mind you, that's not muskrat either. It's genuine seal from the Pacific northwest."

Almira picked it up and buried her face in the fur. Indeed, it smelled of far-off places. "Thank you, Papa, it's a wonderful gift."

"Consider it from me and Loretta both. She specifically instructed me to buy you a muff and to spare no cost in doing so."

"That is so kind of her."

"It is," he agreed. "And I'm gladdened to see your feelings toward Loretta have softened. She does love you, as does little Bertie. He asks incessantly when you are coming home."

"He may have to wait until next summer," said Almira, who continued to run her hands through the muff and brush it across her face. "I've been told that last year Principal Crittenden allowed us scholars but Christmas and New Year's Day off from their studies. The girls were terribly disappointed. Don't you think it was unfair of him?"

There was no response. Hamilton's father's mind seemed to have wandered a long way off, preoccupied, she thought, with business on the lake.

"Father," she said. "I want to thank you. Not just for this, but for everything you have done for me. I know I've caused you some distress since Mother's death, but whatever else may happen, however I might yet disappoint you, I want you to know how much I love and respect you."

Hamilton's eyes welled up. "Dolly, you are my own baby girl," he said. "I would do anything for you. You do know that." He cleared his throat. "Now we must return you to your studies at the boarding house. There is work to do."

111

Chapter 15

September, 1971

David Weis had come to the theory that electro-magnetic fields, such as those created by electrical gadgets—appliances, radios, even battery powered wrist-watches—were incompatible with the ability of ghosts to materialize, either by erasing echoes of the past, or by interfering with the capability of spirit entities to interact with the present. This, he reasoned, was why Almira appeared exclusively in the Quiet Room and could be seen only within that room or from the adjoining room. As undisturbed as a snowdrift at dawn, neither of those rooms had ever been corrupted by electronic appliances or wiring.

Purity had to be enforced. Lots of things could generate disturbing, electro-magnetic fields. Consequently, he adopted a strict policy of no electronics near or within the Quiet Room. David had started wearing a stem-wound watch a long time ago. Once, when Angela brought a transistor radio into the Quiet Room, he'd been so upset he insisted she shut it off immediately and take it downstairs.

When he sought a visit with Almira, David adopted the habit of sleeping in the small adjacent room. Thus, on this first night since the trip to Albany, he found himself retiring by lamplight. He sat on the trundle bed pulling off his shoes, the chirping of a vast phalanx of crickets flowing in through the open window. The sound wasn't just relaxing, it mesmerized him as would the drone of a thousand sitars. Uncertain if his extraordinary patient would appear before dawn, Weis snuffed out the wick and drifted off to sleep.

Sometime during the night, David jolted awake, aware that everything, especially the crickets, had gone silent. His luminous watch indicated a few minutes after one a.m. Lamplight seeped in from beyond the threshold to the Quiet Room. She had arrived and sat patiently waiting for their conversation to begin.

Dressing quickly, Weis rubbed his face with a cold, damp towel. He figured telling Almira about his trip to Albany and showing her the piece of Wedgewood he'd brought back would be exciting. After all, her reaction was a legitimate clinical concern, wasn't it? But David had another, equally strong, more genuine motive. He wanted to please her and gain her approval. Therapeutically it didn't hold water, but who was to know.

A few minutes later, he tapped on the door. "It's Doctor Weis."

"Oh. *Cher Monsieur, s'il vous plaît entrer.*"

Weis smiled and stepped inside. Almira lounged on her daybed, bathed in the warm glow of a wall sconce and candles on the mantelpiece.

"If you don't mind," he said, "I'll get a chair and sit down." David retrieved the klismos and set it a few feet away from her.

"It's good to see you again, miss."

"And you, doctor."

As his eyes adjusted to the dim light, David perceived that Almira wore a dark gray dress with a green floral design. He'd seen her in it before. Draped about her shoulders was a fringed paisley shawl, an open book on her lap. Recognizing the pastel-colored pages, he said, "Isn't that your *Mossrose Album?*"

"It is. I was just reminiscing a little about the academy."

"A pleasant memory, I hope?"

"Very pleasant," she said. "Though it leaves me wondering what happened to these girls. I do so miss some of them."

In recent sessions, it seemed she was becoming more cognizant of her peculiar condition, namely, her separation from living humanity and the afterlife, alike. Presumably, this awareness was helping to move her toward unification with some spiritual host. Bringing up his trip to Albany was bound to contribute to this sense of exile, and that might be uncomfortable for her, but therapeutic progress was rarely made without growing pains. Still, how does one measure therapeutic progress with a ghost?

He was eager to show her the Wedgewood plate, to get her approval and approbation. Any lingering questions could be answered as he went along. David opened the discussion. "I was in Albany last week," he said, taking care to make his elapsed time in transit seem reasonable to her nineteenth century expectations.

"Were you, doctor? Do tell."

"Yes," said David. "I had some people I needed to see in the city, professional appointments."

"Albany is such a busy place. You did not, perchance, have your daguerreotype taken whilst you were there, did you?"

"No. I thought I might, but I had no idea which gallery to visit. Is there one you would recommend?"

"Horsford & Cushman's," she said. "There is none other worthy of one's time. Should you go back, I would suggest you go to that gallery directly. That is where mine was taken."

Horsford & Cushman. Those names weren't among those he'd come up with at Larry Greer's place. David made to write them down and thought to ask, "Is that so? Cushman with a *C*?"

"That's right," she said. "Mr. Cushman was a true gentleman, a poet, and engraver. "It was such a pity when he passed. They say it was the mercury vapors which killed him."

"Then he died while you were in Albany?"

"Yes. He was loved and mourned by very many people."

"So," said David, "would this Mr. Horsford make my image if I went there now?"

"No, I think not. Mr. Horsford is a professor at the academy and does not pose the sitters. I expect it would be Mr. Meade or Mr. Dwyer."

This is becoming very interesting, thought Weis. "I've heard of Meade," he said. "But the other gentleman's name is new to me."

Almira smiled and cast her eyes to the floor. "You truly don't know who he is?" she said.

"No.

"Can you keep a secret?"

"Yes, of course."

She leaned in and whispered, "He is my own Daniel."

Her entire network of relationships in the 1840s world, personal, professional, and academic were coming to light. "Tell me more," he said, trying to conceal his excitement.

"Very well." Almira closed her autograph book and fixed her eyes on the cover, embossed with a rose in gold-leaf. She ran her hand over it as one would the flank of a purring cat. "I have not told you this before, doctor, but I have come to trust you. Can you understand?"

David always cringed when clients asked this question. There was no way to answer it without sounding either presumptuous or ignorant, so he settled on his old standby. "I hope so."

"That's honest of you," she said. "Of late I'm not certain I understand myself."

Almira looked toward the window. "I should tell you more. Daniel and I were very fond of each other. Exceedingly fond."

She seemed to stall, something beyond the wavy panes of glass capturing her attention.

"Yes, go on please," David said, trying to prompt her.

"Very well." She took a deep breath. "When I commenced at

116

the academy, he followed me to Albany. Daniel wanted to learn the Daguerreian arts. That is when he secured a position at Horsford & Cushman's."

All the while she spoke, David scribbled notes. Hearing Almira talk about the past as if it was the present was riveting enough, but to have her illuminating long forgotten details about the dawn of photography made her recollection even more irresistible.

"So, Daniel became a daguerreotype photographer," he said. "What else do you recall?"

"I remember that Mr. Meade was quite enchanted with my friend Rebecca. Who knows, they may already have married."

David made a note to research Cushman, Horsford, and Dwyer.

"He may be in Charleston," Almira blurted out.

"Excuse me, who?"

"Daniel. We had a plan to marry and open a daguerreotype gallery there. It was Rebecca's idea, but her father, Mr. Carvalho, agreed to underwrite us. Daniel would be the first daguerreotype artist in all the Carolinas."

David realized this was another lead he had to research. Daniel Dwyer may have gone to Charleston and opened a gallery in partnership with or financed by someone named Carvalho. It was an unusual name and ought to be easy to identify if such records existed. But David was eager to show Almira what he'd brought back with him from Albany.

"While I was there, I bought something which I think you'd enjoy seeing." Removing the Wedgewood plate from under his legal pad, David held it up in the manner of a shield. "Do you see what I am holding?"

Almira's gaze seemed to pass through him, so he again said, "Do you see this plate?"

Her eyes narrowed, as if focusing on something a long way off.

David repeated the question one more time. "Miss Hamilton, can you see what I am holding?"

"A plate," she said, her voice sounding at once quite near and yet very remote, like patients he'd observed under hypnosis.

Do you recognize this building?" he said, tapping the center of the plate.

"I do. That is my academy."

He decided to test her willingness to interact with the present and held the plate out to her.

"Would you like to hold it, take a closer look?"

Almira shrank back as if from a menacing animal.

Regrouping, David had another idea. He stood, walked to the mantel, and positioned the plate upright against the mirror.

When he looked back at the daybed, Almira had reoriented herself and faced him. Intending to establish in her mind the location of the only object from his world that she'd responded to so far, David remained standing by the fireplace.

"Isn't this plate beautiful, Miss Hamilton?"

"It is."

Her voice sounded a world away, a woman in the throes of some benign trance. She's fixating on it, he thought, she's responding to something in the present world.

"And you can see the academy printed on it?"

"I can, yes."

"I'm going to sit down now," he said. "Then, if you like, you can come and take a closer look for yourself."

As he walked back to the klismos chair, her eyes darted back and forth between David and the mantelpiece. Once he was seated, she stood and, with characteristic silence, made her way across the room. She and the image of her school, standing against the mirror, were only inches apart, yet she was nowhere reflected in either surface.

"Wherever did you come by this?" she said.

"I bought it from a friend in Albany. He has a…a curiosity shop."

Almira wrinkled her nose. Her mouth worked for a moment before she was able to speak. "Did you go by the academy as well?

"I did, yes," said David, thinking back to the sad ruins he'd seen the day before. "I walked right past it. It's a very impressive building."

Almira stood transfixed before the plate. Her attention never wavered, yet she made no attempt to touch it.

"I wonder if many of my schoolmates and instructors are still there. Emily and Rebecca are surely graduated by this time, but the Skinner sisters, and Phebe Gardiner...they are, I should think, not likely finished."

The plate seemed to have a calming effect. Almira looked relaxed and less cautious. Was she projecting herself into the setting?

"Seeing this," she said. "I can so well remember how proud I felt to approach this building and pass between its columns."

For a moment, David had an unsettling vision of Almira in a bonnet and shawl, basket at her elbow, climbing the litter strewn steps and portico of the Albany Female Academy, her skirts sweeping aside empty beer cans, liquor bottles, and cigarette butts.

"Didn't you tell me you lived at a boarding house on Maiden Lane?"

"I did, yes."

"Well, I went there too. It's a very narrow street," David said.

Almira turned toward him. "You found it so? I think no more than any others in the city. Were it wider, it should be named Broadway."

They both smiled at her clever pun, but the cheerful mood didn't last. Almira returned her attention to the Wedgewood plate. "How I should love to go back there sometime," she said, her voice trailing off. "It was a happy place for me, but I am obliged to wait here."

That sounded like a psychotherapeutic opening to David. "That sounds lonely."

"Doctor Weis, you cannot imagine. It is as if everyone has gone off and left me. I've been desperately lonely. It seems like I've been waiting and waiting and waiting forever."

Almira turned back to the plate. Gathering her shawl closer, she said, "Doctor, there is something I must ask you."

David nodded. "Of course, anything."

"Would you leave this plate here on the mantelpiece? For a little while at least? It would mean so much to me if you did. For though it stimulates my loneliness, so it does my happy memories as well."

In the morning David set out to confirm the notes he'd taken during the previous night. He called Larry Greer in Albany. "I've got a special favor to ask you."

"Sure, go ahead."

"Next time you're at the library, could you check out a few names for me?" David gave him the particulars. "I'm looking for daguerreotypers named Cushman, Dwyer, Carvalho, and some guy named Horsford. He might have been a professor at that female academy we talked about when I was at your place."

"It'll take some time," said Larry. "Can you lay some bread on me?"

"Sure. I'll put a check in the mail. And one more thing. I'm interested in whoever opened the first daguerreotype studio in Charleston, South Carolina. Call me collect when you have the information."

That afternoon there was an estate sale in Utica. A disappointment as it turned out, but David couldn't have known that. On the way home it occurred to him that it was Rosh Hashana, the last of the Jewish high holidays, specifically the Day of Atonement. It came early that year. In the past, he'd ignored it, along with all the other holidays, unless forced by unavoidable family obligations.

Wasn't that part of the point of living up here, to be beyond the reach of family obligations. The Weis family wasn't religious. Judaism was seldom mentioned in their home, but of course he'd been taught the basic tenants.

David, don't be such a godless animal, a religious aunt had once told him, and maybe she was right. Maybe atoning was a good thing in and of itself. Didn't we all have something to atone for?

So ran David's thoughts as he parked the truck. The shadows grew long. He'd have to act quickly. According to custom it would be too late once the sun touched the horizon, so he went inside and snatched a slice of white bread from the loaf on the counter. He fled out the back door, letting the screen bang shut behind him. David walked briskly. On the way he rolled the bread between his palms until it was a sphere no larger than a Ping-Pong ball. The last time he'd done this, he'd been what, eleven or twelve? Little more than a kid. He was with his aunt from Crown Heights—she of the godless animal remark. Sin could be washed away, she claimed, by casting bread into the water.

Like pictures in some horrible portrait-essay, the faces of people he'd used flashed before his eyes. Those whose suffering he'd ignored, whose need he'd turned to his advantage. A girl in high school, a student nurse in college, Cheryl Jankowsky. How long had it been since her suicide? He thought about Angela. He'd meant to treat her better but felt somehow incapable of it, or resistant. Perhaps he wanted to test her dedication to him by seeing how much crap she would take. It was kind of sick, he had to admit.

By the time he got to the lakeshore, David felt weighed down by the sins he needed to cast away. The sun was low now, almost set and yet, not quite—not quite too late. The water would have to be deep to accommodate this many trespasses, the laws of displacement absolute. He held the ball of bread in his hand for a moment, then hurled it as far out into the lake as he could.

Chapter 16

November, 1841

Almira's growing uncertainty haunted her like a restless spirit throughout the following week. Her thoughts rarely escaped dread for more than a few minutes, making schoolwork difficult and she, herself, heavy company to be around. Preferring to be alone, she took to withdrawing to her room soon after the evening meal. Once, she even excused herself from the table to rush upstairs to vomit into the chamber pot under her bed.

The only bright moment came the day she received a letter from Sarah Rawson. It didn't offer any advice about her situation—their most recent correspondence perhaps, having crossed in the mail. But a penciled letter from Daniel was hidden inside. Just a note, Almira read it over and over. She was comforted by his strong and loving words, but she knew this would all change when he learned of her shame.

More time passed. A few days later there was a letter from her father and Loretta, but nothing from Sarah. Why? Given the nature of her revelation and plea for help, Almira felt certain Sarah must have been disgusted by her last missive. Yes, she'd suspended their friendship. How could it be otherwise?

Even *The Young Lady's Friend* had abandoned her, for though she searched over and again, she could find no advice about a girl's natural courses, or what to do when they were interrupted.

On Wednesday night immediately after supper, Almira announced that she must succumb to the demands of schoolwork and retire. Emily was still downstairs. Alone in the privacy of her room she undressed and examined her changing body. It was sensitive where it hadn't been before, and there was a swelling to her middle that resisted all efforts to lace her corset stays closely. Almira sank to her bed, her mind rudderless. Why hadn't she received another letter from Daniel? Could it be that he'd forgotten her, grown tired of her? Maybe he'd already found another girl he loved more. A Catholic girl. Someone pure and chaste.

There came a tap on the door. "Who is it?"

"It is I, Rebecca. May I come in?"

"What do you want?"

"Just to talk. May I please come in?"

Almira closed her eyes. "Yes."

Rebecca found Almira sitting cross-legged on her bed, wearing only her chemise, head in her hands. She closed the door behind her, walked across the room and sat on the edge of the mattress.

"Almira," she said. "You've been so quiet lately. What's wrong? What's troubling you?" She didn't respond or even look up, so Rebecca tried again. "Please tell me."

Almira shook her head and whispered, "No, it's too disgraceful."

A strand of hair fell across her face. She brushed it aside. "Rebecca, does your Aunt Flo visit you every month at the same time?"

At first Rebecca looked puzzled by the question, but in the quiet of the room, the implication was clear. "Yes," she said. "Very regularly."

"I thought so."

The sound of Harriet's piano lessons drifted up from the parlor.

The two girls sat together, Almira working a thumbnail, face averted.

"Mirie," she said, placing a hand on her friend's knee, "is your visit overdue?"

Almira nodded.

"How long?"

"Since last summer."

"Do you know why?"

She nodded again.

They sat quietly for a while longer. Rebecca's gaze searched the room, as if looking for words to ease her friend's agony. "May I ask you another question?"

"Yes."

"Does the reason have anything to do with Mr. Dwyer?"

Another nod, this one accompanied by a sound not unlike that of a small, frightened child. Almira looked up for the first time, eyes red with tears. "Becca, help me. I don't know what to do."

This was the first night on which Mrs. Bright allowed a coal fire in the parlor. She sat near it, warming herself and reading her newspaper. Most of the other boarders were scattered around the room. Harriet sat at the pianoforte, playing a darkly romantic piece while little Betty Wheeler looked on. Emily sat at the secretary grading homework. Susannah, crocheting a pair of fingerless mitts, looked vaguely suggestive of a spider spinning its web as she fed silk floss through her needles.

On the settee, Almira lounged with Rebecca. It was the first evening since her confession that she'd felt well enough to be in society. In fact, taking her mind from those worries left her feeling a little giddy.

The girls' idle conversation drifted from the classes of the quarter just commenced to the subject of horseback riding.

Almira thought every girl should know how to ride. "It's superb exercise and builds confidence," she said.

Susannah worked her needles without looking up. "Do you ride?"

"Most certainly. At home I've a pony of my own and ride her almost every day, all about my father's property."

"Has your pony a name?"

"Of course. Ginger Snap," said Almira. "Her color's just like the cookie."

All the girls laughed and pronounced Ginger Snap a decidedly smart name for a pony.

"Well, horses scare me to death," said Rebecca. "When I visit my cousins, we poke around on these itty-bitty donkeys led by our people, but we never ever let them even break into a trot."

"Your people or the donkeys?" Almira teased, alluding to a forbidden subject in Mrs. Bright's parlor, the temptation for mischief too irresistible.

"You wicked girl," said Rebecca, slapping her friend's wrist. "Surely I don't know."

Susannah looked puzzled, but recovered and said, "My father told me riding horses isn't ladylike."

"Not if one rides side-saddle," said Almira. "Riding side-saddle is graceful if you've been properly taught. The son of an English lancer gave me private lessons. Now I can ride like a lady at near a full gallop. It's thrilling."

Mrs. Bright folded her newspaper, got up, and said, "I have some things to attend to so will beg all of your pardons. Also, Almira, I received by today's mail a note from that young man, the daguerreotyper, Mr. Dwyer, requesting permission to pay you a visit this Sunday afternoon. If you wish, I will reply with my consent."

"Yes, please," said Almira, clapping her hands. Harriet paused for a moment, then resumed her piece, the tempo slightly slower now.

"Very well, I will tell him he may arrive at two o'clock and stay for two hours, provided I or Emily are chaperoning at all times."

"Oh, thank you Mrs. Bright. Thank you so much," she said as she and Rebecca squeezed each other's hands.

As soon as the girls were alone, Betty called out, "Almira, he's so handsome. He's so dashing. Harriet, don't you agree?"

"Yes, Mr. Dwyer is handsome in a rugged way I suppose."

"I think Harriet is jealous," teased little Betty.

"I am not. If Almira receives Mr. Dwyer, it is of no consequence to me. After all, he is not of a class."

When she heard this, Almira demanded an explanation.

"Come now," said Harriet, a sly smile creeping across her face. "The fellow is hardly more than a common merchant's clerk selling a chemical novelty."

"Harriet, you surely don't mean that?" said Rebecca, hoping to relieve the escalating tension, but it was far too late.

Almira's eyes went dark. "The daguerreotype is not a novelty," she said, hands on hips. "It is an art, and only a true artist can do the process justice."

Harriet tossed her head and laughed aloud. "*Art?* I hardly think so. No, not an art or an artist. A mere tradesman I should say."

"Well," Almira said, her chin thrust like the prow of a ship, "your ladyship may think him a tradesman if she must, but I have found him a delightful companion and a gentleman of fine character."

All along, Harriet had somehow continued playing, though in the lightest, lilting manner. Now, she brought both hands down on the keyboard. "Dolly, it is obvious you are much taken with him. Maybe someday you and your Irish tradesman will marry, and he can carry you to the alter of Venus. Do let us know if he is all you hoped for."

Betty blushed and giggled nervously at the indecent insinuation in Harriet's remark, but Almira felt embarrassed and exposed.

"I've told you already, he is not a tradesman. And don't call me Dolly."

Harriet laughed as if she were on the stage, having delivered the best line of the evening. Almira saw red.

"I'm warning you. You'd best stop calling him a tradesman. Daniel is an artist, a daguerreotype artist. Do you hear me?"

Swiveling on the stool, Harriet spoke. Her cool voice enraged

Almira, the way it registered clear delight in igniting the ire of her rival. "Dolly," she said, "threatening me is really so vulgar. Besides, we all know I could have your knight on bended knee if I wished. But don't be concerned, your fellow is altogether too, how shall I say it politely? Too rough and ready for someone like me."

She stood, touched her cheek lightly with a fingertip and tilted her head, adding, "On the other hand, maybe I will take an afternoon's amusement with him and have another miniature made."

Almira came up bristling, her face flushed crimson with rage. Rebecca pinched her elbow, in an attempt to hold her back, but it was too late. Almira tore herself free and leaped to her feet.

"I'm warning you, you brazen whore," she snarled, teeth clenched, her fist cocked. "Stay away from him, or as God is my witness, I'll turn your petticoats inside out!"

All activity in the parlor froze. Everyone held their breath except little Betty Wheeler, who burst into tears and ran upstairs.

Rebecca tried to intercede. "Please y'all please stop this," she said. "We oughtn't to fuss like this."

Almira took another step closer. "Did you hear me?"

Harriet went white. She nodded and stepped behind the piano.

Mrs. Bright, already in her dressing gown and slippers, returned to the parlor for her reading glasses. Her intuition hinted that something had shifted while she was out of the room.

"Girls, it is dreadfully quiet in here. Is there something wrong?"

No one said a thing. Mrs. Bright looked from one boarder to the other, but they all averted their eyes. It was Harriet who broke the silence. "Not in the least, Mrs. Bright, no, nothing is wrong."

"That's right," said Almira. "We were just having a conversation about petticoats."

In the morning, around the breakfast table, it was plain that something was indeed wrong. Conversations were artificial and forced. Almira and Harriet refused to acknowledge each other's presence, and little Betty looked addled. As the girls bustled, putting on capes and bonnets to leave for the academy, Mrs. Bright remained seated alone at the table, ominously tapping it with her spoon and brooding over how to handle this latest disturbance in her home.

Outside, the girls separated into factions; those who sided with Harriet, including Susannah and all the younger girls. The only one sympathetic toward Almira was Rebecca. Phebe and Emily wished to remain neutral.

"Well, I've made a smart mess of things," said Almira, starting up the hill. "I can't imagine Mrs. Bright will allow Daniel to visit me now."

"Yes," Rebecca said. "Hush my mouth if there won't be the devil to pay tonight. I'm sure Emily will vouch that you were needlessly provoked, but goodness, couldn't you have called her a hussy and left it at that?"

Rebecca was right. At supper, Mrs. Bright asked all the girls to remain in the parlor after the meal. They sat there, avoiding each other's eyes and saying nothing while Mrs. Bright spoke to Emily in her office. After a while Miss Wilcox appeared in the doorway. "Betty," she said, "would you please come in here child?"

The youngster rose and followed Emily into Mrs. Bright's chambers. She reappeared a few minutes later, clearly shaken. The process was repeated with Rebecca. Finally, Emily asked both Almira and Harriet to come in.

The matron of the house sat in her winged chair by the coal grate, holding her spectacles in one hand and pinching the bridge of her nose. She gestured toward a pair of straight-backed chairs. "You ladies will have a seat."

Almira's heart pounded. As she sat, she cast a sideways glance at Emily, who remained standing by the doorway, wearing an apologetic frown.

"Miss Hamilton," the matron began, "Miss Wilcox came to me this morning, as was her duty, to inform me you had insulted Miss Ames in the worst way imaginable. I have questioned the others who

129

were there, and they all confirm the details of this repugnant story. According to their accounts, all independent I might add, you used the most disgusting sort of language. Little Betty Wheeler is particularly upset. These are the sort of words that should never fall on that child's innocent ears. Your behavior toward Miss Ames was entirely unacceptable to the standards of the Albany Female Academy."

Mrs. Bright took a breath and continued. "Miss Hamilton, do you comprehend how serious this is?"

"Yes ma'am, I do." Almira maintained a downward gaze, all the while aware her nemesis sat inches away, gloating.

Mrs. Bright turned to Harriet. "Miss Ames, twice now the peace in this house has been disrupted. And on both occasions, you were one of the principal parties involved. In my view this is not a coincidence. I am not for a moment excusing Miss Hamilton's choice of words, which were of the coarsest, most unladylike sort, but I am also made to understand that her outburst was at least partly provoked by you, and all over the attentions of a gentleman."

Harriet appeared taken aback, as if she'd never expected this. "Whatever I might have said was, was...pl-playful," she said, "without any malicious intent."

"No, Mrs. Bright. That's not true," Almira said. "Harriet also made a crude suggestion about myself and Mr. Dwyer."

"You lie."

"Be quiet, both of you." Mrs. Bright's voice rose. "The two of you are already in trouble enough." She exhaled and went forward. "Now listen to me, Miss Hamilton, and listen closely. You will beg Miss Ames's forgiveness at once. You will do it now, and so help me, if I do not think you have been sufficiently humble and sincere you will do it again and again until I am satisfied."

"But Mrs. Bright," protested Harriet, "surely, she must apologize before all of us, just as I was made to do."

"No. Almira will make her apology in this room."

"This is unjust."

"Unjust or not, it is my decision. Miss Hamilton will apologize here and now. What is more, if she expects to entertain a gentleman guest this Sunday, she will do so until I feel the propriety of this household has been fully restored."

Harriet sputtered. Her jaw dropped and her eyes blinked as she shook her head and blurted, "I will not tolerate this. When my parents learn of this outrage—"

Mrs. Bright slammed a hand on the table. Both girls jumped in their seats. "Enough! I am thoroughly tired of this quarreling." The room was quiet. "Now, Miss Hamilton, begin your apology."

So, Almira began. She groveled and begged Harriet's forgiveness in the most sycophantic manner she could muster. It was debasing, but she didn't care. After all, her visit from Daniel depended on her performance.

"Are you satisfied, Miss Ames?" the matron asked.

Harriet nodded, though even a blind person could have seen that she did so under duress.

"Very well," said Mrs. Bright. "Let this sordid affair be finished. The two of you will go to your rooms and speak no more of this. Is that clear?"

Almira and Harriet both nodded.

"Good. Now be gone, both of you."

Emily opened the door. They passed through and stepped into what was now an empty parlor. Harriet rushed up the staircase and disappeared into the darkness. Almira meanwhile lingered in the empty parlor. Why Mrs. Bright hadn't prohibited Daniel's visit was beyond comprehension, but whatever the reason, she was exhausted. It was time to go to bed. At the top of the stairs, Harriet suddenly stepped out of the shadows and blocked Almira's way.

"You'll pay for this," she whispered. "I don't yet know how, but you will pay dearly."

Chapter 17

October, 1971

"I have a collect call from a Mr. Lawrence Greer. Will you accept the charges?"

He would. The operator put him through.

"Hey, it's me."

"Did you find out anything?"

"Well, I've got good news and bad news. There's nothing listed for a Cushman, Horsford, or Dwyer in Charleston or Albany as photographers, but I did find a Carvalho. Supposedly, one of the first studios in Charleston was opened by some guy named Solomon Carvalho."

"No one named Dwyer?"

"Nope."

"Anything else?"

"No, except this Horsford guy is probably the same person who made a fortune by inventing baking powder."

"You're kidding."

"Nope," said Larry. "It's the same guy. This dude was into all kinds of shit. Phrenology, Vikings, Indian languages too."

David could barely contain himself. More details related by

Almira were proving to be grounded in recorded history.

"No Dwyer, though?"

"No," Larry confirmed. "No Dwyer. Hey Dave, what's this all about anyway? You mining some big collection of early photographic material up there I should know about?"

David decided to be evasive. "Let's just say I've come across a series of letters, ephemera, stuff like that, and some of it has to do with daguerreotypes."

"And this is connected to that dag you showed me, the one of the pretty girl?"

"That's right," said David, declining to go further.

Greer took the hint. "Okay," he said. "Just don't forget your Uncle Larry."

Reluctantly, David locked the door behind him and started the car. His parents were irked that he hadn't shown up for the holiday. Angela was after him too. A trip down to the city for a few days was unavoidable. He'd do some research, make a business trip out of it, cultivate his network of dealers and collectors.

There was also Dr. Koenigsberg. He hadn't seen his mentor since leaving his practice, and recent rumors had the great man in poor health. As much as David felt he'd been a disappointment to him, he also missed the older man's advice.

"Hello David," said Maureen as he stepped into the very familiar waiting room. "It's good to see you again. Dr. K is very excited about your visit."

"How is he?"

She cupped a hand to her mouth and said, "Not good. He's very weak, and I think he's depressed." Dropping her hand, she added in a louder voice, "Dr. Koenigsberg is doing great. He'll be with you in a minute. Why don't you wait for him in his office?"

David walked in and busied himself. Studying the photographs on the wall was a bit like viewing a gallery of psychology's history over the last fifty years. All the bigshots were there; Freud, Adler, Bowlby. There was even one of Koenigsberg and Eisenhower. He noticed the doctor was in uniform, officers' bars on his shoulders.

At the sound of his name, David turned around and suppressed a gasp. It jarred him to see how much the man had aged over the last year. His entire frame was shrunken, his skin yellowed, and he shuffled more than walked.

"David Weis," he said, wheezing the words more than speaking. "It is good to see you. Please, sit down."

David took a seat on a leather chair. His mentor shambled over to his desk.

"These days, I go to the toilet much too often," Koenigsberg said. He sat with a weary sigh and reached for a cigarette.

"My doctor says I will die if I keep smoking, but I might as well die if I stop, so I see little point," said Koenigsberg, offering his cigarette case.

"No thanks," David said. "I'm trying to cut down. How have you been, doctor?"

"I am afraid not so well, David. The last year has been, how do you Americans say, a real doozy. I had a triple by-pass operation. *Eins, zwei, drei,* you see. It has taken the wind from my sails." Koenigsberg lit his cigarette. "And what about you? Tell me how you have been."

"Well, I took your suggestion and left the psychotherapy field. I bought a piece of property upstate and opened an antique shop."

"Did you? You find this satisfying?"

"I do, and it's safer for me to work with artifacts rather than with people. I think you might agree."

"David," Koenigsberg said, flicking ash from his cigarette. "I have always thought you well adapted to psychotherapy—" The old man erupted in a fit of coughing. Like a wizened traffic cop, he signaled for David to be patient until it passed. "*Entschuldigen, bitte.*" He gasped.

David couldn't remember him speaking so much German before.

"As I was saying, in your state of mind after that unfortunate incident, you would not have been able to apply your skills effectively. You needed to place some distance, you see, but perhaps a time will come when you can resume with a new insight. A *neue Einblick.*"

"Maybe, doctor, I don't know."

Koenigsberg coughed into his fist. "Very well. When you are ready, you will know it. Life, I have found, has a way of circling back on us."

"Doctor Koenigsberg," David said, "I've always meant to ask you about that photograph of you with General Eisenhower. Did you know him?"

"Ike? No, not really. I was working for SHAEF during the war, Allied Headquarters. Eisenhower wanted us to conduct a series of interviews with captured German psychologists. They were all dedicated National Socialists."

"You mean Nazis?"

"Yes, Nazis, of course."

This piqued David's interest. He'd seen plenty of people with numbers tattooed on their forearms. He even had relatives who were Holocaust victims, but he had never considered how psychology may have played a role. "I'd love to hear about that."

Koenigsberg cleared his throat. "I interviewed two in particular. Robert Ritter and his assistant Eva Justin. The funny thing is, I'd actually worked under Ritter before I left Germany in 1935. He was well known in the field at the time."

"He knew you were a Jew?"

"Oh yes, of course. He told me, 'Isaac, I wish you luck, but it is good you leave Germany.' Anyway, this Justin woman, she was from Dresden. She was a doctoral candidate, writing her dissertation about whether Gypsy children could be cleansed of their anthropological handicaps provided they were raised in an Aryan environment. Ritter was head of the racial hygiene office. The *Rassenhygienische Amt*, it was called, so he supervised her research."

Koenigsberg blew smoke through his nose. He reached for a pen on his desk and clicked it compulsively for a few seconds before tossing it aside. "I looked over Justin's dissertation. From a technical perspective it was very professionally done. However, her conclusions were, how shall I say, quite upsetting. *Sehr störend auf Deutsch.*"

He lit another cigarette, took a deep drag, held it in, and

continued. "Justin wrote that Gypsies did not have the intellectual capacity of Jews, and were thus less dangerous to the Reich, or the *Volk*, as she put it. In any case, she recommended they should all be sterilized. Not killed, you understand–just *phased out.*"

"And what about the children in her research?"

"As far as I know, when she was finished with them, they were sterilized and sent to a labor camp."

Koenigsberg ground the butt of his cigarette into the ashtray and cracked his knuckles one by one. David wondered if he was wrestling with more than war time memory. Maybe something was trying to bubble to the surface from deep down.

"This woman, *Fraulein Doktor* Justin. She tried to deny the dissertation. According to her, she was forced to write it. I can remember her saying, '*Herr Doktor, glauben Sie mir, bitte. Ich bin kein Nazi, ich bin kein Nazi,*' but believe me, she was an unrepentant Nazi through and through. She was, I might add, quite attractive, well educated, you see, rather like Garbo." Koenigsberg excused himself and rose from his chair. "As I have said, these days I am often to the bathroom."

While he was gone, David rose to look at the Eisenhower photo. Koenigsberg must have been in his thirties, a young man about his age. He searched for clues that the young doctor's ideals had already been erased. Was it something in the eyes maybe? But no, there was nothing.

Koenigsberg returned, took his seat. After another coughing spell, he lit a fresh cigarette. He took a long drag and exhaled a dreamy blue cloud.

"What did you determine from your interviews with these Nazi psychologists?"

"I will be frank," said the old man. "It left me disturbed. Clinical practice in the service of evil, except that they never saw it that way. They tried to conceal it, of course, but I could see they were convinced in the rectitude of their actions. That was clear to me."

Koenigsberg went silent for a time, before returning to the present. "You know, during the war, I went back to Europe as a thorough atheist, believing that psychology held the only hope for human enlightenment. I returned not believing in psychology either. I'd lost my faith in man's will to work toward what is good." He studied the overflowing ashtray.

"And now?" David said. "How do you feel?"

Holding his cigarette in that odd European way, Koenigsberg resembled a count or baron from some obscure royal family, surrounded by his own fiefdom of smoke and his own thoughts. David was about to pose the question again when the psychoanalyst spoke.

"Now it is, I think, that I have made a mistake."

"What?" David said, startled at the old man's answer.

"Yes. I have devoted my life to a godless discipline, only to think there may be a God after all."

"Then you're saying that you now believe in God?"

"I am saying that the atheism of our science inhibits our ability to understand humanity, or to be therapeutically effective. But David, you cannot trust my belief. Freud would dismiss me as desperate for an omnipotent mother-object to relieve my death anxiety. So you see, my new found beliefs cannot be taken seriously by me or anyone else. That is my dilemma. I believe at once in nothing and everything."

David repeated the words in his head. *Nothing and everything.* He wanted so badly to ask his mentor for advice about the sessions with Almira. If Koenigsberg was as fluid in his beliefs as he suggested, maybe David could raise the question with him after all. This could be the only chance he would ever have. He blurted it out.

"Actually, Doctor Koenigsberg, I have been conducting psychotherapy sessions with one particular patient. It is a highly unorthodox situation, and I need your advice."

The old man lit up with exuberance, as if useful once again. "*Sagen Sie mir.*"

"It's a person who lives in the house I bought."

Koenigsberg's brow furrowed. "A young lady?"

"Yes, but it's not what you think. She's a...well. She's a ghost."

The psychologist cupped an ear and leaned in closer. "*Wiederholen Sie, bitte.*"

"She's a ghost. The spirit of a deceased person."

A broad smile erased the sadness masking Koenigsberg's features. Then he erupted into a booming laugh that degenerated into a chest-wrenching cough. Confused and alarmed, David rose from his chair and began slapping the old gentleman's back in the way one would a choking baby. He felt boney and frail to the touch.

He thinks I'm nuts. I've finally lost the last of my credibility.

After nearly two minutes of coughing, Koenigsberg regained his composure. He looked up at David with glistening eyes and said, "*Ein Geist. Fantastisch.*"

"You don't think I've lost my mind?"

"*Nein, nein.* Perhaps you have, but then, maybe we have both taken leave of our senses."

"I don't understand," David said, bewildered.

"*Fantastisch, simply fantastisch*," Koenigsberg said. "In recent months I have seen them too. More and more. My mother, my Opa Kirschbaum, my brother Jacob. I assumed I have been hallucinating, but now there are two of us. You must tell me all about your ghost."

Over the next hour David recounted the entire story of his relationship with Almira, their conversations, and her psychological problems as he understood them.

Their discussion meandered from the mechanics of psychotherapy with ghosts to the more rarified topics of God, the afterlife, and whether the existence of one necessarily proved the existence of the other.

"I think it must," said Koenigsberg. "If we accept a ghost, *zum beispiel*, as beyond the limits of our natural reality, then isn't God simply a matter of what terminology we use to describe this supernatural realm?"

David nodded with enthusiasm. "That's exactly what I think too."

"*Ja, ja*, continue. *Weiterfahren Sie bitte.*"

"And if that's the case, then the whole psychodynamic model is flawed. It's flawed because it's in denial of half of reality."

Koenigsberg leaned back in his leather chair, crossed his legs and smiled. "David, I have missed you, I've missed our long talks."

The words were so touching, his eyes grew wet with tears. How he loved this old man, admired and revered him.

"So, tell me," Koenigsberg said, after he returned tottering from another trip to the bathroom, "where does your treatment stand now with your new patient?"

"At this point, I think she's ready to acknowledge her spirit-existence. She's on the verge, at least."

"But you must guide her gently," Koenigsberg said, "as one would do with anyone reluctant to accept reality."

David nodded. "I agree. It must be handled delicately. The thing is, I'm not sure I've done her any good. If I hadn't come along, she might have been content to spend eternity reading and sewing in her room."

"You had no choice, David. She is not at peace," Koenigsberg said, leaning forward again and wagging a nicotine-stained finger. "If she is an actual spirit person you must do what you can for her. After all, we agree that she suffers from a guilty obsession. It keeps her imprisoned."

"Yes."

"But even if she is only a hallucination, then she is the symptom of your own pathology, and which case you must treat her in order to

treat yourself."

What a master, David thought. Why hadn't he seen this himself? It was time to go. The old man put his arm around David's shoulder as he walked him through the office door. "You must keep me informed of your client's progress. It is of great interest to me, you see. Until then, *auf wiedersehen.*"

Chapter 18

November, 1841

Almira read aloud, with Rebecca next to her on the settee. The Skinner sisters sat across from her, listening intently. Phebe Gardiner rested in a chair to their left, needle in hand and sewing basket at her feet. Mrs. Bright, as usual, was seated in her wing chair by the hearth, browsing the *Daily Argus*.

"Please, do read us one more passage," begged the twins.

"All right, let me find another," said Almira. She opened the book to a new section, turned the page, and resumed reading aloud from *The Young Lady's Friend*.

> *"If it has been the misfortune of any of my readers to have grown up without being made good needlewomen, the sooner they undertake to supply this deficiency the better. A woman who does not know how to sew is as deficient in her education as a man who cannot write. Let her condition in life be what it may, she cannot*

> *be ignorant of the use of her needle without*
> *incommoding herself and others, and without*
> *neglecting some important duties."*

Feeling observed, she glanced to her right, realizing Rebecca's large black eyes had been fixed upon her the whole time. "Your reading is so accomplished," she said. "I love your voice, it's beautiful, like a song. Please don't stop."

Almira blushed. Rebecca's compliments never failed to elicit in her a queer feeling, like when Daniel spoke to her softly, lovingly, before they would kiss. She resumed reading.

> *"Besides this, there is, in this purely feminine*
> *employment, a moral power which is useful to*
> *the sex. There is a soothing and sedative effect in*
> *needlework; it composes the nerves and furnishes*
> *a corrective for many of the little irritations of*
> *domestic life."*

Rebecca's reputation as one whose sewing skills were rudimentary was already well established. The twins laughed and teased her. "We think this part was written for you."

"*Oui oui,*" said Phebe. "You ought to join our sewing group. We have ever so much fun."

"Well, I've a mind to do just that."

Leafing through her book, Almira checked again the chapter titled "Behavior Toward Gentlemen" for suggestions on how to entertain Daniel the following afternoon, but the passages were all concerned with avoiding intimate conversations or how to gracefully decline a suitor's proposal. Both were contrary to Almira's aims, so she closed the book and turned to her friend. "Rebecca, would you come with me? I want your advice on what I ought to wear tomorrow."

The two said goodnight to the others, but at the top of the stairs, Almira made a hushed suggestion. "Rather than selecting my clothes, might we instead go to your room where we could talk privately."

Inside her room, Rebecca lit a lamp, casting them with a golden light. Almira meanwhile withdrew a small envelope from her dress pocket.

"I received a letter from an older, married friend yesterday. I confided my problem to her, as I have to you, but her advice isn't clear. Would you read this and tell me what you think it means?"

Rebecca scanned through Sarah's letter, reading half aloud. "'Several weeks past their time... restore their courses... a strong tea made of pennyroyal or other mints, mistletoe, foxglove...a mid-wife here in Whitehall...' hmmm." She scanned further down the page. "'Danger if the tea be too strong.'"

When she was finished, she put down the letter. Together within the halo of a lamp turned down low, the two sat in near darkness.

"What ought I to do?" said Almira, speaking just above a whisper. "I don't know if I fully understand what she was telling me, and I should have no idea where to find these things anyway. Even if I did, and I take this medicine and my courses return, doesn't that mean I have done an unspeakable thing?"

Rebecca drummed her fingers on the table while resting her chin in the other hand, deep in thought. "I have an idea," she said as she went to her desk for an envelope and paper. "Mr. Dwyer will be here tomorrow, but for now you will write a note saying it is urgent you speak with him privately, as soon as possible. You get started. I'll be right back."

Almira was glad to do as she was told. It was, after all, exactly what she wanted—someone to direct her and lift the heavy burden of choice from her shoulders. A few minutes later, Rebecca returned with Matilda. "Are you done with your letter?"

"Yes."

"Good. Now give it to me," she said. Rebecca turned to her servant. "Tildie, I have an important task for you."

"Yes'm, Miss Rebecca."

"Almira is expecting a visit from Mr. Dwyer tomorrow afternoon. While he's here, I want you to slip this letter into the pocket of his topcoat. Be absolutely certain no one sees you or knows about this." Rebecca withdrew a silver coin from the miser's purse on her bureau. She held it together with the letter and said, "Do you understand?"

Tildie looked at Almira, then back at her mistress. "Yes miss."

"Very well, Tildie. That will be all. I shall see you in the morning."

Matilda gave an abbreviated curtsey and exited the room.

"Hold still there my boy, I've missed a spot."

Daniel stretched his neck while Jack de Groot pulled the straight razor along its length.

"There, finished," Jack said, rinsing the razor in a basin of warm water. "Your girl will think you're a perfect gentleman. Won't she be fooled?"

"Thanks for everything, Jack. I'm obliged more than you know."

"Just remember that the watch is broken. It's only for show, you can't tell time with it."

Daniel finished dressing. He'd been preparing all week. His best shirt was freshly laundered, and the collar starched stiff as cardboard by the washerwoman. His shoes, used but new to him, were blacked and buffed to a mirror finish just that morning. The satin waistcoat he wore, borrowed from Jack, bless his heart, had embroidered lapels, and with the silver watch chain threaded through the buttonhole, Daniel thought it exceedingly handsome, in spite of being a few years out of fashion.

But it was the pair of dove gray trousers and black woolen tailcoat that gave him the most pride. He'd purchased them with his savings the day before at the new clothing emporium on Hudson Street. They weren't custom tailored for him, both were ready-mades, but they were new. He couldn't believe just the thought of it—new clothes. For the third time, Daniel tied his cravat. He brushed his hair and checked himself in the mirror.

"Aren't you a plunger." Jack whistled. "And that vest looks better on you than it ever did on me."

"Pity I couldn't find a walking stick."

"If she asks why, you don't have one," said de Groot, jokingly "tell her you lent yours to the Duke of Wellington."

According to the clock in the hall it was time to go. Daniel felt nervous, but walking cane or not, he was now openly courting the girl he'd pined over for years.

Downstairs he pulled on his greatcoat and beaver top hat, both borrowed from Meade. "Wish me luck," Daniel said to de Groot as he stepped outside into a westerly November wind.

The bells of Albany's churches chimed as Daniel stepped up to Mrs. Bright's boarding house. Standing at Almira's door, dressed for the first time as a truly respectable gent, and hearing the fanfare as if it were announcing a wedding seemed more than coincidence—it tasted of providence, a sign of encouragement. Just as he reached for the brass door knocker, a gust of wind nearly blew the hat from his head. Daniel caught it, held onto the brim, and was about to try the knocker again when the door opened.

In the entrance stood a maid in gray dress, white apron, and cap. She had a ruddy complexion and was of a sturdy build.

"Good afternoon," he said. "I'm here to see Miss Hamilton."

"Come in, sir. You must be Mr. Dwyer. We are all expecting you. May I take your things?"

As he removed his heavy coat and beaver hat, Mrs. Bright came into the hallway, hands extended. "Mr. Dwyer, welcome to our home. Won't you come into the parlor with me?" Directing her attention to the maid she said, "Rose, do tell Miss Hamilton that her gentleman is here."

Daniel drank in the words like a thirsty man. More than anything in the world, *her gentleman* was what he longed to be.

Following Mrs. Bright, he surveyed the parlor. It was nicely furnished, not elegant in the way the Hamilton's formal parlor was, but very respectable. More significantly, the room was populated with more girls than he'd ever been with at one time, aside from Sunday mass. Including Mrs. Bright and the sturdy maid, nine pairs of female eyes took his measure. They lounged around, adorning the furniture and every architectural feature like so many subjects posing for their portraits. A few looked familiar, but the only one he recognized was Rebecca, the girl from South Carolina.

Daniel bowed, was introduced to each, and bade to take a seat on the only empty chair.

A perfunctory conversation about the unusually cold weather for early November was underway when Mrs. Bright called out, "Here she is. Miss Hamilton, your guest has been kept waiting."

At the rustle of silk, Daniel turned toward the parlor entrance. Almira floated across the room in a frock of pale gray with a gaily embroidered black apron. Her shoulders were bare beneath a lace pelisse. Her hair was perfectly arranged, and the familiar string of coral beads encircled her neck. She looked so exquisite it nearly took his breath away. He almost forgot to rise. In the center of the room they met, he took her hand and kissed it.

"Miss Hamilton," he said, his voice catching like silk on chapped, dry knuckles.

Mrs. Bright stood by with her arm around little Betty, beaming with pride. Rebecca and Phebe commiserated in whispers, assessing every detail of dress and coiffure, but in the face of such a perfect tableau, the other girls were dumbstruck.

"Betty," said the older woman, "I want you and the twins to go and attend to your studies."

"But Mrs. Bright," they protested, "we're thirteen."

"No," she said, her tone as immovable as a barn beam. "Do as you're told. This is a grown up's visit and not for very young girls. Run along and take Betty with you."

Sitting across from Almira, Daniel could hardly take his eyes away from her unspoiled perfection. Except now there was something different, a quality about her now that wasn't there before. She didn't look quite the same. This was a more mature version of the teenaged girl he'd secretly loved for years. She was womanly, a girl no longer.

"Tell us, Mr. Dwyer," said Mrs. Bright, "where do you hail from?"

Daniel felt his jaw tighten. Hopefully it didn't show, but he didn't want to lie. Lying was a violation of the Lord's commandments, but inquiries into his past were bound to expose him for the common fellow he was. "I was born in Halifax, ma'am,"

"And who was your father?"

This was another question he dreaded. "My father was a lieutenant in the British cavalry," he said. It was a partial lie, but the whole truth in this case would never do.

"The lancers?" Almira said, reciting the line as might an actress.

"As a matter of fact, yes."

The idea enthralled them all, but Susannah was unable to subdue her enchantment as well as the others. "How gallant." She sighed.

Mrs. Bright was skeptical. "I am surprised, sir. I did not think the British Army allowed popish officers."

"An exception was made, ma'am. Father's record in India. You understand."

"Of course."

Phebe asked him to explain the daguerreotype. Daniel was relieved. This was something he could talk about safely, without lying or being worried that what he'd say might reveal more about his past.

He walked the ladies through the process, from the buffing of silvered copper plates to the mechanisms of the camera obscura. "You see, as any fine silver platter will tarnish over time, the process simply controls and accelerates what happens through nature."

Phebe sat mesmerized. "You make the miniature sound so simple, sir."

"Indeed, it is—once a thorough knowledge of the actions of the chemicals and light on silver is understood."

Rebecca expressed her parents' astonishment with her own miniature, saying that in their last letter they declared it a perfect likeness.

"That's because it is. The daguerreotype is made by God's own perfect hand, without the distortion of man's imperfections."

Mrs. Bright, who'd been listening to Daniel's every word and observing the subtlety of his smallest intonation, nodded approvingly.

"Mr. Cushman is a true master of the daguerreotype art," said

Almira. "Do tell me, how is his health?"

Daniel frowned. "I'm afraid the gentleman is quite ill. He is not expected to recover."

"How dreadful," said Almira, clasping a hand to her chest. "What will become of the studio should that unfortunate day come? Would Professor Horsford take his place?"

"I don't think so. The professor's responsibilities at the academy are too demanding of his time, but Mr. Meade is thoroughly familiar with the process. I imagine he'll assume the day-to-day operations."

"Might you be brought in as a partner?" said Phebe, having as she did a keen business sense.

Daniel explained it would be indiscrete of him to speculate though, with Mr. Cushman's health deteriorating, he and Meade had for some time been performing all the sittings alone.

"Do extend our regards to Mr. Meade," said Emily.

"Miss Carvalho," Daniel said. "I was asked by that gentleman to convey his admiration to you in particular."

Rebecca inclined her head. "Truly?"

"Yes," Daniel said. "He said that if you were representative of Southern womanhood, it is a wonder any gentleman there would ever travel north of Mason and Dixon's line."

"Did he, now?"

"He did indeed," said Daniel, bearing in mind the strict conditions under which Meade had loaned his coat and beaver hat. Namely, that Daniel arrange an audience for him with the lady whom he called, the *palmetto beauty*.

"In fact, Mrs. Bright, Mr. Meade wondered if he and I might invite the misses Hamilton and Carvalho for a carriage ride someday soon."

Mrs. Bright pursed her lips and momentarily looked away. "Before I could grant permission, I shall first have to meet him personally," she said in a voice teetering on the verge of rejection.

"But Mrs. Bright," said Almira, "it would be so much fun, and of course we would want you to come along with us."

"I, or Emily," she said. "Let me give thought to the matter."

Daniel smiled inwardly. The visit was going exceedingly well.

As Tildie served cups of tea and small cakes, polite conversation continued. Self-conscious of his manners, Daniel sipped his coffee and nibbled on sweetbread the way he imagined a gentleman would. He asked a few questions of Almira, the answers to which he already well knew. She was from Willsborough. Her father was the owner of vessels trading on Lake Champlain. Yes, she had brothers and a sister, but they were all deceased, as was her mother.

Silent as a cat, Betty Wheeler had meanwhile crept into the parlor and taken position on the arm of the settee. With all attention directed at Daniel, no one noticed her, and several minutes passed before Mrs. Bright asked what she was doing.

"I don't know whether to study my sums or my geography."

"Study your sums child and move along. Go up to your room and be sure to take the twins with you. Don't think I'm unaware that they are listening from the foot of the stairs."

Another cup of coffee was served, and then Mrs. Bright stood up saying, "Mr. Dwyer, I do beg your indulgence, but there are some pressing affairs I must take care of. Emily, you stay, but perhaps all you other ladies have compositions to finish before tomorrow's classes."

The parlor emptied. Emily got up from the sofa and went to the piano, where she sat with her back to the lovers, giving them all the privacy a chaperone could allow.

Almira patted the now empty seat next to her on the settee. Daniel joined her. While Emily played, they sat together, half turned toward each other and talking quietly.

"Danny," she said, "you look so handsome today."

"And you," he said, "are so much more than beautiful."

Both directed their attention to their hands, which reclined side-by-side on the cushion between them, inching closer and closer until fingertips lightly touched and mingled. His were boney and calloused, the nails chewed to nubs, knuckles burned by chemicals and skinned by the rough planking of horse stalls. Hers were slender, almost fragile in aspect as porcelain, her nails sculpted smooth as seashell and polished to a high gloss. They looked up, held each other's gaze, and leaned forward into the softest of all possible kisses.

The piano stopped and their chaste moment was interrupted. "I shall get up now and look for another piece," said Emily, reaching for a stack of sheet music with exaggerated deliberation. "There are several here. Have either of you any requests?"

"Please select the liveliest," said Almira.

"Very well then, let's try 'Tippecanoe,' shall we? It is a good Whig song."

Before Emily could begin, Mrs. Bright came into the parlor, announcing that the visit was over. It had been a pleasure, but Sunday calling hours were now ended. "I should like to meet your Mr. Meade. Bring him with you when you next come to see us," she said as she ushered Daniel to the door.

The plan concocted by Almira and Rebecca after luncheon on Saturday used the pretense of discovering they needed to buy some ribbon. They asked for permission to make a quick excursion downtown.

"Very well," Mrs. Bright said with some irritation. "But take Matilda with you, and don't dilly-dally."

The temperance boarding house on Hudson Street was their true destination. It was situated in an older part of the city where many of the buildings were in the Dutch style, with steeply pitched roofs and gable ends of stepped brickwork. The neighborhood wasn't ramshackle, but more than a bit past its prime. Because it wouldn't do for respectable girls to be seen going into a common boarding house unaccompanied, Almira and Rebecca took seats on the bench outside while Tildie went in. A minute later she returned with a portly man who looked to be approaching middle age.

"Good afternoon ladies," he said. "Mr. Dwyer will be right out. I'm Jack de Groot. Danny's a good friend of mine."

"We are pleased to meet you, sir," said the girls.

Rebecca turned to her maidservant. "Tildie," she said, "here is a fifty-cent piece. Make your way to Mrs. Kendall, the dressmaker on Broadway. By ten yards silk ribbon, whatever you think is pretty, and come immediately back here."

"Yes, miss."

When Tildie remained standing, Rebecca urged her on.

"But Miss Rebecca, don't I need a pass from you?"

"No, that won't be necessary."

"You sure, miss?"

"Tildie," Rebecca said, "you don't need a pass here in the North. No one will question you. Now hurry along."

Tildie turned and walked off. As she did so, de Groot stepped down from the stoop. "She shouldn't go alone, miss," he said. "There's all sorts of rascals between here and there. By your leave, I'll accompany her."

DeGroot's kind face and jolly belly made trusting in his introduction as Daniel's friend easy. Rebecca granted permission.

Biting her nails, Almira struggled to contain her apprehension. Daniel would surely be furious, repelled, for it was her animal impulses which had brought this development upon them.

"Almira, darling," said Daniel, appearing at the door. "I'm so glad you could come. And you too Rebecca, thank you. I know she couldn't have come alone."

"Then I'll let you two alone to talk." Rebecca walked a few yards up the street to a milliner's shop. She lingered outside, viewing mannequin heads with their primitively painted faces, each displaying a bonnet or calash.

The lovers sat close together on the bench near the doorway, holding hands. Though they were in the open with innumerable passers-by only feet away, Almira hoped the sound of hooves on cobblestones and teamsters unloading goods would mask their conversation from unwelcome ears.

She took another quick look around to be sure no one stood nearby. "You got my note?"

"Yes," said Daniel. "Well, in fact Mr. Meade found it in his coat pocket and gave it to me the next day."

"Then he must have read it." Almira raised a hand to her forehead and exhaled in exasperation. "I'm sorry, I just had to speak to you right away."

"Never mind, you're here now, and we can talk, but first I have something for you," said Daniel. "It's a birthday gift. I've had it for weeks, but there was no other way for me to give it to you without Mrs. Bright knowing."

He handed her a small package wrapped in paper, tied with a narrow ribbon. "It's not much, but I think you'll like it."

Almira pulled on the blue bow and unwrapped it. Inside were a pair of padded white velvet strips with a spray of flowers painted on them, and a tin catch affixed to each end.

"Can you read what they say?"

Almira looked closely at the tiny script inked onto the velvet. "Think" said one, and "of me" the other.

The thought of wearing Daniel's gift just below her knees, a shared secret so near the palpable memory of an even deeper secret, made Almira blush. "Danny," she said. "This is so sweet of you, and these are so pretty."

"Now, you must promise that every time you put on your stockings in the morning you'll do as the garters say."

"Yes," she whispered. "I'll think of you. I'll wear them secretly, but proudly, as I wear my love for you each day."

Daniel squeezed her hand. "Believe me, things will get better. Now tell me, what is so urgent? In your letter you sounded upset."

Almira hesitated. Though she'd rehearsed it many times in her mind, the words all sounded wrong. She glanced over her shoulder toward Rebecca, who still window-shopped, then turned back to Daniel. Modesty forced her to look downward as she began speaking.

"Danny, you remember our last night together...what we did?"

"Of course. I could never forget."

"What if I—well, I have something to tell you." Her hands trembled.

"You're shaking. What is it?"

"What if I told you, we'd created a baby? What would you think?"

Daniel repeated the words, "A baby. You mean it? My darling girl, you're carrying our child?"

Almira nodded.

He held her close to him, a strong, masculine embrace of the sort she hadn't felt since their union in August. "My Lord, I love you so much."

"You're not angry with me?"

"Heavens no."

"And you're not repulsed?"

"No, I only love you more."

"Daniel, you know that I cannot restore my chastity, but there are still things I could do."

He touched a finger across her lips. "Hush," he said. "God has given us this child. To interfere with His plan would be the greatest of sins. No, you don't need to restore anything. All we need to do is be married as soon as possible."

"Married?"

"Yes, we can't let our baby be born a bastard."

She winced at the word. "But Daniel, if that is the only reason, I don't—"

"Stop it," he said. "It's not. Listen to me. I love you. I've always loved you. For years I've wanted only you for my wife. Only you."

"You mean that?"

"More than you'll ever know."

A freight wagon loaded with lumber rolled by, drowning out any possible conversation until it was past.

"Father will not allow us to marry."

"I know," said Daniel. "We'll have to plan this carefully." He ran a hand through his hair. Almira looked back up the street. She could see Rebecca and Tildie coming down the block, escorted by de Groot.

"Mirie," he said. "Are you willing to be married in a Catholic church?"

"It is Christian, isn't it?"

"Of course it is, and I think I can find a priest who will perform the ceremony for us. Our problem just now is how to make plans. We have to move quickly. Sending letters through Sarah takes too long."

"What about Matilda?" said Almira. "She can be our messenger."

"That's a good idea. If Rebecca will allow it, have her come here later this week. I'll leave a letter with Jack. Hopefully I'll have some plan in place by then."

It was time to go. Daniel and Almira said their goodbyes, and the girls headed back up Hudson Street. On the way, Almira whispered to her friend, "When we get back, come to my room. I have a secret to tell you."

Chapter 19

October, 1971

On the street outside Koenigsberg's office, David found a phone booth, dropped a dime in the slot, and called Angela at work.

"I don't get off for another two hours," she said.

"That's okay. I'll wait for you in the reference room."

David went straight to the reference room's card catalog. Under "Directories, City" he was pleased to find *Hoffman's Albany Directory and City Register, 1840-1841*. The librarian behind the desk reminded him it was a non-circulating item.

"I'm surprised this isn't in Special Collections," she said, probably her way of telling him to be gentle with it.

David brought the directory to a corner table where he wouldn't be bothered and took a seat. There were a few Cushman's, one a dry goods dealer, another the proprietor of a dram house, but the best candidate was a Thomas Hastings Cushman, listed as an engraver. David knew this was a related field at the time, but still no mention of daguerreotypes anywhere in the directory.

He checked for Dwyers. There were some—a carpenter and

another described as a *crier for lost children.* None had any plausible connection to photography.

Horsford wasn't listed, but on a hunch, David found a biographical memorial about him in the 1893 annual of the *American Academy of Arts & Sciences.* Evidently Larry was right; Eben Norton Horsford did teach at the Albany Female Academy, became a Harvard professor, and invented baking powder. It also seemed he had married both Gardiner sisters in succession. *Intriguing.* What strange and unpredictable courses a man's life could take?

Angela pulled out the chair beside him. "Hey doctor, what's happening?"

"Not too much," he said. "You hungry? I thought we could take the subway to Fong's and get some Chinese."

"And then what?"

"Then you come back to my place and let me make passionate love to you all night."

"Hmm, okay," Angela said. "That sounds like a deal."

Once they'd settled into their usual booth, he asked her how the Poe dissertation was going.

"He's far out there, you know, mentally."

"Do you mean creepy and weird?"

"I don't know." Angela's forehead wrinkled. "Weird, definitely. Creepy, maybe." She turned the page of the menu. "There's this one photo of him. If you cover the right side of his face with your hand, he looks happy. If you cover the other side of his face, he looks like the most miserable person on earth. It's something else."

"I know the photo," said David, signaling the waiter. "And what you're saying is absolutely right. I'll check some of the psychology journals I still get. Someone has surely written about Poe and manic depression by now. If I find anything I'll try to get it Xeroxed and mail it to you."

"Thanks, baby," she said, and asked him about his visit with Koenigsberg.

"He's gotten really, really old. I mean he looks like death warmed over. It's sad, because I feel like I'm only now getting to know the man on a personal level."

The waiter brought a pot of tea and took their order—egg rolls, wonton soup, shrimp in lobster sauce, and pork ribs.

Once he was gone, Angela poured David's tea—two sugars, the way he liked it—and placed the cup in front of him. "Don't you think it's ironic getting to know Koenigsberg now, I mean, now that you're not doing psychotherapy anymore?"

"I know. And he's such an interesting guy," David said.

"What did you two talk about this afternoon?"

"He told me about a research project he headed for Eisenhower during the war, interviewing Nazi psychologists."

"Nazi psychologists? Freaky."

"Yeah, freaky," said David. "Can you believe it? The thing is— it really shook him up. Left him profoundly disillusioned about the profession."

"You mean about psychology?" Angela crumbled a handful of noodles into her soup.

"Yeah. He's not sure he really believes in it. He admitted that to me today."

"Wow, that's got to be a lousy thing to come to at the end of a very successful career."

"Tell me about it."

David took a sip of tea, fingers absently working his chopsticks. "Well, according to him his whole purpose in psychology was to confirm that God was an illusion." He closed his eyes and tapped a slow rhythm with the bamboo. "Now he feels the premise itself was the illusion, after all."

The entrees arrived on metallic platters. David took the lid off one and raked a couple of ribs onto his plate.

"Hey, I have to ask you," she said. "Has your ghost been back?"

David dodged a direct answer until Angela lost all patience. "Come

157

on, I don't know any dead people. I don't talk to any dead people. I'm not even on speaking terms with any dead people, so I think you can tell me."

David took a moment to let this settle. "You've got a point. Confidentiality is kind of moot."

"Exactly. If you want me to acknowledge this as real, then you can't play evasive games with me. Otherwise, I'm going to assume this is all in your head."

"Okay, okay, settle down." He glanced around the restaurant, making sure he wouldn't be overheard. "I can say she is on the verge of admitting that she's not an ordinary living person like you and me."

Angela's eyes widened. She brandished a chopstick like a wand. "C'mon, you've got to describe these sessions to me. Are they, I mean, exactly how do they go? What happens? What does she look like?"

David took a sip of tea. "Well, whenever I'm talking with her, she looks solid, like anyone else, except for being dressed in the clothes of her time. I have seen her look transparent, but she doesn't seem to be aware of me when she's that way."

"This doesn't scare you?"

"No, she looks so real, it seems normal. I think the most unnerving part is when she disappears. I mean, she just vanishes—not instantaneously, but over the course of a few seconds."

David took the last spare rib, carefully arranging it on his plate. "As weird as this all sounds, it was even weirder talking about it with Koenigsberg."

"Get out. You talked about this with him? He must think you're crazy."

"That's the thing. He doesn't. He told me he's been seeing his deceased relatives hovering around him recently."

"Man, that's never a good sign." Picking up a tiny fork, she dug meat from a lobster claw. "Hey, I want you to tell me more about this ghost patient, but before I forget, have you thought any more about Christmas? My parents want to meet this phantom boyfriend of mine."

David frowned. "I don't know. It's a risk for me to come down at that time of year. If the weather turns really cold the pipes will freeze and I'll have an enormous mess when I get back. I was kind of hoping this trip would do it for me until sometime next year. Maybe you could come for a while in January. We could run up to Montreal, hit the slopes."

Angela drummed her nails on the table. "This is annoying, you know that."

"Well," he said, "Christmas isn't my bag, being Jewish and all that."

"You know what, David? You can kiss my ass."

"What?"

"You heard me." Angela threw her napkin down. "Listen, you just ate a meal of shellfish and pork. Doesn't that undermine your credibility as a practicing Jew?"

David eased the rib on which he'd been sucking out of his mouth.

"Angie, those are dietary restrictions from thousands of years ago. I'm talking about being culturally Jewish."

"Oh, right," she said, the muscles in her face now rigid. "What the hell was I thinking? Well, rabbi, you let me know when you decide."

He'd hurt her feelings. It didn't take a psychotherapist to see that. It bothered him, yet he felt unable to do more than repeat his rehearsed excuses over and over in his mind. Angela seemed to retreat into herself. With both of them miles away, the conversation lost its momentum, meandered absentmindedly, then died.

They paid the bill, put on their coats, and left without bothering to crack their fortune cookies. Outside, she said, "Hey, look, I think I'm going to go back to my place tonight."

"You're mad at me," he said.

"No, David, I'm not mad. I don't know what I am. I just need to sort myself out."

"You think I'm a pain in the ass."

"Something like that, yes."

159

"Sure, I understand. I'll walk you to the subway."

At the platform they stood shoulder to shoulder, saying nothing of consequence until her train squealed to a stop. He told her he'd call her the next day.

"Sure."

They kissed, the chaste peck of total strangers. Angela stepped into the car and took a seat as the doors closed between them.

Chapter 20

November, 1841

Daniel stood impatiently on the portico of the Albany Female Academy. He had astonishing news to share with Almira. The massive columns left him feeling dwarfed. They stood like gigantic sentries before this bastion of dignity, and the vertical wall of windows, extending across all four stories, allowed only the smallest hint of the world of education and advancement that lay beyond. The idea that Almira would soon have to leave this place, not because they would be married—some of the scholars were already wives–but because she would be carrying and then caring for a baby left him unsettled.

Young ladies exited the building in clusters, getting into waiting carriages, or setting off in small groups for their homes and boarding houses. All were well dressed, bedecked in hooded capes, most with hands protected within a fur muff. Quite unnecessarily, Daniel thought, since the weather that day was hardly cold at all. The front doors opened again. A group of perhaps twenty girls came out, and among them Daniel recognized most of Mrs. Bright's boarders.

161

He tipped his beaver hat and said, "Good afternoon ladies."

"Mr. Dwyer," they all called back. "What a pleasant surprise."

"I'm waiting for Miss Hamilton that I might see her home. Is she inside?"

"She is within," said Emily. "She and Rebecca are lagging behind again, but they should be out soon."

He wished them all a pleasant walk back, asked them to extend his regards to Mrs. Bright, and resumed waiting.

Daniel brushed a particle from the sleeve of his new tailcoat. He had but two thoughts in his mind—a drab color wouldn't show ashes so easily as black did, and soon his work daguerreotyping would have to support Almira and their baby.

Absorbed in thoughts mundane and consequential, a voice caught his attention. "Would the kind gentleman escort two ladies home?"

"He would indeed." He smiled, offering Almira his arm. He positioned himself closest to the street, with her in the center. The three walked toward Maiden Lane.

"I have a lot to tell you," he said. "Mr. Cushman was well enough to be at the gallery yesterday. I had a long conversation with him and explained our intention to marry as soon as possible."

"Danny, you didn't tell anyone about our little stranger, did you?"

"No, no," he assured her. "Only that we have resolved to marry against your father's wishes."

Pleased to see Almira's sigh of relief, Daniel resumed his report. "So, as I was saying, I told Mr. Cushman about us and the gentleman has offered to present us his first camera as a wedding gift. Can you believe it? It isn't the most new-fashioned model, it needs a longer exposure time for the plates than the one we use now, but it will still produce fine daguerreotypes."

Thrilled, Almira pressed herself against Daniel's arm. "Danny, that was so kind of him."

"But there's more," said Daniel. "Mr. Cushman understands we can't remain in Albany, so he's offered to advance me the money to set up a studio in another city. The agreement is, I purchase my supplies through him until the loan is repaid. Can you believe it?"

Almira bounced up and down on her toes at the news. "We could go to Cincinnati. We could even go to Wisconsin. Danny, you always said you wanted to go to Wisconsin."

Daniel was quiet, a shadow cast over the moment. "That could be a problem," he said. "We'd have to take the canal through to Buffalo. Even though we'll already be married, your father could thwart our intentions at any point along the way. He has friends all along the canals."

"Couldn't we go to someplace in Massachusetts or Connecticut?"

"Perhaps, but maybe that wouldn't be far enough from his influence. Besides, there are already daguerreotype galleries open in Boston and Providence, and I think in Hartford as well. It would be best for us to go where there's no other daguerreotype gallery. Mirie, we need to leave New York and get away from this part of the country, but it won't be easy."

"I have an idea," said Rebecca, standing discretely to one side. "Go to Charleston. There are no daguerreotype studios there, and it's surely far enough from Mr. Hamilton."

The couple stopped dead in their tracks. Daniel needed clarification. "Charleston—you mean in South Carolina?"

"There is no other, sir," she said. Take any steamboat from here. The two of you will be in New York City and married before anyone knows it. Then take another ship to Charleston." "My daddy could help you get established. He loves all things scientific, and he loves to invest in new business enterprises."

Almira and Daniel looked at each other.

Although the plan was brilliant, Daniel hesitated. "But your father doesn't know me. Why should he extend us his generosity?"

Rebecca dismissed his fear with the wave of her hand. "Because I wish him to. Even if he says no, I know I can convince him. I shall work on him, and in the end he will say yes."

"And when you're graduated, you'll return to Charleston," said Almira. "Then we'll all be together again. Danny, this is wonderful. You'll be the first daguerreotype artist in Charleston."

"No," Rebecca corrected, "in all of the Carolinas."

Later that afternoon, Almira sat at her writing table, attempting to apply herself to her Latin but without success. Again, and again, her mind went back to the conversation with Daniel and Rebecca earlier in the day. Images of a new life in South Carolina paraded in a loop through her mind. When Tildie came into the room with a fresh scuttle of coal, curiosity seized her.

"Tildie," she said. "What's it like in Charleston?"

"Charleston's a lot warmer than this place, miss. Sun shines there most the time."

"Is it a large city? Is it as large as Albany?"

"I don't know miss. I 'spect it's bigger than this place. There's a lot more black folks there, that's one thing I know."

What would that be like, Almira thought, living among negroes, slaves everywhere? Before the servant could leave the room, Almira took the opportunity to ask one more question. "Tildie, do you ever wish you were free to go where you please?"

"I don't know 'bout that, miss. Except when I was a little girl, I always been with Miss Rebecca and her folks. The Carvalho's been good to me. Where would I go anyway?"

Unsatisfied by the answer, Almira probed further. "You mean you never wished you were free?"

Tildie held the empty scuttle and looked at the floor without answering. "Who's free?" she said, finally. "You and Miss Rebecca, you can't do nothing but Mrs. Bright says it's alright. Ain't nobody free except through Jesus." Tildie shifted on her feet. "It's the way it is, I guess. For me a lot better than for other black folks. Other black folks, they work in the hot sun all the day long. Lord have mercy, not for a high yellow girl like me."

The term baffled Almira. "Yellow?"

"I look black to you, miss?"

"I don't know...sort of."

"Well, real black folk where I from, they black as jet, not like me."

"Oh," said Almira, completely disarmed.

"There be anything else, miss?"

On the Friday following Almira's nineteenth birthday, the boarders concluded their evening meal with a special dessert—apple pie and the last of the oranges from her father. It was customary at Mrs. Bright's to celebrate birthdays in this way.

Mrs. Bright presided over the gathering but did not otherwise participate in the conversation. Her attention was occupied by the newspaper. Every evening it was her habit to read it from front to back.

"Almira," she said, so abruptly, a conversation about young men, school, and all things pretty came to an immediate halt. "Does not your fellow work for Cushman? It says here in the *Argus* that Mr. Cushman died this Wednesday past."

Almira's hand flew to her mouth, her dreams crumbling before her eyes. "Oh, no. Does it say more?"

"Let us see," said Mrs. Bright. She polished and replaced her spectacles. "'Departed this life on Wednesday, the seventeenth of November. He unfortunately engaged in daguerreotyping, then an embryo art, which he introduced into this place in connection with Professor E. N. Horsford. His experiments were made under exposure to the unhealthful fumes of the necessary materials, and in less than a year, he laid the foundation for the total ruin of his health.'"

Daniel had told her of this aspect of the daguerreotype process. It was alarming, but he knew of the hazards. He wasn't careless.

Mrs. Bright looked up from the newspaper. "I do hope your gentleman takes all necessary precautions."

165

Chapter 21

October, 1971

It was going to be a long drive back to Willsboro. That was alright. David's recent conversation with Dr. Koenigsberg begged for deep analysis. He stopped at a Howard Johnson's on the thruway to eat, but the food was tasteless. Thoughts about the Angela situation further soured his mood. Why did things have to be so complicated?

By the time he got back in the car it was dark. David sniffed the air. He judged the temperature to have dropped at least ten degrees— unusually cold for October. And though it had stopped raining, the roads were starting to freeze. A few miles farther, he passed the flashing lights of a state trooper's cruiser. Someone had gone off the road and onto the median. Two hours later it was a relief to hear the crunch of tires on his own gravel driveway. *I should have known better than to leave this place. It's a safe harbor.* He killed the engine and gathered up his things.

Inside, David flicked on the kitchen lights, dumped a bag of groceries on the counter, and poured himself a tumbler of Slivovitz.

At the kitchen table he sorted through the accumulated mail. Some utility bills, but mostly junk. David had just refilled his drink when he became aware that Almira was upstairs. He could feel her magnetic pull like the action of the moon on tides. In a house full of creaking floorboards, he'd never actually heard her make the slightest noise. Nonetheless, her presence was undeniable.

According to his wristwatch, it was just after eleven—early for her to appear. He finished what he was doing and went into the bathroom. Washing the day from his face and hands, David considered the course of his psychotherapy with Almira. He could see the pace of her appearances quickening since she'd first spoken to him over a year ago. Instead of once or twice a month, as it had been for some time, Almira seemed motivated to appear once or twice a week. Most importantly, he saw a growing awareness of her own ethereal nature. If the course of her treatment was at all similar to his experiences with conventional, living patients, she was either building to a breakthrough or nearing a therapeutic collapse. He shuddered, despite himself.

At the doorway to her sitting room David found the usual lamp light absent, though a beam of moonlight fanned the floor. As his eyes adjusted to the dark, he sensed her presence. Yes, there she was, perched, as usual, on the daybed.

Almira would normally greet him cheerfully but tonight her head remained lowered, obscuring her face. Silence vibrated in the air, a lingering melody in a minor chord—clearly a troubled state of mind. At such points in therapy, he'd learned to stay quiet and let silence do the work, so he sat and said nothing at all.

Finally, she spoke. "Dr. Weis, you once told me that our conversations were entirely confidential."

"Yes, they are," he said. They are only between us. You have my professional word on that."

"Then I feel the need to confess something."

"Tell me what is on your mind."

"Very well," she said. "Daniel and I were in love, but love is insufficient to describe what existed between us. Do you understand the words? They have a very particular meaning."

It wasn't hard to catch the subtext. "You and he were intimate?"

She nodded and seemed to shrink further into shadow. *Let her go at her own pace*, he told himself. A full minute passed before she spoke again.

"But there is something more, something with much greater, permanent implications." Almira seemed to struggle for breath, to find words. Finally, she held out her hands in supplication. "Can you help me?"

"Is there another person involved?" he said.

"Yes."

"Was it a baby?"

She nodded—a gesture so slight he couldn't be certain she'd moved at all. "Yes, there was going to be." Hand to forehead and head bowed, it all came pouring out. A dam holding back one-hundred-and-thirty years of shame and secrecy had been breached.

"Daniel said he'd marry me, that he'd love me and our baby forever." Her words came rapidly in explosive bursts. David worried for her sanity. "He said we'd find a Roman priest who would perform the ceremony for us. He'd make me his bride. Do you believe me, doctor? You have to believe me, you just have to."

"Yes, of course I do," he said. "I also believe you both had the best of intentions. You and Daniel intended to marry and raise your child together, isn't that right?"

With great effort, Almira struggled to subdue her runaway emotions in one great gulp. "By my honor, sir, we did."

"It also seems like you're carrying what you perceive as a burden of dishonor all by yourself. Daniel played a part in this, after all. It takes two people to create a child, doesn't it?"

"But I urged him on. A man cannot be expected to...restrain himself as a woman can. I failed as our moral protector."

David was touched by her allegiance to a moral code so different from his own. "I think perhaps both of you were swept away by desire. What happened was altogether natural and not unusual. It isn't a reason either one of you should punish yourselves."

David thought of Angela, the ease with which she gave herself to him, indulged his every whim. Sex without guilt, without responsibility, without children—sex for the mere pleasure of sex—was that an improvement?

There were still questions left unanswered, but before David could compose them, she guttered like a candle in a sudden draft and disappeared.

As usual after these sessions, he felt exhausted. David kicked off his shoes and collapsed onto the trundle bed. His thoughts raced. Guilt over her mother's death. Shame over a pregnancy outside of marriage. Pretty universal human experiences, whether in 1971 or 1841. He wondered if it was sufficient to explain her spiritual entrapment. It didn't seem so. His intuition was that there must be something more.

Chapter 22

November, 1841

Late that month the weather turned colder. With temperatures well below freezing it felt more like the dead of winter than late autumn. In Phebe's suite of rooms, the girls in the sewing circle thanked Rose as she raked out a fresh bed of coals.

"Would the young ladies like a pot of tea?" Rose said.

"Yes, we would," said Phebe. "That would be nice, thank you."

The maid left and the sewing circle picked up their needles, resuming the project of quilted petticoats they had begun the month before. Today the group included Phebe, Emily, Almira, and, for the first time, Rebecca.

"It is our pleasure to have you join us," said Emily.

"Well, my momma only taught me embroidering. We always had our people for plain sewing, so I am all thumbs, but I do think it an art I ought to learn."

"Sewing clothing can indeed be an elegant art," said Phebe. "And as we have read, it's tremendously relaxing to our feminine natures."

Almira sat, trying to summon up every bit of resolve she had within her. "There's another reason Rebecca is here with us today." Her voice trembled, mirroring her hands. She abandoned her needle in the fabric of her work. "I recently discovered that I, well...I...I have an announcement." She threw a glance in Rebecca's direction, searching for guidance, hoping for salvation.

Thank God. Rebecca placed a calming hand on her arm and said, "What Almira is trying to tell you is of a very delicate nature. She came to me in confidence. In the name of our academy's sisterhood, we ask the same of both of you."

Emily and Phebe exchanged glances.

"Of course," said Emily. "Now Almira, do tell us your news."

Maybe if she inhaled deeply, it would instill courage? Almira drew a long breath, then let it out slowly. "I am going to be married."

"Oh, how wonderful. *Tres manifique*," said Phebe and Emily, their faces bursting with joy. "Shall we assume Mr. Dwyer has proposed?"

"Yes, Mr. Dwyer and I are pledged to each other," Almira said. "But there is more. It is complicated."

Phebe nearly jumped to her feet. "No, it's really very simple—we can sew your wedding gown."

Rebecca raised a quelling hand. "You may not understand. Almira needs to be married immediately."

"But why?" said Emily.

When Almira didn't answer, everyone fell silent, a silence that told them all they needed to know. Almira closed her eyes and allowed the wave of shame and embarrassment to wash over her.

A knock on the door interrupted their sad, shocked reverie. Rose entered with a teapot and cups on a tray. As she filled them, Emily said, "Rose, do you know where Harriet is?"

"Miss Ames is in the parlor, miss, giving little Betty and Susannah piano lessons."

"And the Skinner girls?"

"Upstairs, I think."

"Very well. Please see that we are not disturbed before supper, won't you?"

"Of course, miss," said Rose, as she closed the door behind her.

Satisfied that they were alone again, Almira spoke softly. "Your suspicions are correct, I'm expecting a child, but please don't rebuke Daniel, for he is a gentleman. It is I who allowed us to stray from morality's path. But we're trying to set it right. You must believe me. We are so in love."

"But how can that be?" said Emily, trying to comprehend the situation. "You've only just met him a few weeks since. If there has been indiscretion—"

"There is more you don't know," Rebecca said, cutting her off. "Almira and Mr. Dwyer have known each other for a long time. He was a hired man for her family."

"Ah, I think I understand," said Phebe, the sound of the bell ringing in her head all but audible to the other girls. "Your father rejects Mr. Dwyer because he is working Irish and a Roman Catholic."

Almira looked away. "Yes."

"And he has not a great deal to offer for your hand?"

"Yes."

"There, you see?" said Phebe. "It is the same for my sister Mary. Our father will not accept Professor Horsford's offer of marriage, honorable man though he is, because father feels he has little fortune and is *pas de classe*."

"But how possibly can we help?" Emily said.

Rebecca answered for her grateful friend. "Almira and Mr. Dwyer are planning a wedding as soon as can be arranged. If her daddy hears of it, there will be a terrible fuss. We need to help her arrange a wedding without anyone knowing. That includes Mrs. Bright or anyone from the academy."

Emily stood, wringing her hands. "But as an instructress for the school, I cannot be a party to deceit."

"Please, sit down," Rebecca said. "In love's just cause, we need your cooperation. If anyone learns of these plans, Almira's marriage will be obstructed. She'll suffer the most grievous of public condemnation. She'll be ruined for life. We can't allow that."

Gathering herself, head held high, Phebe spoke. "Rebecca is right. We have to help Almira, even if simply by turning a blind eye."

Emily, who had returned to her chair, slowly shook her head, a tight gather stitching her brow. Phebe seized on a moment from the past. "You remember last year Elizabeth Bacon was married here in Mrs. Bright's parlor. You were there. It was a fine little wedding. Why couldn't we have another?"

Almira knew the answer. "Because my father won't allow it. He hates Daniel, and Mrs. Bright would be sure to inform him."

"I see," said Phebe, slumping back into her seat.

Rebecca opened her arms wide. "Can we agree it best that Harriet not know about this? She is ill disposed toward Almira, and we ought to keep this among ourselves."

Emily again stood and paced back and forth—her hands clasped behind her back. After a few circuits she stopped and turned to the group. "You do understand I cannot participate actively in any deception, but neither will I bring anything I am aware of to Mrs. Bright's attention."

That was all Phebe needed. She clapped her hands. "All right then. It's settled. We will unite in the aid of our sister Almira and limit our discussion of this situation to this sewing group."

"Thank you, Emily, and you too, Phebe. I cannot ask for more," Almira said, feeling safer than she had in weeks.

It was getting harder and harder for Almira to conceal her condition as November gave way to December. Sudden, unpredictable attacks of nausea persisted and worse, her corset strained against a considerable gap where it had always been laced tightly. Her dresses were miserably uncomfortable. One afternoon the sewing circle let two of them out. With Phebe and Emily such accomplished seamstresses, they were altered in one session.

Keeping up with her classes and the growing demands of concealing her horrible secret, life was becoming impossible. Emily pulled her along in her second quarter of algebra, and once Phebe dictated an entire English composition for her use. But some of Almira's assignments went unsubmitted or, if completed, were accomplished in a slipshod manner. Miss Meigs had taken to eyeing her coldly, and on another afternoon, Professor Horsford asked that she remain after class to discuss her academic performance.

"Miss Hamilton," he said, "is there a reason your attention of late has been poor?"

Almira lowered her gaze, choosing to be evasive.

"Sometimes scholars can be distracted," the professor said. "I would caution you against the dissipating effects of novels when Latin and the classics ought to be the devotion of your time."

"It is not that, professor, but I will try harder. I promise."

Horsford observed Almira closely, as if he peered into her very soul. She hoped that was impossible.

"I see you are wearing a mourning band on your arm, as I am. May I ask in whose memory?"

"The same person as you, professor—Mr. Cushman, the daguerreotyper." To her Professor Horsford appeared younger than she'd always assumed, maybe only a year or two older than Daniel. "It is my understanding you and he explored the daguerreotype process together."

This seemed to derail the professor's attention. He looked at the floor. "Indeed, we did. As Icarus was drawn to the sun, we were both captivated by the process of painting with light. Though I warned him of the effects of mercury vapors, he ignored my pleas in the pursuit of perfection. Now he is gone."

Horsford paused, absent-mindedly turning a glass paper weight on his desk as if it were a dial to the past. "Thomas Cushman was not just a man of science. He was also an artist, a poet, and a dear friend. I

175

shall feel his absence for a long time." The professor blinked twice and shifted his chair. "May I ask how you knew him?"

"A gentleman friend of mine works in Mr. Cushman's gallery. You have met him."

Horsford lightly touched fingertips to his temple. "The tall Irishman, O'Dwyer?"

"Dwyer."

"Pardon me, Dwyer," he said, clearing his throat. "I do remember him. He is a bright fellow, a capital fellow."

"Thank you, sir."

"You and he are..." Horsford stalled, perhaps searching for the proper term in the language of love.

"Special friends, yes," Almira said.

The professor drew a watch from his vest pocket. "Miss Hamilton," he said, "I have but a few minutes until my next class but let me say this. All of us carry a burden in this life. I know not what yours is, but if it can be relieved by sharing it, I am available to you."

Since their introduction at the commencement of the school year, Almira and Rebecca had grown close in ways beyond their complementary temperaments. They shared parts of their lives which the other girls would not otherwise accept or even tolerate. In private, quiet conversations, Rebecca revealed her unhappy home, how she despised her mother and adored her father. How she felt apart from every social circle outside of Charleston. What Rebecca could not reveal was her longing to be the object of Almira's devotion, as Daniel was.

Meanwhile, Almira poured out nighttime confessions, dreams of a life together with her lover and their child, and her fears that they would never be realized. In these ways the two girls were bound by secrets, secrets which could not be shared without risking gossip's censure.

With growing awareness that within a matter of days they would be separated, perhaps forever, certainly for a long time, Almira and Rebecca resolved to sit for a pair of miniatures. The images would be a preserved moment of their friendship.

A trip to the gallery to accomplish this was planned, but Mrs. Bright insisted on one last minute condition. Susannah Platt would go with them and have her portrait made as well. The girl had begged to go in September, and since that time she'd received written permission from her parents. Mrs. Bright could hardly refuse her again.

Still, taking Susannah along presented problems. They would have to be very careful about what was said in front of her lest word of Almira's elopement escaped.

The girls were about to begin climbing the staircase to Cushman's gallery when Tildie spoke.

"Miss Rebecca. You ladies gonna be awhile? Alright I go visit Mr. Jack?"

Rebecca gave her permission and said, "Be sure to return here before five-thirty. We need to be back at Mrs. Bright's in time for supper."

Tildie disappeared. "Who is Mr. Jack?" said Susannah, as the three climbed the steps to the studio.

Rebecca waved a hand. "Y'all never mind. He's just a friend of hers, that's all."

As before, the strong chemical odor announced with each ascending step that they were nearing the gallery.

Inside, Daniel was finishing with a young couple at the counter, preparing the receipt as they admired their daguerreotype. "Ladies, I'll be right with you," he said.

Another patron sat nearby with a level and masonry trowel on his lap. Though he was well dressed, his rough hands betrayed a lifetime handling bricks and mortar.

Taking seats in the showroom, Susannah's thrill at having her daguerreotype made was nearly too much for her. She got up and flew about the gallery like an uncaged canary, looking first at one displayed image and then flying off to the next. Rebecca remarked about her excited state.

"But you and Almira have both already had your image made. This is for me entirely new. No one in the Platt family has ever been photographed before."

The couple at the counter left, and Daniel had a chance to briefly greet the girls. They were joined shortly by Mr. Meade, who asked Daniel to take the brick mason upstairs and perform his sitting.

Daniel followed instructions, leaving Meade with the girls in the showroom. "It's a pleasure to have young ladies of the female academy in the gallery again," he said. "I have already had the privilege of meeting Miss Hamilton and," he gushed, "the lovely Miss Carvalho, but not you, fair lady."

Susannah seemed to have lost her powers of speech. "I, I am... Miss, Miss Platt."

"Where are you from? Have you ever sat for your daguerreotype before?" said Mr. Meade

"I'm afraid not," she said, her voice dropping to that of a penitent.

"Then we will have to be gentle with you," he said with a wink that made Susannah blush.

He turned to Almira. "Let me be among the first to congratulate you on your nuptial, miss." He took her hand and added, "Danny is a fine fellow. You are both very lucky."

Almira responded at first with a blank stare, trying to give the impression she didn't know his meaning. "I think you must be mistaken, sir. There are no such plans as yet."

"Is there a wedding being planned?" the suddenly aroused Susannah said, looking from one to the other. "This is such wonderful news."

At once, and a bit too abruptly, Almira corrected her. "No Suzie, there's no wedding planned. I'm sure Mr. Meade has misunderstood."

Daniel reappeared downstairs. "Mr. Woodruff is finished, sir. I'll develop the plate."

"Excellent Dwyer," said Meade, who turned to Susannah and offered his arm. "Are you ready, Miss Platt?"

As they were about to climb the stairs to the studio, Rebecca called out to him, "Excuse me, sir. Might we have a word with you privately?"

"Of course." Mr. Meade turned to the young boy who assisted in the shop and said, "Sam, would you take Miss Platt upstairs and make her comfortable?"

As soon as they were alone and Rebecca felt secure her words would not be overheard, she explained, "We have something to ask of you. It is important that Almira's marriage remain, shall we say, a surprise to her parents. We would be much obliged to you, and I would regard it as a personal favor to me, if no further mention were made of this to Miss Platt whilst you make her image, or to anyone else."

"Yes, please, Mr. Meade," Almira said. "You've helped us so much, but no one, not Miss Platt or anyone else can know about the plans Daniel and I have made. I'm already afraid she'll divulge something."

"My apologies for speaking out of turn, miss," said Meade, fist pressed to his forehead. "You may both rest assured. From this point forward my lips are sealed."

Almira released a deep breath of relief. Perhaps the intoxication of Meade's attentions would cause the giddy girl to forget everything she'd heard.

Almira and Rebecca were left alone in the showroom, save for the bricklayer awaiting his finished portrait and the sound of Daniel in the developing chamber. They sat together on the now familiar settee.

Almira whispered, "Susie will tell every girl in the academy. I just know she will."

Rebecca agreed it was a problem. "Let's see if she says anything about it on our way home. We may be forced to bring her into our confidence if she does."

The two said nothing more. Almira's thoughts drifted back to the way Tildie had seized on the chance to visit Jack de Groot. She was stealing away every moment to be with him—that was obvious. And what about her previous conversation with Tildie about life in Charleston and whether the girl ever longed for freedom? Like the flash of lightning which reveals all which is hidden in darkness, a sudden insight told her Tildie and Mr. de Groot would soon elope, like she and Daniel.

"Rebecca," Almira said. "You don't suppose Tildie and Mr. de Groot would run off together, do you?"

"Don't be a silly goose. She'd be a runaway, and Tildie would never do that to me. It would be most ungrateful of her."

The comment, rather than explain anything, only deepened the mystery of the complex bond between Rebecca and her servant.

"It's hard to believe you'll be gone within a fortnight," said Rebecca. "You do promise to write to me?"

"Of course."

"And in another year or two," Rebecca said, "I'll return home to Charleston where you and Daniel will be waiting. Won't that be wonderful?"

Almira nodded, but her eyes welled. "I shall miss you, Rebecca. You've been my true friend."

"Cousin Dolly, you'll be too busy for that. It is I who'll do the missing for us both."

By now, Susannah's sitting was finished. Meade called for Sam to bring Miss Platt downstairs and return with Almira and Rebecca.

Susannah was stimulated beyond composure. "Mr. Meade was so kind to me," she said, her words coming as rapidly as starlings. "And I know he took special care. He posed me three different ways, and in the end wished me standing, gazing into a volume of Shakespeare. He said it would best exhibit my scholar's status. He is a true genius, isn't he?"

Rebecca winced. "He sure enough is."

"And you, Almira, you and Mr. Dwyer are about to be married.

This is all too, too exciting."

Almira moved closer. "Susie," she said, "this is to be a surprise wedding. You mustn't breathe a word of this to anyone."

Bewildered, the Platt girl looked back and forth between Almira and Rebecca. "But why not?"

"Because my father will not approve," Almira said. "He will in time, but right now this must be our secret."

"We are very serious," Rebecca added. "No one can know. Can you be trusted not to tell?"

"I think so, yes."

"No, you have to be certain. It's very, very important," said Almira.

Susannah nodded. "I will, I promise."

"Cross your heart and hope to die?" said Rebecca, invoking an oath to bind her to secrecy.

"Cross my heart and hope to die."

"Stick a needle in your eye?" Almira said.

Susannah hesitated.

"Say it," Rebecca said, taking the girl by the shoulders. "Say it."

Susannah shrank back but repeated as told. Short of a threat, which might cause the younger girl to run to Mrs. Bright, there was little more Almira or Rebecca could do.

In the rooftop studio, Meade led the girls to a deacon's bench situated between a pair of reflecting panels. Behind it was a curtain pulled tastefully to one side and a Doric pedestal with a book lying upon it.

"Do remove your bonnets ladies and take a seat side-by-side on the bench."

Almira and Rebecca followed his directions, sitting with arms crossed on their laps, left hand holding left and right hand holding right. Meade adjusted the drape of Rebecca's paisley shawl, stepped back, and returned to arrange the geometry of their arms to be exactly symmetrical.

"Ladies, lean into each other, please."

They did so. Temples pressed together Almira detected a hint of lavender soap. Her curls fell in a cascade on Rebecca's shoulder, their soft cheeks almost as one.

"Next week you will be gone," Rebecca whispered as they settled into position. "I want to always remember us like this, until we meet again in Charleston."

Meade took position beside the camera. "Chins down please, just a little," he said. "Excellent. Now, look up into the camera. Fix your eyes on this brass point just below the lens."

As they held their pose, he took out his watch. The exposure time, he explained, would take a little longer on this late autumn day than it had during the girls' visit in September. "So, do hold still now," Meade said. He removed the lens cap and counted off the seconds remaining.

Chapter 23

November, 1971

He was surprised to find himself outdoors, walking barefoot through wet grass. In the dead of the night, the light from the Quiet Room cast a sickly glow through the trees. Through the darkness, Almira's voice called out to him. Sometimes she cried for help or spoke indistinctly—somehow simultaneously near and yet far away. She was in distress, in some kind of danger. David knew it in his bones.

Now, as if a page had been turned in some strange photo album, he stood at the lakeshore. The water, smooth as glass, reflected the starlit night sky.

Almira cried out to him again, but this time her voice more desperate, like someone struggling for their very life. "Doctor Weis, please help me!" The sound coming from every compass point, a chorus of Almira's harmonizing as one.

Nearly mad with frustration, David pulled at his hair, a strange, metallic taste in his mouth. Sensing a presence behind him, he spun around. He came face to face with a man holding a horse by the bridle.

He seemed young, with brilliant blue eyes and a distinctive cleft chin.

"Can you hear her? She needs our help," David said.

The figure nodded. "I hear her eternally, though she does not know it."

Almira cried out again. They turned toward her at the same time. Oddly, this time David could see the house as if he hovered above it. He saw Almira clearly, standing at the window, arms raised, palms pressed against the panes of glass.

The perspective changed once more. David viewed the room from within. Almira sat on her daybed, embroidering. He saw himself, seated a few feet away on the klismos chair, yellow legal pad on his knee and a cup of coffee on the floor beside him.

"She is trapped," said the man. "But you can save her."

"How?"

"Help her to reunite with God. Bring her to the lake where I wait for her. It is the only way."

"I don't understand," David said.

The scene changed and he stood once again on the lakeshore with the stranger.

"Hold out your hand," the man said.

When he had done so, the man released a handful of black beads into his cupped palm. David noticed a tiny gold crucifix nestled among them.

"Throw them," the figure said.

David hesitated. "But they'll be lost if I do."

"Not if you have faith," said the man, waving his hand toward the water. "Do not fear. Toss them into the air."

David hurled the cross and beads into the sky. Miraculously, they aligned themselves into the shape of a serpent with the cross at the leading end. The shape soared into the night. Ascending by some unseen force, the cross climbed higher and higher. The trailing beads moved like the tail of a kite, until it took position overhead, among the canopy of stars.

Dazzled, David peered into the night sky. The stars began to rush away, and the trees closed in, spinning as if he were at the center of an accelerating whirlpool.

He bolted awake to find himself in bed, entwined in a tangle of sweaty sheets. Except for his own heavy breathing, the air was still as a graveyard at midnight. David sat up and rubbed his face.

His wet and cold feet drew his attention. There was mud between his toes. The hairs on his neck stood and his heart pounded wildly. It took time, but once he regained his composure, David picked up the notepad and pen he kept by the bed. As fast as possible, he wrote down every detail before they faded. Fragments of dialogue, what the man looked like, emotions, and any content regardless of how meaningless it seemed.

All through breakfast the next morning, David thought about dream. His training had taught him that they were full of symbolism. Freud called them the "royal road to the unconscious" but never acknowledged them as having significance beyond one's own internal, subjective meaning. If he assigned an external origin to the content of his dream, David would be wading into the collective unconscious. That was a Jungian concept, and Jung had a bad reputation as a mystic among fellow Freudians.

David absently played with his mustache, his thoughts outpacing his ability to keep up. Ordinary dreams don't leave tangible, material evidence. He peered at his filthy feet. No, this was no ordinary dream. He got up and dropped another slice of bread into the toaster, refilled his cup of coffee, and went back to the table, his thoughts careening from one improbability to another.

The personal, psychodynamic symbolism seemed clear enough. Almira, trapped in her ghostly existence. Him, trying to rescue her. That was easy. The big question was the man at the lake, the one who tossed the cross into the heavens. Who or what was he? God? Jung? Daniel? All three embodied as one? And that cross, climbing into the night like a firework. What did that mean?

185

What if this dream was different? What if it meant Almira could only be released by reuniting with God? That this could only be accomplished by returning to the lake with him. Was he willing to accept the premise? It seemed as if a door had opened, an invitation to step through and devote himself to serving God. He need only speak the words, surrender his self-absorbed narcissism, give himself unreservedly, for once, to someone or something other than David Weis.

After a year of psychotherapy with a ghost, maybe clinical practice had played itself out. David's last conversation with Koenigsberg haunted him. His mentor had already crossed that boundary from atheism to one that accepted God as inevitable. Maybe it was time for him to follow in the great man's footsteps.

Though it seemed theatrical and corny, David looked upward. After all, isn't that where God resides? It took a couple of false starts to summon the courage, but finally he managed to say the words aloud. "God, I need your help. Will you help me?"

Divulging her secret seemed to have lightened Almira's mood, but the psychotherapist in David believed significant distress remained just below the surface.

In spite of this, his patient this time gave little evidence of wanting to pursue uncomfortable questions. They followed perfunctory greetings with small talk, until David asked, "Miss Hamilton, do you believe in dreams? Do you think they have meaning?"

Almira tilted her head one way, then another, as if weighing a response. She seemed to relish the possibilities.

"It is a romantic notion, this idea that dreams are more than a folly, but I think it must be so."

"Well," he said, "I had an odd dream about you."

"Oh, do tell me."

Almira listened, enraptured, as he told her about wandering barefoot, her voice calling out in the night, the man with the horse, and the way the cross soared into the night sky.

"This man," she said, "what did he look like?"

David tried again to envision the mysterious figure. "He was tall, with very blue eyes."

"Is there anything more?"

"Yes," said David. "He told me you could be saved by meeting him at the lake. That's all I remember."

"Nothing else?"

"No, except that the man had a distinctive cleft chin."

Almira's eyes grew wide. "That is him. That is my Danny. He is returned." She clapped her hands together and bounced on the daybed.

David couldn't recall seeing Almira this happy. Her joy seemed to radiate out into the room, rendering everything vivid to him, as a child's first glimpse of the sea.

"Please. Tell me again what he said."

Almira's excitement was contagious. David allowed himself to be drawn into events that had taken place over a century before. He couldn't help it—the seduction was overwhelming. Against his professional judgment, he reiterated once more what he remembered. "He had a horse. He said I could help you. That you needed to reunite with God. He said he'd wait for you at the lake." When he was done, Almira's gaze seemed to pierce deep into his eyes. David had never felt so unsettled, or exposed. Her expression had changed from unbridled joy to one of abject confusion.

"Then who am I to be reunited with? God, Daniel, or both?"

Maybe telling her about the dream had been a mistake? After hearing the words spoken out loud, all this business about reunification with God seemed of dubious clinical value. Therapeutically, it was sloppy and called on her to do something of which she might not be capable.

"I don't think I can answer that," David said. His earlier request for God's assistance seemed so distant now and more than a little embarrassing. He decided to return to familiar psychotherapeutic tactics.

"The main message in the dream seems to be that you should return to the lake. That's the one detail I feel certain about, but I can't say what it means. I think only you can supply the meaning."

"But Doctor Weis, it frightens me. I have not left this room in such a long time. I feel safe here."

He found significance in those words. Was Almira beginning to grasp the sad reality of her imprisonment within her endless waiting. "Are you really safe? Or are you trapped?"

She seemed to gnaw on the proposition, her expression weary. She rested her chin heavily in her hand. "I must give thought to this. I must seek wisdom upon this question." She looked up and fixed him with a lingering gaze, her face never more beautiful than in that moment. "Where ought I to seek wisdom? Do you know?"

Before Weis could respond, she flickered and disappeared.

Chapter 24

December, 1841

Mrs. Bright made her way to the second-floor landing. "Mr. Hamilton, it is against house rules for you to be upstairs."

Standing in the doorway of Almira's room, Hamilton turned on his heel. He looked disheveled, a stubble of beard on his face and fury in his eyes. "I don't give a two-penny damn for your rules, madam," he said. "I am packing Almira's things, and she is leaving with me at once. That is all you need to know."

Her sudden excitement at again hearing his voice in the house gave way to hurt and confusion. "What is going on here? Why is my home being overrun in this way?"

"You don't know why? Well, let me enlighten you. I've learned through a reliable source that Almira has plans to abandon her studies and elope with a common, uneducated scamp."

"I assure you sir I have no knowledge of any such thing."

"Then you've been quite remiss in your duties, haven't you?"

Mrs. Bright bristled. Any affection she had felt for Hamilton, drained away. "I doubt that," she said. "Very little takes place in this household but that I am immediately aware of it."

"I'm sorry, madam," he said, "but you've proven to be a disappointment. I once confided to you that my object in sending Almira here was to remove her from certain undesirable situations in Willsborough, and this is the very circumstance with the same individual."

"Do you mean that young man, the daguerreotyper?" she said. "You know him?"

"Daguerreotyper, indeed," Hamilton said, with a dismissive snort, his voice rising. "Yes, I know him. I know him far too well." Redirecting his attention to the boy struggling to drag Almira's trunks into the hallway he ordered, "Take them both down to the coach, and be quick about it."

When she tried to speak, Hamilton cut her off. "Be quiet, woman. You're becoming an annoyance."

Mrs. Bright fell back a step, gasping. "I will not be spoken to in this way. I demand an explanation."

"Very well," said Hamilton. He took a deep breath and lowered his voice to that of a lecturing academic. "This fellow Dwyer is a wastrel from the Burlington docks. Some years ago, I foolishly took him in, hired him on my property. My generosity was betrayed when he took liberties with my daughter. I dismissed him at once."

He closed his eyes and inhaled deeply. The words came slower now, almost at a whisper. "Of course, this level of deceit is more than I thought him capable of, but I was obviously mistaken. That is why Almira was sent to the academy, so she would see there are other, much more worthy fish in the sea. There. Now you know it all. Are you satisfied?"

Mrs. Bright reeled. She rested her forehead against the wall and closed her eyes. The front door opened, and a flurry of excited feminine conversation poured inside.

Even before she reached the boarding house, Almira had noticed what looked like Loretta's trunk loaded atop a coach parked in front. When she encountered a porter carrying her own of cowhide through the door, she said, "Where are you going with that?"

"The gentleman says to load it," said the boy, as he walked past.

Gentleman? Alarmed, she ran inside. Her father was descending the stairs, followed by an upset Mrs. Bright.

"Mr. Hamilton," the oblivious Skinner twins said, blind to the glowering man who strode past them. "Will you be our supper guest tonight?"

"Step aside, you chattering magpies," Hamilton growled as he strode up to his daughter. He pointed his finger in Almira's face. "All your things have been packed. If anything has been overlooked, it will be sent. Now turn around, we're leaving this instant."

Across the vestibule the other girls, the joyous racket of removing cloaks and bonnets, interrupted, stood frozen in shock. Pushed to the doorway, Almira twisted her head around, searching for Rebecca. Instead, she came face to face with Harriet standing to one side wearing a satisfied smile, hands folded serenely in front of her.

"Goodbye Almira," she said. "I do hope things work out well for you."

Before Almira knew it, she was outside in the cold again. Twilight had descended and the gas streetlights burned bright. Hamilton pushed her up into the coach. In a flash, she found the window latch and unfastened it. Poking her head through, she determined to fix the last sight of Albany onto her memory as one might an image on a daguerreotype plate.

A few of the other girls spilled out onto the front steps. Rebecca ran out of the building, pushing her way through them. A handkerchief streamed from her hand.

"Dolly, don't go!" She clung to the coach.

"Everything will be alright. I'll be fine." said Almira. "Don't cry. I'll send you a letter."

"For God's sake, miss," the driver said, waving her away. "Stand clear of the wheels."

"Goodbye dear friend," said Almira, as the coach lurched forward. "Thank you for all you've done."

Father and daughter sat across from each other, glaring in the dim light of the lanterns mounted outside the coach. It threw ever changing, grotesque shadows across her father's features. He didn't speak and neither did she, not even to the other passengers.

They crossed over the Hudson to Troy and stopped to pick up more travelers before continuing onward, more or less following the route of the Champlain Canal. At Fort Anne, the coach stopped to exchange horses. It was past ten o'clock by now. Jostled for hours, Almira was hungry, tired, and despite the tin foot warmers which were renewed at every station, benumbed with cold.

At an inn, a greasy bowl of stew was indifferently placed in front of her. The smell turned Almira's stomach. She forced herself to take a few bites while the lodging was prepared.

The dreary room she found herself in with her father only had one bed—nothing like the Albion hotel. Once the door closed, Hamilton uttered his first words since they left Maiden Lane.

"I've rescued you from a life of penury, which is all you could ever have expected with him. Someday you'll be grateful. Someday you'll thank me."

Almira didn't dare look in her father's direction, her jaw set in fury. She ground her teeth to point of almost cracking them. "You don't understand. You don't understand anything."

"Oh, I understand very well," he said, tugging off his boots and dropping them on the floor. "I understand a great many things. I understand that grand institution of yours neglected to instill in you any sense whatsoever."

Broken in body and spirit, Almira hung her bonnet from a peg on the wall and sat on the bed to unlace her bootees.

Hamilton emptied his pockets onto the bureau. "Thank God I received a letter from Miss Ames, informing me of your foolhardy intentions."

Almira stopped in the middle of removing her cloak and spun around to face him. "You received a letter from Miss Ames? You mean Harriet Ames?"

"Yes, Harriet Ames. Who else? She learned through the Platt girl that you were about to run off with Dwyer." Hamilton peeled off his tailcoat and untied his cravat. He laid down with his back to his daughter and covered himself with his winter coat.

Fully dress, she laid awake with her face to the wall. Using her own cloak as a cover, Almira's mind raced in spite of its fatigue, reviewing the events of the last ten days. Harriet's surprising and uncharacteristic kindness. *Mirie, let's do be friends again,* took on a new and sinister meaning. Susannah had also averted her eyes whenever Almira looked in her direction. Now these things made perfect sense.

In the morning, the weather was even colder than the night before, and a light dusting of snow had fallen. After a cup of coffee with fried hash in the dining room, Almira came to learn that, due to the onset of deep winter weather, both the canal and the lake were already closed for the season. Their journey back to Willsborough would be entirely by coach. Almira wasn't pleased to learn this, but the other travelers, drovers and teamsters alike, seemed thankful for the hard freeze.

In the crowded coach, Almira surveyed her fellow passengers. All of them men, except for a middle-aged woman and her teenage daughter. Normally, she would have welcomed the opportunity to talk, but there seemed too great a gulf of experience between them. She tried reading a novel instead. Jolting over frozen ruts made that impossible. In the end, Almira buried her hands in her muff and watched the bleak landscape go by.

She contemplated the new life she would have had with Daniel in South Carolina. They would have been boarding the steamboat Columbia by now, on their way to New York City then Charleston.

Now what would she do? Perhaps more to the point, what would her father do? Send her to another academy, or imprison her at home until he found a man he regarded as suitable? It didn't matter. Once her condition became known, as it must in a matter of weeks—days, perhaps—there would be no more academies, no more Daniel, and no more happiness.

When Julia met Hamilton and his daughter at the door it was already dark. Sandborne and Jeremiah carried the trunks up to Almira's chambers. Egbert meanwhile hugged Almira about the skirts of her dress, nearly disappearing within the voluminous material. She'd bent down to kiss him when Loretta came in from the parlor.

"My dear Mirie, it's good to have you back with us."

Hearing a kind voice felt wonderful. Hamilton made no gesture toward his wife, other than to say, "For God's sake woman, bring me a brandy, won't you?"

Loretta ignored him, turning her attention toward Almira. "Goodness child, you look exhausted," she said. "I'll have the girls start a fire in your room. Would you like a hot meal, a cup of tea?"

"Tea would be nice, yes, but I must go directly to bed, I'm exhausted."

As she entered her sitting room, Almira sat wearily on her daybed without removing her cloak. Sally had already lighted a lamp and was starting a fire in the hearth. It was still terribly cold, but even under these circumstances it felt good to be in familiar surroundings, among the stenciled Grecian urns, her daybed, the klismos chair, and her writing table.

There was a rap on the door. Julia brought in a tray with a small teapot and cup, asked if there would be anything else, and left with Sally.

Taking in the warmth of the fire, Almira took a satisfying drink. After opening her trunk, she viewed with irritation the way her clothes, hairbrush, and other sundries had been thrown in haphazardly by her father. Tomorrow she would unpack them slowly and inspect each item for signs of rough handling, but for now the hairbrush was all she required.

In her bedroom Almira unlaced her bootees, removed her dress, petticoats, and corset. In her bureau she found a flannel shift, one she'd deemed too old and threadbare to take to Albany, but an old favorite, nonetheless. She put it on and sat at her dressing table.

She let her hair down and was about to start brushing it, when she heard the sound of paws paddling the door. Almira's heart leapt.

"Wigwam, is that you?"

She unlatched the door, and he scampered in with his tail pointed to the ceiling, weaving himself in and out between her ankles. Almira scooped him up. "How is momma's little lion?" she said over and over as she rubbed his coat and massaged the skin between his shoulders. "How is my little sachem?"

Putting him down on her bed, Almira finished combing out her hair, extinguished the lamp, and crawled under the cold covers. It took but a moment for Wigwam to settle himself flat on her chest, his captured prey. "Ah, Wigwam," Almira said. "You've missed me, haven't you?" He rubbed his face across her chin, warming her through the blankets. The vibration of his purring on her abdomen was deliciously relaxing. Soon she was fast asleep.

Chapter 25

December, 1971

The house had gone silent, and cold like the dead of winter. Angela called occasionally, though those conversations didn't go well. She'd been very put out—more than David expected—that he wouldn't travel down to the city over the holidays.

Despite the disagreement, she still came up to Willsboro when the fall semester finished. She had said she wanted to enjoy a long weekend skiing in Vermont and a night or two in Montreal, but David suspected Angela was after something. A long talk culminating in a clear commitment—wedding plans, no doubt.

In truth, the distraction wasn't welcome. Clinically, things with Almira were heating up. And even when he wasn't focused on her, he had plenty of chores and the antique shop to keep him busy.

The moment Angela stepped off the bus in Willsboro, it became clear the visit would not go well. She seemed to be holding something back. He certainly was. Love making felt forced—two people simply going through the motions.

In the morning on their way to the Killington slopes, they took the toll bridge over Lake Champlain near Ticonderoga. Midway across, David glanced down at the water. It was a menacing dark gray with large chunks of ice bobbing in the wake—broken off from the shoreline. He couldn't avoid comparing the imagery with his overall mood.

Angela remained unusually quiet, which only added to his tension. He switched on the radio to lighten things. Some guitar riff was playing.

"I've never heard this particular Beatles song," David said.

"It's not the Beatles, it's Bad Finger," she said, her tone curt.

Okay, something's eating at her. Probably something to do with not going to her parents for Christmas.

Outside of Rutland, Angela turned hostile, argumentative. She kept going on about politics, but David wasn't the slightest bit interested in the invasion of Cambodia.

"You don't give a shit about the war, do you," she said. "You don't know anybody who went to Vietnam, do you? Well, I do."

"C'mon, Angie. Give me a break. Demonstrations aren't my bag, and you know I was too old for the draft. You can't blame me for that. I would have had a college deferment anyway. Right now, I want peace and quiet. Is that okay with you?"

He got a wicked glare for a response. David switched off the radio. "Something's bugging you, and don't tell me it's Nixon. What is it?"

"You're right. All you care about is that spooky old house and your stupid ghost." Angela ground out her cigarette in the ashtray. "You're not ever coming back to the city, are you? Go ahead, David. You can say it."

"To live? No, probably not."

"What if I told you, I was pregnant? Would that make any difference?"

Even if David could have conceived an answer, he was too flabbergasted to form words.

"Well, don't get uptight, I'm not. I just wanted to see how you'd take it. Now I know. And the thing is—" Her voice broke. "—I really love you. I'd have a baby with you just like that." She snapped her fingers. "Even if we weren't married."

"I'm sorry." His words sounded pat and emotionless, like something he'd say after brushing against someone on the sidewalk. Trying to explain himself in conversations like this got David tangled in words he didn't like to use.

"I know you love me," Angela said, through tears. "In your own selfish way, but what good is it? There's no future for us the way things are. Not for me anyway." She cried hard, something he'd only seen her do once or twice before. "So where does that leave us? Because I'm not going to wait forever, and I'm not going to live up here in the middle of nowhere, I'll tell you that much."

Silence stretched between them until Angela reached down under the dashboard and retrieved her purse. Rummaging around, she extracted a disk of Johnson & Johnson birth control pills. She held it up.

"You know what this is, right? Well, watch me, just so you don't think I'm playing games with you." She pushed a tablet through the foil in the back and made a show of swallowing it. "There. Now you can relax."

A few awkward minutes later, she said, "Take me back."

"What?"

"You heard me, take me back. There's a four-thirty bus back to New York. I want to be on it."

He did as she asked. Neither of them said anything else for the rest of the ride. All the way, she sat looking out the window. At the house, Angela gathered up her things. She kept her distance until it was time to leave. David made sure to carry her bags out to the truck. It was the least he could do. Who knows, maybe it would buy him some goodwill.

"So," he said, on their way into Willsboro. "What's coming up for you this week?"

Angela sat with her eyes closed, head against the window. "Nothing. The usual stuff."

At the depot, the few minutes of awkward silence felt like an eternity. Finally, the bus pulled up.

"All right," David said. "I'll call you and make sure you got home, all right?"

Angela shook her head. "No, please don't. I need some space." She turned and climbed aboard the bus without turning around, vanishing into the shadows.

Back in the truck, he fought against an urge to take a valium, something he hadn't done in a long while. But Angela...it killed him to see her cry like that. She used to be so carefree and confident. Now she seemed beaten down and depressed.

Some psychotherapist you are. You expect everyone else to spill their guts, but you can't talk about your own feelings.

"96 Tears." That was it, the song they danced to on the night they met—three, almost four years ago. Now they stood at a horrible impasse.

"Great." He sighed. "Another relationship down the drain."

At home, David cracked the seal on a new bottle of Slivovitz and poured himself a stiff drink. He found it funny that this was the only habit of his father's that he'd picked up. Though probably better than the valium.

He took a seat on the sofa, thinking about their aborted weekend. What a debacle. The whole ride back from Vermont, Angela's lie about being pregnant kept running through his mind. It was a lousy trick, but it worked. It exposed him for the heel he was. He had been fooling himself. Aside from sex, his relationship with Angela wasn't as important as his conversations with Almira in the Quiet Room. Though ethically wrong and physically impossible, Almira had replaced her as his primary love interest.

Chapter 26

December, 1841

As Almira entered the dining room, Loretta greeted her. George Hamilton looked up stone-faced from his newspaper.

"Good morning Loretta, good morning Father."

The two women engaged in small talk about Egbert and how much Dorothea had grown until Hamilton interrupted.

"Well," he said. "What are we to do with you?"

"George, please, not now," said Loretta from the sideboard, preparing her morning toddy of gin, cream, and nutmeg.

Hamilton grunted and went back to his newspaper.

Returning to the table, Loretta tried to recover the conversation. "Did you enjoy your education at the academy, my dear?"

"I did," said Almira. "Very much so."

Hamilton gave his wife an irritated glance. "For God's sake, Loretta. Haven't we had quite enough of girls' academies for the present?" He dabbed his chin with a napkin, threw it down, and announced he had work to do. The atmosphere at the table grew immeasurably more relaxed with Hamilton gone.

"He's furious," Almira said.

"Yes, of course. That's how he is. In a few days, maybe a week, the storm will have passed. Let's give him time. We all need some time to settle ourselves, and then we can have a civilized talk about things. Until then, I'm sure you need to unpack, sort your things out, and think about the future."

"Future?" Almira cradled her head in her hands. "There's no future for me."

"Almira, I know you aren't pleased with things as they are, and I wish your homecoming were a happier one, but let us try to begin anew."

Almira nibbled on her buttered bread and took another sip of coffee but didn't answer.

"It seems Mr. Dwyer succeeded in entering the business of likenesses—I cannot remember the word..."

"Daguerreotype."

"Thank you," said Loretta. "The daguerreotype business. Despite everything, I must say it's commendable."

"It doesn't matter." Almira let the words fall as Sandborne might a plank. She stared out the window. Yes, Loretta was trying to be kind, but Almira was in no mood for conversation. "There is yet little snow. If you'll excuse me, I think I'd like to take a walk, maybe see Ginger Snap."

While dressing in her sitting room, Egbert poked his head through the door. A bristling fan of turkey feathers stood up in his hair, a streak of yellow war paint spanning the bridge of his nose. "I come in?"

"Yes, but I'm going for a walk. Do you wish to come with me?"

He nodded.

"Then, Chief Egbert, you'll have to take off your headdress."

A few minutes later, the two exited onto the back steps. Taking Egbert by the hand, Almira strolled across the yard. In daylight, she surveyed the surroundings. Though over three months had passed, everything looked as it had when she left for Albany, only now it was winter, always cold and most of the time dark. "Did you take good care of Ginger Snap while I was away?" The boy nodded. "And Wigwam too?" Egbert nodded again.

"Sandborne let me ride," he said.

"Ginger Snap? He let you ride Ginger Snap?"

"Uh-huh."

Hammering sounds came from the carriage house. Almira and Egbert went to the side door and peeked in. It was Sandborne with his old dog asleep on the floor beside him. He drove pegs into a slab of lumber with a mallet. She watch as he mark the wooden board with a pencil, took a drill and, pressing down with one hand began cranking vigorously with the other. Removing the drill, he blew away the wood shavings and inspected his work.

"Mr. Sandborne," she said, "whatever are you doing?"

He looked up and smiled. "Fixing up some benches for the new sugar house, miss."

Almira noticed that his whiskers had turned completely white while she was away. "Sugar house? Is this something new?"

"It is. There's a nice stand of maples at the edge of the property. I'm going to tap them in the spring."

Sandborne asked Egbert about his war paint and demonstrated the hand drill. He even let the boy help tamp the next peg into place.

Almira needed the old man's advice. When Egbert wandered off to explore the workbench, she took the opportunity. "Do you think I will ever see him again?"

Sandborne scratched at his whiskers. "Don't lose heart, miss. When I heard that your father was going to fetch you home, I didn't need to be told why. I thought to myself, never has a man loved a lady more than Daniel does her. If there is a way, then he will return for you."

"Do you really think so?"

"I do. He knows how to reach me, and if he does, then I'll let you know at once. You do remember our signal, the taper in my window?"

"Of course, I do."

"Then have no fear, but trust in the Lord, Almira. He knows your heart."

"Bless you, Mr. Sandborne," she said. "I knew I would feel better if I sought you out." Almira smiled for the first time since leaving Albany. "There is one other thing."

"Yes, miss?"

"Do you think I might see Ginger Snap this afternoon?"

"That is certain. I'll need an hour or two to finish this bench. Come back after dinner and I'll have her here for you. Will you want her saddled? It is very cold, but you may not be able to ride her much longer."

Ginger Snap had grown shaggy, Almira observed as she walked into the carriage house that evening.

"She's been well taken care of," Sandborne said, "but she misses her mistress, that is plain to see."

Ginger Snap snorted in agreement.

"See, she's telling you herself," the old man said.

Pressing her cheek to her pony's forehead, Almira petted her neck. Ginger Snap had been a silent witness to the love she had shared with Daniel. Seeing her again wearing the familiar side saddle made her ache for him.

"I gave the boy a few lessons while you were gone," Sandborne said. "He gets on bareback and holds onto her mane while she's led around the paddock."

"I haven't ridden since last summer," Almira said.

"Don't worry, miss, I'm sure she'll enjoy it as much as you."

Though it did feel good to ride Ginger Snap again, Almira found the unseasonable cold had a sharp bite when she sat in the saddle. She dismounted and led Ginger Snap on foot. They ambled along the course she and Daniel had taken so many times in the past. Each turn in the lane recalled for her particular conversations they'd shared over the seasons. Almira had intended to visit the promontory and sit on the rock ledge as she and her lover used to, but when she reached it, the clover was dead, and a cruel wind made it impossible to stay.

"I shall be sick," Almira blurted, leaping, one hand pressed to her mouth, from her chair.

"This is ridiculous," Hamilton said.

"I think I should check on her," said Loretta, concerned.

"Sit down and let her be. Can't you see this is another piece of her chicanery?"

Easing back into her chair, Loretta drained her glass of wine, took another bite of her roast, then dropped her utensils on the table as if they were hot from the forge.

"No George," she said. "Don't be angry, but I must satisfy myself that she's all right."

Hamilton made a face. He looked like a petulant child. "Go if you must. I intend to finish my meal in peace." He'd taken on a flinty edge as of late.

Being a mother and having experience with sickness, Loretta held onto her napkin and grabbed the one Almira discarded as she exited the dining room. Moving swiftly up the stairs, she hadn't yet reached Almira's door when the sickening sound of gagging erupted. Without bothering to knock or say anything, she entered the sitting room where Almira kneeled over her chamber pot, one hand flat on the floor, the other at her heaving chest.

Ignoring the foul air, Loretta glanced around. On the daybed lay an open sewing basket and the disassembled parts of a dress. To any mature woman, it all made perfect sense. All knew how to alter an ordinary dress, with its tightly fitted bodice formed over a corseted figure, into one intended for maternity use. In the course of her own pregnancies, she had performed the same alterations many times.

Almira looked up only to have another surge of sickness erupted, racking her body violently. Once the spasm passed, she made no move to stand. Remaining prone, she gasped for air, a thick rope of spittle dangling into the pot.

Loretta joined her on the floor. She wiped Almira's face clean and rubbed her back. "Tell me child," she said, her voice soft as a spring shower. "Tell Loretta what's wrong."

Almira shook her head and looked away. She scrambled across the floor and threw herself onto the daybed, hoping to hide her secret.

"It's no use, Mirie," said Loretta. "I understand why you've been unwell."

If Almira heard Loretta, she gave no indication, but burrowed deeper into the crook of her elbow.

Loretta knelt by her side and placed a hand on her shoulder. "Daniel is the father?"

Almira nodded into the disassembled parts of the dress.

Loretta stroked her hair for a long time. "Does he love you?"

Almira raised her head, her eyes swollen and red. "Oh yes. He does, and I him. We were about to be married." Almira gulped and brushed a stray tear from her cheek. "Now I don't know what will happen, except that I shall die without him."

"My dear girl," Loretta said, her eyes welling despite herself. For she knew that people could indeed die of broken hearts.

"When Father learns I am with child, he will be in a rage. He'll lock me up in this house and I'll never see Daniel again."

Almira's stepmother stood. "Wait here."

Loretta went to her room. She returned with a tumbler of water and a peppermint candy. "Here," she said, "refresh yourself with this."

Almira thanked her. Kneeling side-by-side on the floor with their elbows on the daybed, the two women talked quietly for a long time. To an outsider, they could have been lost in prayer. How often did she feel nauseous? How far along was she? Had she felt the baby move yet?

"Do you feel better now?" Loretta said, rubbing her back.

"I do, but I'm so tired."

"Almira," said Loretta. "It is correct that your father will be quite upset. I have learned he is a man who doesn't like surprises. Let me tell him. Will you let me do that?"

"It won't matter, I know it won't. He despises Daniel, and I've disgraced the family name."

Loretta envisioned her husband's face going red, his fists searching for somewhere to land. She had to agree. "I can't promise a thing. As you know, your father has lately been in an unpleasant mood. Nonetheless, when the time is right, I'll try to tell him as tactfully as I can. Will you let me do that?"

Almira nodded.

"Get some rest," Loretta said. "I'll take this pottie and have Julia bring you a clean one, but you should go to bed and try not to worry. Everything will be alright, you'll see."

Chapter 27

December, 1971

Almira appeared twice over the following week but only in translucent form. In this state, she wasn't available to David. He could only be satisfied with observing her through the open doorway of the Quiet Room, reading or sewing. Even if he had the will to venture a soft, *Miss Hamilton, would you like a visit tonight?* he knew better than to expect an answer. But on her third appearance, she was fully formed. From long experience, this meant she was ready to talk.

"Good evening, doctor," she said, as he entered the sitting room.

He detected more apprehension than usual. Positioning the klismos chair, David took the opportunity to study the anguished features of Almira's face. A storm cloud of emotions seemed to be building inside. Considering the content of their last session, it wasn't surprising.

"We discussed some important things when we last spoke," David said, after settling on the klismos chair. "Do you remember what we talked about?"

She remained so still David feared her image had somehow frozen.

"Yes. I told you about me and Daniel."

David nodded. "That's right."

"You must surely think ill of me now."

"No, I don't," he said. "But I must ask you a direct question." Almira said nothing, so he took it as a silent assent. "Miss Hamilton, do you understand your situation?"

Almira plucked at the divan cushion. "Doctor Weis, I only know I'm so very confused. It's as if I'm caught in some horrible dream. Everything is at once familiar, yet changed and strange."

"Tell me, what year is this?"

She wrinkled her brow. The question seemed to have left her befuddled and unable to speak. After what seemed at least a quarter of an hour, she finally spoke. "1841? No, no...1843, I think. Is that correct?"

"I'm afraid it's not. I know this will sound strange, and it may be hard for you to accept, but the year is 1971."

"Please, Doctor Weis. Do not toy with me." Almira squeezed her eyes shut, tucked her chin, and pressed the palms of her hands to her temples.

Nothing in his training had ever prepared him for this. Under any normal circumstance, belief that the year was radically different from the actual date would indicate dementia or, in a person Almira's age, psychosis. This, however, was no ordinary circumstances by any stretch of the imagination. Wasn't at least part of her problem being stuck in time? Didn't she need to somehow be shaken loose to join the cycle of life and death? Wasn't that part of what being a ghost was all about?

David's mind raced. Therapeutically, he may have ventured too far, too fast. Without some proof, she might simply deny what he told her and retreat into her spiritual prison—the only reality she could accept. An idea seized him. It was a gamble, but maybe one he needed to take.

"Almira," he said, standing. "I want to show you something. Will you promise to stay in this room? Will you promise not to leave? I swear I'll be right back."

At her nod, he ran from the Quiet Room, bolting down the stairs to his office where her memorial hung. Snatching it from the wall, David ran back, taking the steps two at a time. The whole way he plead with God that she would be there when he returned.

Relief washed over him to still find her on the daybed. She had her knees pulled up and her face buried in her skirts, like someone cowering in a collapsing building.

"Thank God you're still here," David said, slightly out of breath. He placed her memorial on the klismos chair and crouched beside it. Miss Hamilton, please open your eyes and tell me what you see."

Almira raised her head and read her own memorial. Her face turned ashen, and a hand went to her mouth. "Please no, don't force me to look at this again."

"Again? You've seen this before?"

"Yes, once before. You were gone. I left my chambers in search of you. When I saw it, I ran. I've since told myself it must surely have been a bad dream." Almira looked at him, her eyes dark wells of desperation. "Please. Won't you help me to wake up from this nightmare."

He couldn't turn back now. But rather than answer her directly, he pressed ahead with another question. "Almira, what happened to you?"

Her reaction was unprecedented in his practice. David had never witnessed such a violent display of shaking. He feared for her sanity. He doubted his own. Koenigsberg would have been gentler, he was certain of that. Unable to stand the suffering, he violated his professional training. David reached out for her hand.

Something in the air shifted, the atmosphere becoming charged with a powerful current. The hair on David's arm stood on end.

She drew her hand away. "No, you mustn't touch me."

"I'm sorry, I'm sorry. I won't touch you, but please try to calm yourself. Breathe deeply," he said. "This isn't a nightmare. I don't think so anyway. I'm not sure what's going on, but I suspect you are caught between—"

"Life and death?" Her words hung in the air between them like ice fog.

"Yes, I think so—something like that." With no real way to make sense of what should have been an impossible predicament he ended with a quiet, "I'm so sorry."

They sat together for a long time. David feared she would dematerialize at any moment, but Almira seemed to regain her composure. She turned toward him.

"You asked what happened to me. I will tell you. After Father brought me back from Albany, I was sure I would never see Daniel again. But he did return for me. He sent me a note saying I should meet him by the carriage house at midnight. He said everything would be all right, that we could slip away unnoticed and escape across the frozen lake."

The events of that night in December 1841 were becoming clear to him. "Tell me," David said, "did you and Daniel reach the other side?" Almira's pretty mouth went awry, her eyes sadder than the saddest song he'd ever heard.

"No. The ice was too thin," she said. "Before we were halfway across, we fell through."

David's heart broke for her a thousand times over. He'd brought her to this point. Could he ever forgive himself? "Was that the end?"

"No. I was able to climb back onto the ice. I reached into the water again and again, thinking I might feel him and pull him up, but my dear Daniel was gone." Almira hid her face behind her hands. Her body heaved, gently rocking back and forth.

"Please. Try to go on. It's important."

She pulled her hands away. Her eyes angry and red, yet she spoke slowly and clearly. "I stood beside the place where we'd fallen through. I shook my fist at the night and cursed God until my voice gave out. After that, I remember only cold, then the sweetest drowsiness you could imagine. I woke up here in this room, one final curse on my lips.

"Then you survived. You didn't..."

"Die?" Her voice shifted, coming as if from the depths of a bottomless chasm. "I do not know. I only remember falling asleep."

An emotional surge grew within him. In David's view, having controlled emotions at all times was essential to conducting effective psychotherapy, but how could he go on now? He swallowed back tears, trying to admonish himself to keep his composure.

"Doctor Weis," Almira said. "Please don't be sad for me. As you have shown me, this has all been a long time since."

Could she read his every thought? The idea pleased him to the core. "What happened next?"

"At first, nothing. I tried to speak to Father and Loretta, to console them, but neither would answer. When Wigwam ran from me, I knew something must be wrong. I soon grew fearful of leaving this room."

"And you've been here ever since?"

"Yes, certain God would never accept me. I have since spent endless hours waiting for something, or someone. It's as if a spell had been cast, and now I am awakened. Can you see now why I've been so grateful to have your company?"

David let the tears run down his face, unable to restrain himself any longer. "I didn't know. I didn't realize." He wept as a child, ashamed that he could have imagined, even for one moment, that he could treat her with such dispassion, hiding behind the curtain of professional distance. "Now I understand."

Watching her vanish with the breaking light of dawn, the mysterious contours of Almira's life had become distinct. The circumstances of her death revealed. Despite their love for one another, their hopes for the future, Daniel and Almira had never made it to the other side.

Chapter 28

December, 1841

Over the following days, Almira rarely left her sitting room except to comb Ginger Snap and take evening meals, during which her father remained uncommunicative. As long as she remained within her chambers, she could stay comfortable in her dressing gown, surreptitiously letting out the remaining pieces of her wardrobe while the rest of the household was occupied.

Feeling tired all the time, she napped often. She spent some of her time at her writing table, penning letters to Rebecca or Sarah. She also read, there being three issues of *Godey's* which had accumulated in her absence. But mostly she waited. Waited for Loretta to break the news of her pregnancy; waited to learn from her father what he intended to do with her; waited for a letter from Rebecca or Sarah—for a sign that Daniel had returned.

Later in the week, Almira overheard Julia mention that Sandborne had gone to Willsborough Falls. Knowing he'd stop at the post office, Almira sought him out after he returned, asking that he fetch her pony later that afternoon. An hour later, she waited impatiently at the carriage house.

Sandborne led Ginger Snap in from the paddock. "I imagine you'd like to brush her down a little."

He handed her a curry comb and with it a small envelope. Almira's heart raced with excitement but forced herself to secret the letter in her dress pocket and attend to Ginger Snap first. Looking on, it must have been obvious to Sandborne that she was distracted.

"Go ahead, miss. Why don't you run along? I'll finish brushing her down."

Almira apologized to her pony and thanked Sandborne, handing him the curry comb. She strode back to the house, dashed up the stairs and, taking care to lock the door behind her, sat at her daybed.

> *Darling Almira,*
> *I send this by way of Sandborne. Be on the lookout for a candle in his window. It is the signal that I have come for you. That night, you should meet me at Midnight once you are sure everyone is asleep. I will wait for you by the carriage house. Do not pack anything you cannot wear or put in your pockets. Trust me for this is my plan. With God's help, we will be husband and wife very soon.*
>
> > *I am yours forever and ever.*
> > *Daniel Dwyer*

Almira closed her eyes and pressed the letter to her chest. He did love her and had come back for her, just as Sandborne said he would. She took the note, looked around the room for a place to conceal it, and finally reached for *The Young Lady's Friend*, where she tucked it safely between the pages.

Over the following days, Almira retrieved the book numerous times, read the note, kissed it, and returned it to its hiding place. Never straying long from her vigil of watching for a candle in Sandborne's window. Her anticipation grew as she prepared her heart for leaving but dared not make any outward preparations for fear of tipping her hand. Until, on the fifth night, after the sun had set, the flame of a single candle glowed in the window of the carriage house.

At that night's meal, Almira could barely bring herself to eat. Supper seemed a lifetime away from her meeting with Daniel. She picked at her food and looked around the room, aware that this would be her last meal in this house.

Hamilton watched his daughter from across the table. "What the devil is the matter with you?" he said, always sounded like he had no more patience for her. "Why don't you dress properly for meals anymore?"

"George," Loretta said, "Mirie isn't feeling well today."

Hamilton scowled. "Perhaps this will enliven your mood. After the first of the year, I intend to engage tutors for you. That Frenchman, Descharmes, will be back, as well as another pinhead from Burlington named Gibson. He'll live with us until spring and instruct you in whatever it is he instructs."

Almira didn't respond.

"Well, have you nothing to say?"

"Nothing Father. I'll do whatever you wish."

After the meal, Loretta joined her husband in the parlor. He was slouched on the settee, legs outstretched, his cravat limp and drooping, forlorn as wilted flowers. He looked in a surly mood, but the subject of Almira's condition could no longer be avoided.

"George," she said, "I must tell you something very important."

"What is it?"

Loretta went to the sideboard and picked up the brandy decanter. For this conversation she'd best steel her nerves—and his as well.

"Almira is going to have a baby."

Expecting an explosion of anger, she kept her back to him and held her breath. When no reaction came, she turned and handed Hamilton a brandy, then took a seat on the wing chair, opposite him. Her husband swallowed much of the drink but continued to stare into the fire. After eight months of marriage, she'd grown to realize that George Hamilton was far more complicated than the hail-fellow-well-met associate of her late husband. No, George wasn't always gregarious, good-natured, or even happy. He had another side. Dark moods exposed a place inside him where something had been hollowed out and never filled.

"Did you hear me?"

"Yes, I heard you," he said, his voice flat as a flagstone. "How long?"

"It is hard to tell, but I think her baby will come in April."

He made no sign of acknowledgment, just sniffed, sipped his brandy and continued staring into the fire.

"I think you already know who the father is," Loretta said.

"Yes, isn't it obvious," he said, lifting his eyes to her for the first time. "I never wanted this. Of all the things for my girl, this was not what I wanted."

"George," Loretta said, "God gives us so much we do not ask for. We're tasked with making the best of what He gives us."

Hamilton scowled. "Is that so."

"It is. You know it is."

Hamilton raised his glass in a mock toast. "As you say, madam." He drained what remained in one gulp.

"George, you told me once how fond you were of Daniel," said Loretta.

"My God, woman. Will you never relent?"

The grandfather clock in the hallway chimed eight. It was joined by the one in his office, striking the hour until both fell silent. She sat for several minutes more, saying nothing.

"I'm going to ask you something," Loretta said, unable to stand the silence any longer. "Please answer me truthfully." Hamilton made no response, but Loretta knew he'd heard her. "How long after you and Gloriana were married was Almira born?"

Hamilton pinched the bridge of his nose and squeezed his eyes shut. For what seemed like ages, he rocked, his face flushed bright red, sweat beading his forehead. At the sight of tears running down his face, Loretta realized that this proud, proud man's heart was breaking.

"Two months," he said. "This isn't what I wanted for her. I wanted something better for my girl, not this."

Hamilton brushed his cuff across his nose. "I was young then, young and too ardent. But we were in love, so in love."

Loretta got up and sat beside him on the settee. She placed her hand on his arm.

"Almira was the product of my failure to control passion," Hamilton said. "And that same weakness has been within her always. The van Elsts could never forgive me. That is why they turned their backs on us and why Gloriana and I came up here."

She stroked his shoulder and lowered her voice to a whisper. "George, don't condemn Almira for your own sins. Can you not see she so loves Daniel, and he loves her? Open your heart to them. Don't deny them the happiness you enjoyed with Gloriana. Let them marry. Let them have their child together as man and wife."

Hamilton bowed his head. He cradled his brow in one hand and pulled absently at his hair with the other, weeping as she had never seen. After a while, he managed to compose himself. He blew his nose. Loretta took his glass, refilled it, and was about to pour more for herself, but put the decanter down.

"George, do you remember a conversation we had this summer just past? That day you described Daniel as a good fellow. I think your words were, *he's no scallywag.* Do you remember that?"

"I do."

"Give him a chance, George," she said. "I know he's low-born Irish and Catholic, but he loves your daughter desperately, and look at all he's done, establishing himself among these daguerreotype people, learning the process, the chemicals, the camera obscura, all with no education. These things call for a great deal of intelligence and determination. Surely you recognize those traits in him, as I recognize them in you."

Hamilton drew a deep breath and let his head fall back. The muscles of his face relaxed, like that of a soldier after the battle. She could almost hear the groan of long held tension, released at last. Surprisingly, he fell asleep.

Loretta took the glass from his hand and placed it on the mantel. She stayed near the fire, allowing it to warm her. She observed her husband sleeping in the candlelight and reflected on the Hamilton family. The bull-headed George, his daughter, if anything even more so, and Gloriana's museum of memory dedicated to her lost children. Her thoughts drifted back to her own lost husband and her darling little Tommy. She missed them so. She missed Plattsburgh as well. This place in Willsborough was picturesque, but so very lonely.

Hamilton had been asleep for perhaps twenty minutes when he awoke and looked around with eyes bright from some inner light. "It is decided. We'll have a large wedding here. We'll invite everyone, even these daguerreotypers Daniel works for, all your friends from Plattsburgh too, we'll invite them all. And if anyone doesn't like that these youngsters have already started a family, well, they can go to the devil."

Hamilton sprang to his feet, walked to the mantelpiece and emptied his glass. "By God," he said with a grand gesture. "This will be a happy home once again." Tightening his cravat and buttoning his tailcoat, he said, "Let's wake the girl up and tell her at once."

Loretta rose to her feet and raised a hand of caution. "George, the poor thing is exhausted. She needs her sleep. In the morning, we'll tell her the good news."

"You're right, as always," Hamilton said, his eyes welling again.

"George Hamilton, you are a good man."

"Only, my dear, because you've made me one."

Chapter 29

December, 1971

It took more than a week for Almira to reappear. David had noticed that, like a cat hiding under the bed, she stayed away when there was discord in the house. His simple theory figured her ability to materialize was dependent on the quality of energy around her.

At one a.m. on a winter night in mid-December, David entered her sitting room. Without any exchange of pleasantries, Almira said, "Doctor, have you seen Wigwam?"

The lapse of etiquette struck him. So unlike her, it made him think that perhaps she was disoriented or even regressed.

"No," he said. "Have you looked everywhere?"

"I think so. I'm not sure. You will tell me if you see him?"

David studied the way she held herself. Was there something different about the set of her shoulders, the curve of her back? "Of course, I will."

Since the subject of her relationship with God had been broached, David thought it time for Almira to further explore her feelings.

Besides, he was full of questions, and not just for clinical purposes. The whole experience with his ghostly client had eroded his atheistic assumptions. If anyone could convince him of a reality beyond the material world, Almira Hamilton was that person.

"I'm curious, Miss Hamilton. What do you do with your time? Where do you go when you're not here speaking with me in this room?"

Almira, barely audible, repeated the phrase to herself. She seemed to be considering the question but also avoided his eyes. "I mostly read. I practice my needlework, write letters, and I wait for an answer."

"Isn't there anyone for you to talk to, other than me? Daniel? Your father? Your mother?"

"No, they have all gone on. I'm not at will to join them, as much as I long to."

"You make it sound as if you're prohibited from contact with them," David said. "Why?"

"Isn't it obvious?" she said, a crimson mask of anger flaring on her face. "They are all at peace with the Lord while I am not." Before he could formulate another question, Almira changed from helpless and confused, to defiant and confrontational. "I have already warned you that I am a troubled person, doctor. Perhaps now you can see it plainly."

Her pale gray eyes, so often averted in avoidance, fixed on him. They had grown dark and penetrating. The shimmering aura forming around her was as vivid as the Aurora Borealis.

"Yes, I can see that. But I don't understand what troubles you so deeply. Can you explain it?"

"That is a simple matter." Her voice changed yet again, becoming robotic, soulless, devoid of warmth. "I am estranged from God. He hates me, and I hate him. This is why I am as I am."

She pinned him to his seat with her glare, her blasphemy hanging sooty in the air. Except for one foot which bounced rhythmically on the divan, Almira sat utterly motionless. Almost as if she dared him to speak. Would she lunge at him, envelope him in an icy mist from which there was no escape? For the first time in their long association, David feared her presence.

"You hate God?" he managed to say.

"With my very being. Why should I not feel so?" Almira said. "God has taken everything and everyone from me."

"Yet…knowing you has restored my own faith that God exists." He could hardly believe the words coming from his mouth. David Weis, clinical psychologist, man of science, confessing his faith in God? Something in her seemed to slacken. The weight of the awful fury bearing down on him softened.

"I don't understand," she said.

"Well, I wasn't raised in a religion. Most of my parents' family were killed in the war. They saw things that destroyed their belief in God as well. I guess they were angry with Him too. Isn't it ironic you should feel the same way?"

Almira leaned forward, hands tented beneath her chin, her anger melting away. "What happened?"

"You don't know much about me, the awful things that I've done… still do. If you did, you probably wouldn't like me very much."

"Tell me, please."

David took a deep breath. "Well, to start with, I'm self-centered. I use people. Not in a predatory way, but once I've gotten what I want, I lose interest in them." He let this sink in for a moment. He yearned to read her mind, but Almira's eyes were opaque as sea glass. "Do you want me to stop?"

"No, please go on."

"Alright," he said. Had confession ever felt so good? "I've wasted a lot of time chasing after material things; alcohol, drugs, shallow relationships, hedonistic stuff like that. Diversions that, in the end, don't amount to anything. It's hard to explain, but when the chase grew meaningless, my actions became…"

"Careless?" Almira said.

"Yes, you could say that. Careless, yes, but worse. I started to believe I was set apart from people—smarter, better. The point is, I really messed up, and now someone is dead because of me."

She encouraged him in much the same way he'd been trained to work with his patients. How ironic? Both Almira and Angela had innate talents as therapists. Was that what he'd been searching for in a woman all along? Someone to whom he could unburden himself. Someone to mother him, kiss his scrapes.

"I got into this thing where I thought I could look at someone's problems from a comfortable distance. Say more—do this; do that."

He took a deep breath, but Almira said nothing, so he continued. "Anyway, I quit my, well...my practice—if you want to call it that. At the time it felt like everything I did was a failure. I couldn't face it. I had to get away, and that's how I ended up here."

"I had no idea, Dr. Weis. To think, you of all people, a haunted man." She paused, as if listening for something off in the distance. "You found...refuge here."

"Yes, that's a very good way of putting it. Something about this place calms me. I can't explain it, and I don't expect you to understand what I'm saying, but our conversations have forced me to consider the idea of something larger than myself. Don't you see that it's impossible to talk with you and not conclude there must be a God?"

"I do not doubt that God exists, doctor," Almira said, looked away, "only that regards me as one worthy of forgiveness."

"If we ask, aren't we all worthy of forgiveness?" David said. "You've even forgiven your stepmother."

"That is a different matter," she said. "Loretta was a sad woman, another one of God's victims. She meant me no harm. Indeed, she was kind to me when I deserved no such consideration. No, it isn't her for whom I've withheld my forgiveness."

"Who is it? Your father?"

Almira seemed becalmed by sadness, a small boat adrift on a trackless sea. "For a long time, I hated him, but not anymore. He was but a man, a lonely man at that, subject to all the corporal desires of men. He needed the moral guidance of a wife, and I cannot begrudge him that."

"Then who? Who is it that you can't forgive?"

Almira looked up, her eyes shining like beacons. "God, Himself. And not only for what He has taken from me and done to me, but for everyone else as well. He torments us. Toys with us for his own amusement. Surely you can see that. And yet God expects us to thank and adore Him. Well, I choose not to." Almira sat erect, shoulders back, head held high, a woman in possession of her voice, perhaps for the first time. "Doctor Weis, I've known so many saddened people. Not just me, but my mother, Daniel, Sandborne, even my father. God has been heartless with us. He has been heartless with everyone."

"Then the reason you're here with me, in this room and not with those of your time, is that you refuse to forgive God? Doesn't that make you a prisoner of your own design?"

"Excuse me?" she said, leaning back. "What do you mean?"

"I mean, that as things are now, your imprisonment depends on your own decision to withhold forgiveness."

Almira eyed him, guarded, it seemed, by suspicion.

"Could it be," he said, "that the easiest part for you is insisting God could never forgive you? Is this a strategy which allows you to avoid forgiving Him? Could that be?" It was like speaking a foreign tongue, in a language he couldn't remember learning. As if someone was speaking through him. Almira seemed to have stopped breathing. David, in fact, couldn't remember ever having seen her take a breath before now.

"You challenge me," she said, the lovely crease above her eyes breaking his heart in a thousand ways. "But I will give consideration to your idea."

"Of course," said David. "If you'd rather, we can talk more about this another time."

Later that night as he unlaced his boots and undressed to a sense of satisfaction. Perhaps he'd finally penetrated the origins of Almira's psychopathology. Jealousy and guilt, sure, but the true origin of her dilemma was something much more profound—her separation from God. Wasn't this the issue which exposed the rage within her?

Almira had acknowledged she was not alive in the present. From his professional point of view that was an enormous admission. But therapeutically speaking, where did it leave them? The absence of any roadmap for this kind of work was frustrating. Freud, an atheist, still dominated the parameters of psychology, maintaining ghosts were hallucinations, nothing but a sign of psychosis. But the more he thought it through, the more David could see Almira's underlying condition had to be described as a spiritual, not a psychological, disorder.

It was an idea worth writing down. David retrieved his legal pad and put thought to paper as fast as he could. Not until dawn's first light, did he put his pen aside and lay down to sleep.

Chapter 30

December 21, 1841

As midnight drew nearer, Almira slipped out of her bed. She put on her quilted petticoat and warmest dress. Her thickest wool stockings came next. As she clipped the garters Daniel had given her just below her knee, Almira thought of the inscription, smiled to herself, and turned the top edges of her stockings over to hide them.

Working quickly, she put her hairbrush, toothbrush, and a small bottle of lavender into a silk reticule. She picked up *The Young Lady's Friend* and removed the tiny braid of her mother's hair pressed between the pages. Taking the miniature of herself and Rebecca in hand, Almira opened it and, with a sigh, placed the braid within, closed the case, and slipped it into her skirt pocket.

Arranging the bolster of her bed underneath the blanket would give the impression of someone sleeping. Stepping back to admire her ingenuity, she sculpted the pillow for better effect. Satisfied with her ruse, she took a last look around. Except for those recent months in Albany, this was the only world she had ever known. Now she was preparing herself to take leave of it—perhaps forever.

Almira struggled with her mixed emotions. She loved this place, even with all its sorrows, and she was developing a genuine affection for Loretta, but stronger was her excitement. She had great anticipation for her new life in Charleston with Daniel, the joys of marriage and motherhood. True, a nagging fear at her movements. What if Daniel wasn't there waiting? She would be left to face her future as a mother alone without a husband. *No, have faith. Daniel will be there. Hasn't he always been? In a few minutes he will take you away from Father's unbending ways.*

Almira buttoned on her riding habit and sat on her daybed. She put on her heaviest pair of leather shoes then pulled a pair of old stockings on over them. There, she thought. That will muffle my footfalls until I am outside.

Wigwam slept on the cushion beside her. Almira knelt and woke him gently.

"Wigwam, my little sachem," she whispered, fighting back a well of tears. "Wakey-wakey. Momma has to tell you something." Almira caressed his entire length. She scratched his jowls, patted his belly, and brought her face close to his. "I have to go away now. I wish I could take you with me, but I'll be back for you someday very soon, I promise. Momma loves you. Be a brave boy." She kissed the top of his head and whispered, "Goodbye Wigwam."

Almira tied on her bonnet, pulled on a woolen shawl, and drew her cloak around it. Her muff was at her wrist. After taking a last glance around the room, she blew out the candle and stepped into the hallway, pulling the door behind her until the latch clicked.

At the foot of the stairs, Almira waited several seconds, listening for the sound of anyone awake. There was none, only the clocks ticking, so she opened the rear door and went outside. In the perfect quiet of the night, she stepped off the porch and into the snow. The moment she peeled the stockings off her shoes Almira knew she'd have to run. Someone stood near the carriage house. Yes, it was Daniel holding

Marcus by the reins. She ran to him and threw herself on his chest.

"Mirie. Mirie, you came. I didn't know if you would. God, I love you so much." He squeezed her to him. "Are you sure you're ready to do this?"

"Yes," she said through a flurry of kisses. "Danny, I want only to be with you, you and our baby. Take me away with you. All I want in this world is for us to be together."

"You're sure?"

She nodded. It was all very frightening, yet exciting and wonderful at the same time.

"All right," he said. "Listen closely. Marcus is going to take us away from here. We'll ride to Split Rock Point. The lake's not even a mile wide there. We'll cross it tonight, and once we're on the Vermont side, it's on to Middlebury. I've been told about a Catholic priest there, Father Daly, who will marry us."

His nose running from the cold, Daniel sniffled and paused as if listening for something in the distance.

"And then?" Almira said.

Daniel sniffed again. "Then I'll sell Marcus and we'll take a stage to Boston. We'll get on a steamer there and go on to Charleston."

They stood in the darkness, facing each other.

"Do you trust me?"

She smiled and pressed herself against him. "With my whole life."

"Then let's go."

Daniel mounted Marcus and pulled Almira up in front of him where she perched in a side-saddle position, partly on the saddle and partly on his lap. She was reminded of her mother's prescient admonitions about riding alone with Daniel. Yes, Mother had been right. Side-saddle lessons had brought her to this point. But what a wonderful point it was, enveloped together in their desperate, private world, at once more alone than they'd ever been, yet undeniably together.

Marcus, nudged by the sharp kick of a boot heel, trotted off. At the road, Daniel coaxed his horse along more stridently. "Get on there, my boy. Show us how you make tracks."

They'd gone nearly a mile when Daniel relaxed the horse to a more comfortable canter. "I haven't told you that I saw Rebecca before I left Albany. She received a letter from her father. He's fascinated by the daguerreotype and excited to underwrite our gallery in Charleston. Her cousin Solomon is interested in helping too."

"I've sent her letters every day," Almira said. "Has she gotten them? I haven't gotten one reply."

"Rebecca told me the same thing."

"It's my father, I know it. The drunken wretch has withheld them from me. I hate him."

"Don't say that Mirie, you might regret it someday," Daniel said. "We're leaving the road now. Hang on tight."

Her left arm was tucked under his sleeve, around his body, and her right, still within the seal fur muff, protected her face from the cold. She saw little even when she peered from behind the fur anyway.

The ground changed, taking a sharp angle down a ravine toward the lakeshore. At the bottom, Daniel dismounted. There was a steady, damp breeze blowing up the lake from the south.

Daniel sniffed the air. "Mirie, the lake is narrow here. We're going to cross it. Horses don't like walking on ice, but Marcus is wearing special shoes, so you needn't be concerned. Just remember what I've told you. Don't be scared or he'll sense it. Do you understand?"

"I do. I'll be brave."

"Good. We'll go slowly. Once we get to Thompson's Point, we'll be in Vermont and it'll be too late for anyone to stop us."

Daniel petted Marcus's nose. "I've already arranged with Meade for the camera and apparatus to be shipped to Charleston, and I've got my letter of introduction to Mr. Carvalho right here," he said, patting his coat pocket.

Almira was ready then to set out, but Daniel stood, shifting from foot to foot for a long while.

"Danny, is there something wrong?"

He looked at her for a long moment, as if for the very first time. "No. No, nothing at all." Daniel took off his hat and removed something from inside his clothing. "Here, I want you to wear this. Put it around your neck."

"What is it?"

"It's called a rosary."

Almira took off her bonnet and put it on. When she looked back, Daniel stared at her intently. "Whatever happens," he said, "I want you to know that I will always love you."

Daniel led Marcus by the bridle, speaking to him softly. After a few hundred yards Almira felt the muscles in her legs, arms, and stomach ease. The frozen lake was strangely beautiful. The smooth ice was clear of snow except for occasional small drifts. Overhead, the sky was black as ink with countless stars twinkling like diamonds above them. Any ambivalent feelings she'd had when they rode off from the house were gone now, replaced with optimism at what lay ahead.

"Are you all right, dear?"

"I am very well, my young swain," she said. "I presume you are taking me to your favorite spot?"

Daniel laughed. "Yes, that's right, my favorite spot." A little further on, he began to murmur what could have been a prayer, though it seemed to Almira as much to the wind as to God. "The canal has been closed for a month. All the steamboats have quit for the winter. Even a steamboat can't break through lake ice once it's frozen."

Almira supposed they'd gone a half mile, though it was difficult to judge distance on the lake, especially at night, but Thompson's Point was definitely growing closer. Marcus hesitated, then stopped.

Daniel patted his flank. "Come on boy, don't be stopping now. Let's keep moving."

Marcus started again but seemed to lose his footing. Before Almira knew what was happening, the horse reared.

Daniel tried to steady him. "No Marcus, whoa boy, whoa."

The horse rose again, this time more wildly. Horse and rider

231

plunged into the frigid water as the ice collapsed beneath them. The freezing water swallowed Almira's shocked scream. She had never felt such sudden bitter cold. Marcus thrashed half submerged, desperate to climb out, but breaking off more of the ice shelf as he struggled.

"Mirie," Daniel shouted, "let go. Grab on to the ice."

Holding fast the reins, Daniel had been yanked into the water too. There was enough air trapped under her petticoats to buoy Almira, giving her a chance to reach for the ragged edge of the ice. She tried to pull herself up, attempting to swing one foot onto the frozen surface, but she kept slipping back into the lake. Daniel gulped water in his panic to find a breath of air.

"I'm caught," he yelled.

Marcus whickered. Almira felt Daniel's hand pushing her up from below. She flopped onto the ice and plunged her arm into the lake, groping until she felt Daniel's sleeve. Almira grasped his hand tightly, but his fingers pulled free, and contact was lost. The last thing she saw was the water close over Marcus's madly rolling eyes.

She looked up into the night sky. "Why, why, why did you do this to us?" she screamed. There was no answer.

Though her clothing was heavy and soaked through, Almira stood up. With her face turned to the heavens, she shook her fists at the stars. She tore the rosary free and hurled it in God's face, showering the ice and water with beads black as night.

"I. Hate. You!" Almira raged, spitting each word out clearly. She wanted there to be no mistaking what she had to say. But to anyone who might have been standing on shore, some mythical animal, blind with fury, howled in pain from out of the black void of the lake. Her bellowing echoed across the ice until all fell silent.

Almira sank to the ice, soaked to the bone, a spreading pool of water freezing around her, holding her fast. It was over. Utterly alone, she stared at the hole where Daniel and Marcus had disappeared. All that remained was her lover's hat bobbing gently on the surface.

Chapter 31

December 21, 1971

In the days following their breakthrough session, david sensed they would be terminating therapy soon. In truth, he wanted to savor every hour they had remaining. Rather than passively wait for almira to appear, he made the decision to seek her out. That night he went into the quiet room and lit the candles on the mantelpiece. He built a fire in the hearth, a pot of coffee on the floor. He positioned the klismos chair across from her daybed, took a seat, and waited.

He opened his eyes to a fire burned down to glowing embers. He must have fallen asleep. Rubbing his eyes, he strained to hear any sound in the pervasive silence. After several minutes, he noticed a subtle change in the room. For the first time, david watched the lamps light themselves as almira shimmered into fullness on the daybed.

"I was hoping we could visit tonight," he said to her completed apparition, resplendent with its comforting accessories.

"Doctor," said almira, forgoing the usual formalities. "Do you

233

remember your dream?"

"I do, yes."

"Since you told it to me, i've contemplated its meaning."

"And have you reached a conclusion?"

"Yes," she said. "I think it was about crossing from life to afterlife." Almira stood and glided to the mantle. She moved with purpose, as if taking center stage to deliver the denouement in some strange play. He noticed with astonishment the faint outline of her reflection in the mirror for the first time.

"You say i must return to the lake, that by returning to that place i can be released."

"I think so," he said. "I can't say for certain. I can't promise anything."

She rested a hand on the mantelpiece and laid her wistful cheek upon it. "And if it does not work? Am i to be forever imprisoned here in this room, with my needlework and my books, writing letters never sent and never answered? What will become of me? Would you promise not to leave me?"

"I promise," said david. "I won't leave you all alone."

Almira glided back to the daybed, sat, and smoothed the skirt of her dress. "I will confess to you, doctor. That having been able to meet here as we have, i've become so fond of our conversations that i do not think i could bear it be otherwise."

For the past year, the quiet room had been a sanctuary for both of them, a place to seek secret refuge together. A wave of sadness washed over him at the thought of their meetings ending. Somehow, he'd won her heart. He imagined what might have been, and still could be. Meeting with her in this room decade after decade—him slowly growing older, her forever young. David shook off such thoughts, recovering his professional sensibilities. "All right, how can i help you?"

"Go with me, please. Meet me at the carriage house tomorrow at midnight. Then all will be as it was."

All the next day, david isolated himself, immersed within thoughts of almira and accompanying her to fulfill her destiny. He didn't go out to get the mail, and when the telephone rang, he ignored it. He didn't care. His world, angela, the antiques business—those things were of no consequence.

At midnight, he pulled on his duffel coat and walked outside. The weather mild for december. A low ceiling of clouds scudded by overhead. With only a trace of snow and the ambient light, walking to the carriage house was easy. Sure enough, as he neared, she emerged from the shadows. Almira wore a long, dark, hooded cape, and a gray bonnet decorated with a black ostrich feather, her hands buried deep inside a muff.

He approached her, careful to stop a few feet away. "You don't have to do this."

"No, doctor weis, i must. You see, i've learned something. To live is hard, but to die and yet go on existing in some twilight world is harder still."

"Are you ready?"

"Yes."

She looked nervous, but he knew better than to offer his arm. The two walked together in silence until they reached the path down to the lakeshore.

Before descending almira stopped. "Doctor, might we wait here a moment?" She looked around, the light wind smelling of snow. "This has been my home these many years. I shall miss this place."

Finally, they went on. At the water's edge, almira turned toward him. A break in the clouds allowed the nearly full moon to shine through. Her face glowed in the light, surrounded by the delicate silken flowers decorating the brim of her bonnet. The moon disappeared behind a cloud. A squall erupted, blowing a million snowflakes around and between them. A few clung to her eyelashes, played across the bridge of her nose like a spray of glittering freckles.

David fought the impulse to kiss her, to tell her he loved her. He opened his mouth to ask her to stay with him in his world until they could be together in hers but noticed something dark on the frozen lake—just offshore. A man stood holding a horse by the bridle. Any chance he might have had was gone. He'd waited too long.

"I think perseus has come," david said.

Almira cast a glance over her shoulder. When she turned back her face beamed like that of a june bride. "Thank you, doctor weis. You are my true friend. You've been so kind to me. You've helped me live again, but i have to go now. Daniel is waiting." She leaned forward and placed a hand on his shoulder, brushing her lips to his cheek for the briefest instant.

"You're real." David blinked, trying to comprehend the implications of this surprising change. "You're not a dream...Not a hallucination. Are you even a ghost?"

"I cannot be certain. A ghost? Once, perhaps. But not anymore." She smiled. "Goodbye doctor weis, i shall miss you." She turned away and stepped onto the frozen lake.

David counted the footprints she'd left in the snow. He watched daniel advance and take her hand. They kissed and embraced, light reflecting off the snow turning them alabaster. Daniel took a glittering string from around his neck and lowered it over her head. He helped her onto the saddle and, taking hold of the bridle, they vanished into the storm.

Snow came fast now, wet and heavy. It made walking back much harder. Even before david opened the rear door into the kitchen, he heard the telephone ringing. Picking up the receiver he heard the operator say, "i have a person-to-person call for david weis from angela bellasaro."

David needed time to think. He wasn't in the mood to deal with angela, but it was too late now. Reluctantly he told the operator he'd take the call.

"David, where the hell have you been? I've been calling you for two days. Why don't you pick up the phone? We're supposed to get clobbered down here in the city, and you're up there in that house all alone. What've you been doing that you don't even hear the phone?"

"Nothing," he said.

"Nothing?" She yelled. "What the hell does that mean, nothing? I've been worried sick."

"You wouldn't understand."

"Oh, is that so? Well maybe you'll understand this." There was a click, and the line went dead. David cradled the receiver, surrounded by silence, except for the hum of the refrigerator. He walked over to the kitchen table and picked up the transistor radio. On winter nights like this, am reception could be exceptional.

Chapter 32

December, 1841

In the morning a posse of neighbor men assembled to help search for Hamilton's daughter. The weather had turned colder overnight, bringing with it a cruel wind from the north. Even as the sun rose, the temperature plummeted to zero.

Though they stopped at every house and questioned the inhabitants, no one in Willsborough or Essex had seen any trace of Almira. Early in the afternoon, one of the men noticed a faint set of hoofprints leave the road in the direction of the lake. "Gentlemen," he called out, "there's an odd set of tracks this way."

Assembling on the roadside, they followed the trail to the water's edge and dismounted. Standing among the other men blowing into their hands and stomping their feet, Sandborne feared the worst. He had known Daniel and Almira might try to run off together, but he didn't think they would try crossing the lake.

The man on his left held up a spy glass. Suddenly he shouted, "Look, there's something out there." Hamilton snatched the glass away and sighted along the man's pointing arm. "Can you see it, sir?"

Hamilton uttered a barely audible, "I can."

The search-party stepped onto the ice. Cautious, they spread out, keeping a wagon's length between one another, advancing toward the dark form. As they drew closer, they could see it was a bundle lying near the edge of a frozen blemish on the smooth surface of the ice. Hamilton recognized Almira's cloak. Breaking into a run, he slipped and stumbled. He scrambled to his feet—lip now bloodied but desperate to close the distance.

"No, no. Dear God. Please no." He reached her and dropped to his knees. He tried to gather her up in his arms but found it impossible; she was frozen hard to the ice. "My poor girl, my poor, poor, poor girl. What have I done, what have I done?" Inconsolable, his sobs and cries of agony rang out across the frozen lake.

One of the men tried to pull him away. Hamilton shrugged him off. "Leave me with her," he yelled through ragged sobs.

"Come George, there's nothing more you can do. Come away. Go back. We'll bring her to the house." The other men milled around. Sandborne watched from the edge of the gathering until he could bear it no longer. Looking down, he spotted a small gold cross on the ice and slipped it into his pocket.

One January afternoon in early 1842, Julia knocked on the door of Hamilton's office. "Sir, Mr. Sandborne is here. He wishes to speak to you."

"Very well Julia, show him in."

Sandborne limped through the door, leaning heavily on a hickory cane.

"Sandborne, please take a seat."

"If it pleases you, sir, I'll stand."

"Very well. What is it?"

George Hamilton had been reduced to a shell of himself. Once magnificent in stature and bearing, he appeared as a man who had survived, just barely, banishment to some far-flung penal colony. The change had shocked Sandborne.

"It's about Almira, sir."

Hamilton sat expressionless, betraying no more emotion than Pharaoh's sphinx. "Yes, I thought it might be."

"There's something you should know," Sandborne said. "I knew that Daniel and your daughter were in love and had plans to marry one day."

"I see," said Hamilton. "How long were you aware of their intentions?"

"A short while, sir. But for a year or longer I knew they fancied each other."

"And why did you not bring this to my attention?"

"Because Almira and Daniel were truly in love as no others I'd ever seen. So happy were they together, I could not bear to see them separated. I couldn't. But it...I was wrong. I see that now, and maybe if I had done right by everyone, things would be different today."

"Those same thoughts," said Hamilton, "have haunted me without ceasing these last forty days and nights."

Sandborne sagged on his cane. "I have wronged you, Mr. Hamilton. And am sorry, through and through, for what I've done. I'll leave this afternoon, or I'll stay until you have a new man if you prefer, but in the meantime, the boy can do nicely without me."

"That will not be necessary, Sandborne. I can't hold you responsible. You've been honest. Now let us go forth from this point as before."

Astonished, the old gentleman wasn't sure he'd heard correctly. "Excuse me, sir. I don't understand."

"I said we should go forth as before."

Sandborne hadn't considered the possibility that he might be allowed to stay on after all that had happened, but here was an invitation to do exactly that. "Bless you, sir. You're a true gentleman." The old man closed his eyes and gripped the head of the cane until his knuckles turned white. For what seemed an eternity he stood, rocking gently back and forth. "But I have to say no. I cannot stay."

A look of disappointment unfurled like a flag of defeat across Hamilton's face. "Emmett, please reconsider what I'm saying. I want you to regard this place as your home."

"That's kind of you, sir, but no."

"Won't you reconsider?"

"It's hard to explain," Sandborne said. "But if you had seen them, sitting hand in hand on the clover hill by the lake, your heart couldn't but rejoice in their happiness as mine did. Now my heart is broken, as I can see yours is too."

"I understand," Hamilton whispered. "This place has become a garden of broken hearts."

Chapter 33

April, 1972

It was spring again but early in the season, before the budding of the leaves or the peeping of the tree frogs. Almira had been set free, reunited with her Daniel. David returned frequently to the Quiet Room to read late into the night or sit contemplating the frescoed urns, the klismos chair, her trunk positioned exactly in the way she had favored.

On the wall above the daybed, locus of so many restorative conversations, hung Almira's memorial. Its placement pleased David. He was the sole occupant of a silent memorial to the waking dream of his lost love. He even gazed for hours at the mantelpiece where her daguerreotype was displayed beside *The Young Lady's Friend*, the *Mossrose Album*, and the Wedgewood plate. Almira was gone. Save for these fragile artifacts of her life, she might never have existed.

Angela was gone as well, except for some stray articles of clothing, a few lipstick-stained cigarette butts, the odd hairpin now and again, and one false eyelash discovered frowning on the tiled floor of the shower. These were the only reminders of their time together. He tried to telephone her once, but she wouldn't say anything more than to ask him not to call again.

More than lonely, his life had become a scoured emptiness he'd never felt before. Like a melancholy tune echoing in the nameless canyons of some trackless wilderness.

With the snow melted away, the lengthening days called for long walks along the lake. This afternoon he'd gone farther than usual and crossed the property line onto LeBerge's dairy farm. Gary didn't mind, knowing his neighbor's habit of solitary wandering.

Bare trees revealed the lay of the land. On one hillock beyond the rock ledge stood a small copse. He'd seen it many times before, but always in full foliage. This time, denuded of leaves and undergrowth, he discerned an unnatural quality. He studied the confluence of angle and cove. Something man-made loomed within. He approached the little grove to investigate, a pattern revealing itself. The center of this cluster of trees had once been cleared. David stepped inside and plunged toward the heart of the grove. He found himself looking at a skeletal graveyard, the tombstones tilted and covered with moss, the little shrine contained within a decrepit iron fence. From the rusted railing he counted the granite markers. Two, three—no, six in all.

It took great effort to pry open the rusted gate, and even greater fortitude to approach the mute sentinels within. Once there, he read.

George Washington Hamilton, Born September 9, 1796, died February 12, 1842. Glorianna Olcott van Elst, wife of George Washington Hamilton. Born August 8, 1801, died October 12th, 1840

Three small, identical markers leaned tumbling nearby. *Daughter Flora, Son George Jr., Son DeWitt.* All had dates of death within a week of each other. The last grave was marked by a larger stone. It was almost entirely hidden beneath what looked like a rose bush, judging by the thorns and rumor of dead flowers. David knelt before the stone. Like a man frantic to unearth buried treasure, he clawed at the tangled branches, oblivious to the agony of his own torn flesh and bloodied hands. After long moments of single-minded effort, the face of the monument was revealed. A thick impasto of lichen covered the marble. Still, he could make out a lamb resting in the shade of a weeping willow. Beneath it, an inscription.

Daughter Almira, born November 16, 1822, Died, December 21, 1841

The dates bracketed Almira's short life with immutable finality. He knelt by the grave, studying the epitaph in silence. A solitary crow called from the trees above. It was answered by a distant cousin. David saw traces of yet one more line, another clue in Almira's long journey. He ripped away the birth and decay of countless seasons until the half-legible inscription was revealed.

Sweet thought, to meditate the day when we shall meet our friend again.

To Be Continued...

A long time ago, **Joseph Covais** enjoyed a successful career producing precise replica clothing for museums, historic sites, and the movie industry. He was an avid collector of early American antiques –especially photography.

In his mid-30s, blindness presented Covais with a challenge. It was also an opportunity many of us don't get. He dismantled his life and rebuilt it from the ground up. Today Joe is a psychotherapist, work he finds immensely rewarding--and teaches psychology--which he is surprised to find he loves.

A third career is as historian/writer. In 2011, Covais self-published *Battery, a non-fiction account of the glider service in WWII,* based on in-depth interviews conducted with surviving veterans. The focus of his current historical research involves the unpublished personal papers of one of America's first daguerreotype artists. Its working title: *Love, Science, and the Albany Female Academy.*

Today Joe lives with his wife, Donna, in Winooski, Vt. He works as a psychotherapist with blind and visually impaired persons throughout Vermont, teaches psychology classes at St. Michael's college, writes novels, and welcomes correspondence from readers, through Facebook, Good-Reads, or through direct email at josephcovaisauthswor@gmail.com.